THE SUMMER OF SECOND CHANCES

NAN REINHARDT

The Summer of Second Chances

Copyright © 2015 Nan Reinhardt

Published by Fine Wine Romances

ISBN-13: 978-1-7336913-0-7

ISBN-10: 1733691308

Cover art by Chipperish Media

Cover art and logos Copyright © 2015 Chipperish Media

For Kathi, with love—thanks for always being my cheerleader—I miss you.
And to my other cheerleaders—Pam, Connie, Dee, Harlene, Liz, Moe, Patt, Patty, Lani, and Cheryl—thank you all for your support, advice, encouragement, and love! I'm one lucky lady!

CHAPTER 1

"There!" Sophie Russo brushed her hands on the butt of her jeans and gazed around the living room of the Sandpiper, her guest cottage on the shore of Lake Michigan. The place fairly sparkled—all ready for the new summer renter, her colleague and friend, Henry Dugan, right down to a lovely spot on the screened porch, where he would be able to set up his laptop and work in the breeze off the lake. She and Henry had been working together for years and he was setting aside his publishing empire to write a novel. If he couldn't get some serious writing done here this summer, it wasn't going to happen at all.

They'd never met in person, but Henry published the famous GeekSpeak books and as his freelance editor, Sophie had worked on nearly all his computer how-tos over the last ten years. She enjoyed his chatty, familiar voice, and wondered if his fiction had the same easy quality. She hoped he'd let her read the novel. He'd never mentioned using her as his fiction editor, but it made sense. She knew his writing style and they already had a good working relationship. He hadn't even told her what genre the novel was, but she assumed it was guy-type fiction, political suspense, crime drama, or maybe a mystery.

Even though she still had her own cottage to deal with, she was grateful the Sandpiper was all finished. Henry was due sometime tomorrow afternoon, arriving on a one p.m. flight that no doubt made a couple of stops before landing at Cherry National in Traverse City. It was kind of an off-the-beaten-path airport. His plan was to rent a car and drive down to Willow Bay. In a text earlier that week, she'd told him she'd leave the cottage door unlocked so he could just come in and make himself at home. No doubt a comfortable, clean place would help him settle in. Maybe he'd want a nap. She couldn't recall how the jet lag time zone thing worked.

Laden with cleaning supplies, she crossed the wide flagstone patio to the Firefly, her own cottage, and hurried back to the utility room to pull sheets and towels for the Sandpiper from the dryer. Dusk settled over Willow Bay as she folded the fresh linens and stacked them on top of the washing machine, and she debated whether to take them over immediately or wait until morning. Tired from unpacking, she shuddered at the thought of all the boxes she still had to unload from the back of the Jeep and the U-Haul. She'd sold most of the furniture and lots of other items from the house in Indiana, but she'd still had plenty of stuff to cart up.

She glanced in the door of the microwave as she passed through the kitchen with the armload of laundry and scowled. Forty-five was more than evident on her face in spite of a smudge of dirt across her cheek that made her look like a kid who'd been playing in the mud. Setting the towels and sheets on the table, she gazed in the glass at the dirty blouse she'd deliberately left untucked to hide the slight thickening of her waistline. Damn baking frenzies. Food, both preparing it and eating it, had become her comfort during Papa Leo's arduous last days.

She wasn't as toned as she once was either. But the only exercise she'd gotten in the past year had been yoga in the living room or the occasional walk around the neighborhood while Papa Leo slept. She'd also allowed her dark hair to grow long simply because pulling it up into a ponytail was so much easier than trying to style it each morning. Doing her hair and makeup became a tiresome and unnecessary ritual when Papa Leo needed a bath or help eating breakfast.

Speaking of food, her stomach was growling. She hadn't eaten since breakfast and it was well past suppertime. Damn. Too bad she hadn't stopped by the market on her way into town—all she had here was whatever was left in the freezer from last fall. Certain it was empty, Sophie yanked open the fridge anyway. Maybe... just maybe... and then she chuckled. Sure enough, just as she'd hoped, her dear friends, Jules and Carrie, had left her a welcome back gift. A casserole of some sort, a green salad, and what looked like... *please god, let it be...* she pulled the foil off a round dish. Oh yes! One of Carrie's homemade apple pies.

She spooned a generous portion of the casserole onto a plate to zap it and frowned again at the woman reflected in the door of the microwave before giving herself a little shake. Being depressed about her appearance was no way to start her new life in Willow Bay. First thing in the morning, she'd call Jules to find out who cut her hair, which was styled in a long layered pageboy that Sophie liked. A new life meant new hair. Her curly tresses cascaded down her back as she yanked the cotton scrunchie out, releasing her boring old ponytail. Running her fingers through the thick mass, she toyed with it, imagining a more stylish cut, maybe some layers or even a short, flirty cut like Carrie's. Perhaps a few highlights to hide the gray threads. Different. That was the main thing.

Just the idea of making a change put a little spring in her step as she walked down the hallway after her impromptu dinner. She was more than ready to get into her pjs and wash her face. She dug in the hallway closet for her favorite summer quilt and spread it over the fresh sheets she'd put on the bed in the larger bedroom earlier. The fan swept around in a lazy circle above the bed, the quiet hum providing soothing white noise. She gave a satisfied sigh, confident this move to Michigan had been exactly right—a new town, but familiar. Even making herself at home in Papa Leo's old bedroom brought comfort instead of sadness. She gazed around the room that was still so much his, right down to the pipe rack on the tall dresser and the family pictures hanging on the wall by the door.

She pulled the chain on the fan light as she approached the display that Papa Leo always referred to as his "rogues' gallery." The wall had always fascinated her. Sepia-toned photographs the Italian great-grandparents she never knew bumped against black-and-white photos from pre-WWII when those Russos had first bought the two cottages in Willow Bay. A pastel-tinted print of Papa and Nonna's wedding back in the sixties hung in the center —a place of honor surrounded by old photos of the two of them down on the beach, in Paris and London and Venice and even waving from the top deck of a cruise ship. Several pictures of her and Nonna and later ones of her and Papa Leo brought a lump to her throat. So many dear people already gone from her life. One picture of a dark-haired, green-eyed, teenaged beauty sent a frisson of annoyance through her. Impulsively, she jerked the frame off the wall.

Eva was the last person she needed in her head right now. She tossed the picture in the bottom drawer of the dresser, then slipped into the bathroom to get ready for bed. A quick glance at the clock told her that it was really too early to fall asleep, but the bed was so inviting... She'd started reading a new novel on her Kindle at the hotel the night before. An hour or so of reading would be a great way to settle into a good night's sleep.

Moments later, a clang outside brought her bolt upright and sent her sprinting to the window—a skunk scampered away from the tipped trash bin, dragging a limp asparagus stem. Damn critters had already discovered the unlocked shed.

She grabbed her hoodie off the chair and shrugged into it. All the old food she'd cleaned out of the freezer earlier would be strewn across the patio and down the beach steps by morning if she didn't go secure that door.

On her way through the cottage, she nabbed the pile of linens from the table. Might as well take them next door as long as she was up. Crossing to the Sandpiper, she set the sheets and towels inside the screened porch before cleaning up the trash mess and securely latching the shed doors.

The cottage still smelled fresh when she opened the French doors and switched on the overhead light. Standing for a moment in the open living room with the armload of sheets and towels, she took another look around to make sure everything was perfect for Henry's arrival. It was. In the morning, she'd get some flowers at Anna Porter's farm stand and set them on the table to complete the homey scene she'd created.

The mantle clock chimed eleven as she hung fresh towels on the rack in the bathroom and then began making the bed. With the windows open slightly, the crisp May breeze had aired the coverlets nicely, and she smoothed Papa Leo's favorite log cabin quilt over the clean sheets. She'd never thought about it before, but with the tall pines and spectacular lake views, this cottage was the ideal place for a writer.

A loud noise at the back door nearly sent her sprawling across the bed. Whatever was back there was way bigger than a skunk or raccoon. Apparently, she'd forgotten to lock the door when she left earlier. Great. A break-in and it was only May third! Of course, Beach Road was practically deserted. She'd been the first to open up this season. None of the other summer folks had even arrived yet.

Hands fisted at her sides, she peered into the hall, assessing whether she could get to something she could use to defend herself before the prowler stepped inside. What that would be eluded her completely. Maybe the oar hanging above the fireplace or a badminton racket from the closet in the second bedroom or the hairdryer here on the dresser? All good options except that heavy footsteps sounded in the utility porch and the kitchen suddenly flooded with light.

Would a thief switch on the brightest light in the place, knowing she was right next door? Maybe a dumb one who didn't bring a flashlight…

Oh, screw it.

Sophie grabbed the hairdryer and brandishing it like a pistol, jumped into the hall with a loud shout. She recognized the intruder immediately. His graying hair was longish, soft, and slightly tousled. Small rectangular wire-rimmed glasses gave him a rather intellectual air. He'd grown a goatee since the last publicity photo, but it was unquestionably Henry Dugan gazing around the cottage before his eyes lit on her.

He had a canvas messenger bag slung over one shoulder, a large duffel in one hand, and a guitar and a brown paper bag that emanated the heavenly scent of onions and fries in the other. Obviously, he'd found Swenson's, the only fast food place in Willow Bay open after ten p.m.

Her heart pounded and her mouth was dry with residual fear, or maybe it was simply dismay that he'd caught her with her wild hair streaming down her back, no makeup, and clad in pink polka dot pajamas. Shouting and waving a hairdryer at him probably didn't help either. She couldn't tell. Whatever, one of them needed to speak. In what was probably a futile attempt to regain her dignity, she set the hairdryer on the table, stopped a few feet away from him, and gave him a tentative smile. "Hello, Henry."

He let go of his duffel to reach out to her with one hand. "Sophie?"

She nodded, took another couple of steps forward, hand extended, and with a very unladylike, "Oof!" promptly stumbled over the duffel and landed in Henry's arms. In one smooth move, he set the guitar down and tossed the sack of food on the counter as he caught her. He held her so close she could feel his heart beating under the soft cotton of his light blue shirt.

"Oh god, I'm such a klutz, sorry." She struggled, pushing against his chest with both hands as he tried to maneuver them around his luggage.

"Hey, stand still." With one arm around her waist, Henry pressed her to his chest. "Your foot's caught in the strap. Here, hold on a sec."

She gripped his shoulder as he grabbed her knee and lifted. "Okay, shake your foot," he ordered, and when she did, first the bag and then Henry released her.

"Hello." He grinned. "I can't believe I'm finally here."

Shock and humiliation kept her from guarding her tongue. "What are you doing here? You aren't due until tomorrow."

"I caught an earlier flight out of San Jose. Anxious to get here, I guess." He picked up the duffel and moved it out of the center of the kitchen. "I hope that's okay."

"Of course it's okay." Her cheeks burned as she realized how brusque she sounded, so she pulled a plate out of the cabinet in an effort to cover her embarrassment. "You must be starving. I see you found Swenson's." She handed him the plate. "Here, let me take your jacket and you can eat while it's still halfway warm... or there's the microwave. You can zap it if you need to. How were your flights? Did you come through Detroit? Oh, here let me get you a drink. You want water or... um, water?" More heat rose in her cheeks as she realized she was chattering. Henry merely gazed at her with an enigmatic smile on his face. She clamped her lips closed and turned away to straighten the perfectly straight place-mats on the kitchen table.

Idiot. Shut up. The poor man's just flown over twenty-five hundred miles and then driven another forty to get here. You've already fallen all over him. Last thing he needs is you hovering like a damn helicopter mom.

She had to go before she started babbling again. "Well, I'll let you get settled in." Sophie wrapped her arms around her waist and backed toward the living room. "Welcome to Willow Bay. Goodnight, Henry."

"No, wait." He followed her, dragging the wheeled duffel behind him. "Don't go. I texted you that I'd taken an earlier flight and would be here tonight. When I didn't get a response, I just figured you'd leave the door unlocked for me like you said earlier."

"Oh, damn." Sophie released a frustrated breath. "My phone's still charging in the Jeep. I didn't see your text."

"Are you sure you're okay with me being here early?" Henry glanced around. "I can maybe go find a hotel and come back tomorrow." Clearly he was tired and his words didn't sound all that sincere.

A pang of guilt shot through Sophie. What kind of welcome had she offered? First she nearly knocked him over and now he gets nervous blathering from a middle-aged landlady in a ratty sweatshirt and pink fuzzy slippers. She was fairly sure she'd seen this whole scene on a bad sitcom several years ago. Good God, she was a damn cliché. He deserved better after a long flight from California.

"Don't be silly. That's not necessary. You just surprised me. I'm all ready for you." She offered a genuine smile. This was Henry, her colleague, her friend. No need to be all flustered. "Truly. Actually, I was just making up the bed."

"Okay. Great." Relief washed over his features as he tugged the messenger bag over his head and set it on the table. "This way?" A little jerk of his head indicated the back of the cottage and he headed that way with the duffel.

She nodded and followed him, pointing out the second bathroom, linen closet, and spare bedroom along the way. He dropped the duffel on the floor while Sophie smoothed the last few wrinkles out of the quilt on the bed.

"Wow, this is nice." Henry eyed the beamed ceiling as they made their way back into the main part of the house, making her glad she'd swept the cobwebs. "I really appreciate this, Sophie."

"I'm glad you're here. I hope you can get some writing done."

"Me, too." He wandered over to the French doors to peer out into the screened porch to the trees and lake gleaming in the moonlight beyond. "We're pretty high off the water."

"It's sixty-seven steps down to the beach." She couldn't help noticing that he looked older than his picture on the book covers. His hair was more gray than blond, a few lines that had probably been airbrushed out of the photograph creased his cheeks, and although he still appeared fit, he did have a slight paunch. Sort of a much tidier sober version of Jeff Bridges' character in *Crazy Heart*... god, she loved that movie. Maybe Julie's husband Will would help her set up the TV and Blu-ray player tomorrow...

He turned to face her and caught her staring. She blinked and shook her head. *Focus, Sophie!* Sheesh. She needed to escape before she set his hair on fire or slipped on a rug and landed on her ass. "It's late. Your supper's probably cold by now. I'm going to go. I'll see you in the morning."

"I'll heat it up." But this time he didn't stop her and could she blame him? He probably wanted her the heck out so he could eat and fall into bed. "Goodnight, Soph. Thanks again."

"'Night, Henry." Gratefully, she slipped out into the cool moonlight

CHAPTER 2

Henry watched Sophie Russo cross the patio and enter the other cottage, but as she disappeared into the darkened screened porch, the scent of onions drew him back to the kitchen. He unwrapped a double cheeseburger and dumped a large order of French fries onto the plate Sophie had left on the counter. Thirty seconds in the microwave had the sandwich and fries reheated and smelling even more delicious. What was it about reheated fast food that was so irresistible?

When he sat down at the table with the plate and a bottle of expensive airport water he dug out of his bag, he heaved a sigh of relief. Alone at last and with a meal that would've sent his ex-wife into orbit. In addition to being a world-class shopper, twenty-nine-year-old Kristie was also a vegan and had spent a good portion of their short-lived marriage trying to reform what she referred to as his "diet of death." He bit into the burger, savoring the taste of fat and salt and blessed calories. No more diet sheriff, no more yoga, no more raw cauliflower and jicama (he never did figure out what that shit was). Not that he didn't like vegetables—he certainly did. Just not for every fucking meal, and sometimes it was nice to actually have them cooked.

He closed his eyes, leaned back in the chair, and relished the flavor of deep-fried potatoes as he thought about the world he'd left behind in San Jose. Henry loved his work as publisher and main author for GeekSpeak Press, and he enjoyed writing his syndicated computer Q&A newspaper column. However, his life's passion was to write a novel—novels, actually. He had so many characters and stories in stuck in his head... but the computer books were lucrative and had made him into a multimillionaire in ten short years.

GeekSpeak was in the capable hands of his staff in San Jose now, and the column was on hiatus for the summer. Maybe, just maybe, it was time to stop writing computer how-to books and finally realize his life-long dream—to make it as a serious novelist. When his favorite freelance editor offered him one of her lake cottages in Michigan for a few weeks of peace and solitude, he knew he had to take the chance.

He glanced up at the clock on the microwave just as his cell phone went off. It had to be his nephew, Peter, calling from California. A junior at San Jose State, Peter was earning summer money housesitting for Henry and interning as a publicity assistant at GeekSpeak Press.

"Hey, Uncle Hank, it's me, checking in. Didja get there? How's the editor?" Henry heard the creaking sound of the kid settling into the leather wing chair in his living room, probably slinging his long legs over the upholstered arm. "Did she meet you with a sledge hammer like that chick in *Misery*?"

"I never should've introduced you to King's early work." Henry reached for a napkin from the basket on the table. He was so tired, he chose to ignore Peter's use of the hated *Hank*. "Your imagination is working overtime, kid."

"All your fault." He heard Peter take a long slug of a beverage before he continued. "So, what's she like? Spooky old spinster? Maybe just little crazed?"

"Seriously?" Henry ate another fry.

"Well, you're up there in Bumfuck, Egypt with a woman you've never met in person. Just sayin'…"

"Okay, back to reality. She's my editor, not my number one fan. I've been working with her for over ten years. Don't you think I'd know by now if she was a nut job?" Henry shook his head. "We exchanged about six sentences when I arrived. She seems very nice, not at all spinsterish or crazy." He smiled, remembering Sophie leaping out of the bedroom with the hairdryer. Peter didn't need to hear about that.

"How's the place?"

"Pretty nice, what I've seen of it in the dark." Henry heard him take another deep drink. "Hey, are you drinking *my* beer? My Founders?"

"Of course I am." Peter smacked his lips. "And man, is it good."

"Buy your own, you little shit. I can't just get that beer at the Safeway, you know. I have to order it from Michigan."

"Yeah, well, you're *in* Michigan, Unk, so go buy yourself some."

Henry rolled his eyes. "How's the Press? Everything okay?"

"You mean since you left less than twenty-four hours ago? Yeah, it's all good. One thing though."

Oh, god. Henry was almost afraid to ask. "What?"

"There was a note on the door from Kristie when I got home today. She wants the treadmill."

"You didn't tell her where I was, did you?" Henry shoved the half-finished plate away and focused on deep cleansing breaths. "Do not tell her how to find me."

"Even if she shows up on your doorstep and flashes those amazing boobs?"

"Oh, you mean the ones I paid for?" Henry rose and dumped the rest of his food in the trash, his appetite suddenly gone. Who knew that the sweet little blonde marketing assistant who'd swept him off his feet five years ago would turn into such an avaricious bitch?

"Don't worry. I promise I won't say a word." Peter stopped laughing. "Do I give her the treadmill?"

"No, you don't. Don't give her a damn thing. Don't let her in the house. Don't even talk to her. If she shows up again, tell her to call my attorney."

"Okay, okay, chill." Peter said. "I promise I won't tell her a thing or give her a thing."

After making his nephew swear again that he'd keep his location a secret, Henry ended the call and wandered around the cottage. It was nice—homey and old-fashioned with knotty pine walls and wide-plank floors—but updated too, with a shiny stainless steel kitchen and modern bathrooms. The perfect place to finish his novel.

He shut off the lights, leaving the one above the stove burning in case in he needed to get up in the night, and then wandered back to the bedroom and unpacked, hanging shirts, jeans, pants, and jackets in the narrow closet and tossing the rest in the empty drawers of the old oak dresser. He set his shaving kit on the sink in the master bath and dropped his toothbrush in the empty cup.

Debating a shower, he was stripping out of the clothes he'd traveled in all day when the sound of a car backfiring took him to the bedroom window. Peering between the wide slats in the blinds, he caught a glimpse of a beat-up old Honda Civic as it passed under the sodium vapor light that cast a circular pattern on the parking area behind the cottages. The car crept around the corner, but it was still moving, so it must have been night owls out cruising. If it was someone who needed help, surely they'd have stopped and knocked. He shut the blind and crawled beneath the warm quilt.

∽

Sophie peered into the window of the Daily Grind and saw exactly whom she was hoping to see—her old friends, Carrie Reilly and Julie Miles. When she shouldered the door open, the aroma of fresh-brewed coffee nearly sent her into a paroxysm of joy. She inhaled deeply. God, how she'd missed this place.

Perry Graham, the owner, let out a joyful whoop when he glanced up from the milk he was foaming. "Sophie!" He held up the metal beaker in salute. "You're back early!"

"Time to get away, Perry." She gave him a wan smile. "Nothing left for me down in Indiana anymore."

He handed off the steamed milk to a barista and came around the counter to tug Sophie into a giant bear hug. "Baby girl, we were all heartbroken to hear about Leo. Your grandpa was one of Willow Bay's favorite people. We all thought of him as a villager even though he was summer folk."

"Thanks." Sophie returned the hug, knowing this was highest compliment he could've paid to her grandfather. "Baby girl? Really? You're only about ten years older than me."

"Twelve, and I remember when you were born." He loosened his hold and hurried back around the counter. "To me, you'll always be that freckle-faced girl who followed me down the beach all summer, begging to use my metal detector. I hear you're here permanent." He grinned down at her. "Couldn't be happier if my own baby sister moved back home. Now what can I get you?"

She gave Perry another squeeze before placing her order. "A cappuccino, please, with two raw sugars in the bottom and—oh —" She spun around as someone grabbed her from behind.

"Soph! You made it!" Carrie Reilly enfolded her in her embrace as she pressed a kiss to her cheek. "How are you, sweetie?" Her big brown eyes were so full of concern Sophie nearly lost it.

She swallowed hard. "I'm… I'm okay." Tears stung her eyelids and she blinked them back, determined not to start blubbering in front of her friends and the whole village of Willow Bay, Michigan. "So very glad to be here."

"Sophie!" Tall, willowy, and more beautiful than ever, Julie Miles reached in for a hug, too. "Welcome home."

Sophie lingered in the group embrace before stepping back and straightening her shoulders, more metaphorically than literally. "God, it's good to see you guys. And if I didn't say it while you were down in Poplar Hill, thanks for coming to Papa Leo's funeral."

"Oh, please, like we wouldn't be there? Besides, you said it about sixty times." Julie waved away her thanks and led her to the table while Carrie stopped by the counter to pick up Sophie's order. Julie and Carrie met at the Grind almost every morning at nine. It was tradition. Summers, she usually joined them for coffee, food, and fellowship.

"So you're really here to stay?" Carrie gave her an affectionate smile.

"I am." Sophie gave them a firm nod. "Oh, and thanks for the food. You saved my life last night. I've got to hit the market today."

"Our pleasure." Jules bit into her muffin, scattering crumbs all over her blouse. "So, tell us about the new guy renting the Sandpiper. When's he due? What happened to the Olivers?"

"Actually, he showed up unexpectedly last night. He's one of my clients." Sophie stirred her coffee, basking in the warm glow of familiar surroundings and good friends. "His name's Henry Dugan—"

"Henry?" Jules brushed at her blouse. "Really? That's his name? *Henry*?"

"What's wrong with Henry?" Sophie asked. "It's a perfectly good name. Indiana Jones's real name is Henry." She lifted her chin, surprised at how Julie's comments brought her defenses up. And what made her bring up Indiana Jones of all people? Henry Dugan didn't resemble Harrison Ford in the slightest. She shook her head and gave Jules a smile. "He's the publisher of the Geek-Speak books; I do a lot of his copyediting work. It was kind of a fluke that the Olivers decided to spend the summer in California with their new grandbaby just as Henry needed a break from corporate life. I was glad he was interested in renting the Sand-piper so I didn't have to vet any new summer renters."

"The GeekSpeak guy, really? Liam loves those books," Carrie said. "They're hilarious and they explain all that computer crap to non-techies like us." She snapped her fingers. "Yeah, I remember now that you work on those."

Sophie nodded. "I've been working with him for about ten years. Henry made a fat fortune very fast with GSP. Anyway, he's writing a novel and needs some peace and quiet to finish it. Apparently, he's just out of a bad divorce."

"Oooh, Soph, a newly divorced rich guy? So what if his name is Henry. Is he hot? Look at Indiana Jones. How old is this guy?" This from Julie, who was madly in love again after being widowed a couple of years earlier. She was an incurable matchmaker.

"Ah, we add the divorce and the big bank account and suddenly Henry's not sounding so bad—is that how we're playing this?" Carrie threw Jules a pointed look.

"Just let her answer." Jules said.

Sophie couldn't help chuckling at her two friends. God, how she'd missed this. The gentle squabbling that came with long-time friends. The familiarity. The girly teasing. "He's in his early fifties, I think. Kinda nerdy, but a very nice man."

"Nerds can be sexy, even nerds named *Henry*." Jules smirked. "Look at my Will. Major nerd, hot as hell."

"Jules, don't even go there, okay?" Sophie held up one hand.

"Last thing in the world I need or want right now is a man. I just want to get settled in here. Besides, he's only staying until August, then he's back to California."

"What about a quick summer fling?"

"I'm a little old for that, don't you think?"

Julie smirked and waggled her perfect brows. "You're never too old for a steamy romance, sweets, any time of the year. Trust me on this one."

"No, thanks." Sophie sipped her beverage with an appreciative slurp. Nobody made a cappuccino like Perry.

"So..." Carrie's hesitation was evident. "Did you ever hear from your mom?"

"Nope."

"You're kidding." Carrie's brows knit as she tipped her cup and drank.

"Not a word. I called her cell before and after the funeral and left messages, but I never heard from her." Sophie glanced longingly over her shoulder at the case of baked goods, but then thought better of it. Her ass truly didn't need more carbs and fat.

"Did you really expect to?" Julie gave her a probing stare. "I mean, honestly?"

"You know, I thought she might react to the death of her father. A normal person would." Sophie shrugged. "Dumb, huh?"

"No, babe, not dumb," Carrie said. "But why did you think she'd behave any differently than she ever has? It's expecting 'normal' that might've been a little naïve."

"I kinda half expected her to at least show up for the reading of the will. I know the attorney contacted her." Sophie gave a grim laugh, then chewed her lower lip for a moment. "Eva bugged Papa Leo for money all the time. He'd send it to her, wherever she was, and she always let him know where she was. That's how he knew she was okay. She'd call for money and the checks got cashed, which was about the extent of their relationship."

"She's never tried to communicate with you?" Julie took another bite of muffin and wiped her fingers on a napkin before looking expectantly at Sophie. "She's your mom, for God's sake."

Sophie met her gaze with a wry smile. "No contact. Nonna was my mom, and then Papa Leo was all things parent after she passed. As far as Eva's concerned, I don't exist."

"Sophie..." Carrie leaned forward to place a solicitous hand on Sophie's knee. "Honey, I know how hard losing Leo has been on you and Eva's not showing up didn't help, but there's something..."

"What?" Sophie didn't like the I-have-something-to-tell-you-that-I-don't-really-want-to-tell-you expression on Carrie's face.

"Noah told me she was up here over the winter."

"You're kidding. When?" Sophie felt the shock of Carrie's words all the way down to her scruffy tennis shoes. She dropped back in her chair and blew a frustrated breath into her bangs. What the hell was Eva doing in Willow Bay? "Did he talk to her? What did she want?" Tension crept up her spine and stiffened her shoulders.

"She came up in February, just a few weeks after Leo's funeral." Carrie swirled the foam in her drink. "She wanted the key to your place."

"He didn't give it to her?" Sophie couldn't help the alarm that colored her tone, even though she knew that was a silly question. Of course Noah would never give Eva a key to the either of the cottages, at least not without Papa Leo's permission... or hers, now that they belonged to her.

"Of course not." Carrie's brows furrowed. "He sent her away. Told her to contact you."

"Well, she didn't." Sophie scowled and smacked the table with her open hand. "Dammit." Frustration laced her voice. "How typical. Papa Leo's gone and *she* finally decides to make an appearance."

"Relax. As far as we know, she left again." Carrie's voice held the same soothing note she used with her five-year-old. "I just thought you should know she'd been sniffing around. Nobody's mentioned seeing her since."

"Like anyone up here besides Noah would even know her at this point." Sophie's stomach roiled at the thought of running into the mother who'd abandoned her as a baby. "God knows *I* couldn't pick her out of a lineup."

Julie's eyes narrowed and Sophie could almost hear her mentally debating with herself before she asked, "Did he leave her anything?" Then she shook her head and held up one hand. "Wait. Don't answer that. I'm being too nosy."

"I don't mind telling you." Sophie waved away her concern. She didn't have any secrets from these two. "He left her five thousand dollars, which the attorney sent her. Otherwise, everything came to me."

"Are you rich now? Dripping in diamonds and thinking about a Bentley?" Jules teased, obviously trying to lighten the tense atmosphere that had settled over the table.

"Hardly." Sophie's mouth curved up at the twinkle in her friend's eyes. "Remember Papa Leo was a retired college professor—he lived on a pension and social security. There was few thousand in the bank that paid for the funeral, and the life insurance was a bit more. He owned the house in Poplar Hill and the cottages free and clear, but he liked to spend money."

Carrie sipped her coffee and licked foam off her upper lip. "I remember how much he enjoyed good wine. Gosh, the very last time I saw him, he'd brought over some fancy French wine for Liam to taste. They finished the whole bottle out on our deck."

"He taught me to love wine." Sophie nodded. "And traveling. Remember two years ago in October, he and I went wine tasting in California? That was so much fun. He rented a convertible, and we drove all over Napa, Sonoma, and the Sierra foothills. I begged Tom to come along since it was quarter break, but he wouldn't. Then he was pissed we went without him. I never imagined at the time that it'd be my last trip with Papa Leo."

"Tom's a dick." Julie pronounced around a mouthful of blueberry and crunchy topping. "He's always been a dick, even the PhD didn't fix that. Thank god you never married the schmuck. You're well rid of him."

"Jules!" Sophie made a half-hearted attempt at indignation, then chuckled as she met Carrie's eyes over the napkin dispenser. "Oh hell, when you're right, you're right. Almost fifteen freaking years and the most commitment I ever got from the professor involved him graciously allowing me to leave a toothbrush in his bathroom. *I* was the schmuck." She gave them a self-deprecating grin. "Honestly though, I'm really glad we broke up before Papa Leo died. It made moving back home and taking care of him so much easier." An onslaught of melancholy forced her to swallow hard as she settled back into her chair.

"Ah, Soph, I'm so sorry." Carrie tugged her into a sisterly hug. "I know you really miss him."

"More than you can imagine." Sophie let herself sink into the embrace, struck again at how lovely it was to be back among her dear friends. The time since her grandfather's death had been arduous as she sold the house in Indiana and most of its contents, and closed up Papa Leo's estate. For several months it had seemed as if all she did was sign papers and sort through boxes.

Carrie's arms tightened around her, and she stroked her hair as Sophie finally let the tears she'd held in for so long flow freely. Julie patted her shoulder, and handed her a few napkins. Fortunately, it was late enough that only a few patrons lingered in the coffee shop. Sobbing in front of the morning crowd would've been deeply embarrassing.

After a few cathartic moments, she stopped, blew her nose noisily, and then gave each woman a hug. "I'm okay. I am. I'm here now. I'm home."

"You know what you need?" Julie tugged the lid off her coffee and tipped it to get the last few drops.

"No, but I bet you're about to tell me." Sophie sniffed and wiped her eyes again.

"You need to get laid."

"Jules!" Carrie gave a disgusted sigh and rolled her eyes. "Cripes. That's your answer to everything. You are a horny old woman."

"First of all, what makes you think I haven't gotten laid recently?" Sophie dug a pen and paper from her purse. She needed to make a list if she was going to the market. "And second, even if I haven't, just who in the village do you have in mind for that job?"

Julie shrugged and raised one elegant brow. "First of all, I know you, and second, I'm thinking..."

"Frankly, my most recent affair has been with apple pie and snicker doodles. Do you suppose there's a single man in town who's looking for middle-aged and round?" Sophie glanced down at the curve of her belly. Whoever Julie decided to fix her up with had better appreciate curves because she was curving all over the place.

"You're adorable and you know it," Julie said. "That lush librarian vibe rocks—and hey, big boobs are very in right now."

"Well, then I'm all set, aren't I?" She pushed out her ample bosom and grinned. "Find me a man, Jules, and I'll give it some serious thought. Now, I've got to hit the market and then empty that stupid U-Haul. I got almost everything out of the Jeep before I came here this morning."

"Can we help?" Carrie stuffed the pile of used napkins in her cup, busily policing the table while Julie applied a little extra lip gloss. "We can meet you at the Firefly after you get done shopping."

"I'd love some help," Sophie said. "Just getting the trailer unloaded and returned to the rental place in Traverse City would be huge today."

"I'll help, but only if you promise to meet Will and me for shrimp at the Fishwife tonight," Julie said. "Our treat. A welcome home dinner."

"Are you ever going to marry that poor guy?" Sophie grinned and lifted her arm in a farewell wave to Perry. She grabbed her keys and led the way out the door.

"Maybe one day." Julie shrugged. "But he so loves being a kept man."

They chuckled as they went their separate ways and Sophie smiled after them, affection filling a place inside her made empty by loss and grief. Her friends were so much in love—Carrie with her symphony conductor husband, Liam Reilly, and Julie with Will Brody, whom she referred to her as her "gentleman friend." Both women had found love later in life. Carrie was forty when she reunited with Liam after a sixteen-year separation. Julie, widowed at fifty-one, had found romance with a sexy younger man. Her friends proved it was never too late for a second chance at romance. But for now, Sophie was perfectly happy beginning her new life on her own.

CHAPTER 3

The breeze off the lake ruffled Henry's hair and it flopped in his eyes, reminding him that he should've gotten a haircut before he left San Jose. He shoved it off his forehead, pressing his fingers against his scalp as if that would magically hold his hair back. The words weren't coming today. Oh hell, the words hadn't come since he'd arrived in Willow Bay, and the whole getting-away-to-write-in-seclusion idea was starting to feel bad. Really bad.

First of all, he was homesick. Fucking homesick at the age of fifty-one. He looked forward to Peter's inane text updates the same way a kid at camp looks forward to care packages from Mommy. He'd checked in with the press so many times in the last two weeks that his assistant had started letting his calls go to voicemail. Hell, he'd even called his ninety-four-year-old grand-mother just to see how she was doing back in good old San Jose. The only thing he *didn't* miss from home was the drama from his ex.

Second, this place was seriously remote... like, hell and gone from any big city. Even though he had cable TV and Wi-Fi, he still felt cut off from civilization. He'd driven to the market in town to grab some groceries, but he couldn't find the Founders beer he loved so much and had counted on having in endless supply in Michigan. He hadn't tried any of the restaurants in town yet because he hated eating at a table by himself in a strange place, although the coffee shop in the village did make a decent cappuccino and killer muffins. He'd made a couple of trips down the sixty-seven steps to the beach and walked along the hard-packed sand a mile or so. But the water was frigid and he wasn't sure enough of what part of the beach might be private and what wasn't to go too far.

Third, he'd barely seen anything at all of Sophie Russo. Not that he expected her to entertain him, but he'd kinda thought she'd drop by, say hi, and maybe offer a tour of some of the interesting places in the area. But no. She was clearly involved in clearing out her dead grandfather's things from the cottage next door. He'd seen her bustling around, hauling boxes out to her Jeep, and filling her trash barrels. He'd watched discreetly from the screened porch as she laughed and chatted with a couple of friends who'd come to help—a tall blonde and a short, curvy brunette.

Worst of all, every time he sat down to write, he drew a complete blank. He'd tried his old trick of rereading the stuff he'd already written, hoping to get some inspiration, but he came up empty. He couldn't even write in his journal, and the journal was sacred—he'd written in it nearly every day since his freshman year in high school. He had writer's block—something that had never happened when he wrote his computer how-tos. He needed to write and yet, he was sitting on his ass, watching World War II documentaries on cable, drinking grocery-store beer, and eating junk... he glanced down at his belly, half-expecting to see it over-hanging his belt like a watermelon.

Of all the things he'd anticipated when he planned this trip, writer's block hadn't even occurred to him. The story of his great-grandparents' migration to California, how they'd started a news-paper together in San Francisco during the glory days of the Gold Rush, had practically written itself back in San Jose. The ease of the first few chapters was what had convinced him to turn the press over to his employees and take this sabbatical in the first place. But now, fuck all, he was lonely, demoralized, and getting downright depressed. This was his big chance to do what he'd always dreamed of doing and he was blowing it.

What if he wasn't a writer at all? What if he was nothing more than a goddamned computer geek who had a knack for explaining complicated programs? What if his ex-wife was right and he should just give up the novel and concentrate on keeping the money rolling into GeekSpeak Press? He shoved away from the pine table that Sophie had arranged so nicely for him as a writing corner, nearly knocking his notes off in the process.

Well, at least Sophie seemed to believe in him. She'd been unfailingly generous and gracious in her support of his choice to take the summer off to write, to the point of offering him this cottage and making him a special place on the porch to do it. He straightened the stack of notes before wandering out onto the patio. He really wanted to nosh on some corn chips, but he'd do better to take a walk on the beach. The exercise would do him good.

"Hey." His editor opened the door to her own screened porch and backed out carrying a large trash bag stuffed full.

"Soph!" Henry was unreasonably glad to see her. She'd gotten a haircut, but her dark hair, which was falling out of the clip she'd used to pull it off her neck, still touched her shoulders. "Let me get that for you." He hurried over, took the bag, and carried it to the shed.

Sophie ran ahead to yank open the door and pull the lid off the already-overflowing trash can. "Yikes. Looks like I've filled this one." She scooted another dented metal bin forward from the back of the shed. "Okay, stick it in here, I guess."

Her teeth worried her lower lip, and Henry couldn't help noticing she had a little gap in her front teeth, kinda like that famous model from the seventies—Laura or Lauren... whatever. It was cute. He watched as she secured the lid on the garbage can and then carefully latched the shed doors.

"How's the writing coming?" She stood with her hands tucked in the back pockets of her jeans.

"Good. It's good," he lied. No way was he going to admit how bad things were on his side of the patio. Maybe it was best she hadn't stopped by. If she walked through his cottage, she'd know in a heartbeat. Empty beer cans on the coffee table in front of the TV, dishes in the sink, and a trash can full of chip bags would be a dead giveaway. He didn't want her to know he was blocked. Not after she'd been so kind to offer her cottage to him.

She led the way to a round, glass-topped table, stopping to yank cushions from a covered box and toss them into a couple of chairs. "Do you want some supper? I think I'm about done for the day."

"Um..." he hesitated for moment, thinking about the entire package of chocolate chip cookies he'd downed throughout the morning.

"No worry if you need to get back to work."

Suddenly he was way too aware of the fact that he needed a shower and a shave. His beard felt scruffy, and his hair was no doubt sticking up in all directions. Shoving his fingers through the tousled mess, he shifted from one foot to the other. "You don't have to feed me. I bought my own groceries. Besides, I don't want to eat up your food."

"Whatever." Sophie shrugged. "It's no biggie—I went to the

farm market this morning, so I made a salad. Cut up some straw-berries and peaches. Opened some cheese and crackers. I don't want to interrupt you, but I have plenty. I thought I'd bring it out here on the patio where it's cooler. You're welcome to join me... or not."

The menu actually sounded really good. It would be the first fresh vegetables and fruit he'd had since he arrived. He was prob-ably on the way to scurvy by now... or was it rickets one got from not eating fresh vegetables and fruit? No, that was from a lack of calcium...

"Henry?"

He was doing it again. Drifting off—a habit that had driven Kristie crazy. He blinked and nodded at Sophie with a sheepish smile. "Well, okay, thanks, if you're sure you don't mind sharing."

"Not at all." Sophie ambled into the kitchen with Henry tagging along behind her. She washed her hands and then reached into the dishwasher for another wine glasses and a plate. He washed his hands too as she picked up a tray of food, and nodded toward a bottle of chilled white wine and the glasses and plates on the counter. "Want to grab that stuff?"

Oh, god—she has wine, and is that brie? He peered over her shoulder as she carried the tray out to the table on the patio and set out plates, napkins, and silverware. *Does she know I've eaten nothing but crap for two weeks?*

Brie was one of his favorites (he *was* from California, after all), and the fruit would be perfect. He sniffed the open wine bottle—apricots and some other crisp, cool essence—it might be tasty.

She lit a couple of citronella candles before she poured wine into the glasses and passed one to him. "To your book." With a warm smile, she tipped her glass toward his.

Grasping the glass, he clinked with her and took a sip of wine.

It still wasn't the time to admit that he hadn't actually written a word since he'd arrived. She'd asked about the book first thing, almost as though she was invested in his success. Admitting he was blocked was simply too humiliating.

"This is great." Henry took another taste. "Frankly, I don't know that much about wine," he confessed.

"I can't believe you were born and raised in California and you don't know about wine. I thought everyone in the state was an expert."

"I come from a big Irish Catholic family of beer drinkers."

"Ah, I see." Sophie grinned as she offered him the plate of cheese and crackers. "Here, try it with the cheese, it's wonderful." He accepted it eagerly, salivating over the brie. She took some herself and added succulent berries and peaches to her plate.

He filled his plate and began eating slowly. Watching Sophie —how much she enjoyed each bite—reminded him of his younger sister, Chloe, who always ate with great relish. The memory brought another wave of homesickness.

Sophie tucked a stray curl behind her ear and took a bite of a strawberry. "Mmmmm, this is so good. Annie's farm stand always has the best produce in the county." Juice ran down her fingers as she took a slice of peach in her hand and nibbled at it. She licked the nectar off with a guilty little smile. "Try the peaches, they're great."

Henry forked up a couple of peach slices—they were fantastic. As he chewed, he continued to eye Sophie. After years of being around women who barely nibbled at their food, it was delightful to watch a woman actually eat. Sophie brought such pleasure to the table, abandoning her fork, using her fingers to pluck crisp lettuce and cucumber slices from her salad bowl, dipping them in a puddle of ranch dressing she'd poured on the side of her plate. She mixed and matched—first fruit, then cheese, a bite of cracker and then salad. Each tidbit was savored. With a blissful sigh, she sipped the white wine between bites. It was a sensual experience simply sharing a meal with her.

That thought surprised him. He'd only ever thought of Sophie as an editor and friend, which made sense because they'd always worked via email and phone. It was an odd relationship—colleagues and friends for years, yet this was the first time they'd even shared a meal. They'd talked frequently and exchanged details about their lives, but they'd never laid eyes on each other until two weeks ago.

Heat rose to his face when Sophie glanced up and caught him staring. "What?" She gave her chin a quick swipe. "Is there something on my face?"

"No. Nothing." He scooped up some more fruit.

"You were staring." She smoothed a hand over her chin again. "I really don't have anything on my face?"

"No, your face is... fine." Her face was great actually—rosy cheeks, full lips, dark brows, and the greenest eyes he'd ever seen. He avoided her gaze, disconcerted about the direction his mind had taken.

"Is your wine okay?"

"It's very good." He took a gulp before shoving a forkful of lettuce into his mouth, then refilled his glass. He already had a slight buzz going from drinking the first glass on an empty stomach. It felt good. Damn good.

Shadows filled the patio as the sun set over the lake. The light from the candles on the table glimmered. They chatted about the area, about the other cottages. As she made him laugh when she described the neighbors and small town life in Willow Bay, he began to loosen up. Pointing out the distant flashing beam from Willow Point, she invited him to walk down the beach to the old lighthouse with her the next morning. He said he'd see how his work was coming. He didn't need her handing him any more excuses to avoid writing.

"Tell me about your novel." She licked salad dressing from her fingers. "Is it a mystery? Political suspense? Stephen King-type horror?"

Henry hesitated a moment. What was she going to think when she found out his book wasn't typical guy fiction? He took a deep breath. "It's a love story actually, based on my great-grandparents."

"You're Nicholas Sparks?" She teased, her green eyes twinkling. "*The Notebook*?"

"Hardly." He gave her a dismissing wave. "More like Louis L'Amour meets Robert James Waller meets... I don't know..." He was at a loss. The wine was loosening his tongue. If this conversation went on much longer, he was going to spill his guts about not being able to write. He opted for humor. "Dr. Seuss?"

"Dr. Seuss?" She laughed. "So like *The Cat in the Hat* goes west, becomes a cowboy, falls in love, but then gets in a shootout on a bridge?"

"Sure. That works." He grinned, reminded of how much he enjoyed her quirky sense of humor and intelligence. "Seriously, my great-grandfather, Henry, for whom I'm named, came out to California for the Gold Rush and ended up starting a newspaper. He met my great-grandmother when she brought him some photographs she'd taken. They were married for sixty years and ran the paper together all that time. Their story's pretty cool and was turning into a good novel—" He took a long slug of wine. "It's an amazing time in California history. The research has been fascinating."

ophie caught the *was*. Past tense. Was he having trouble writing here? How awful if his muse had taken a hike after he came all this way to finish the novel. She drained the wine bottle, dividing the last of the Riesling between them and he downed it in one long gulp. "It sounds interesting," she said. "You going to need an editor?"

"Absholutely," he slurred and his grin was a little crooked. Funny he was getting buzzed from a perfectly harmless Riesling. Apparently, he really *wasn't* much of a wine drinker.

When they finished eating, she cleared away the dishes, while, on slightly unsteady legs, Henry helped her carry things into her cottage. As she set her tray on the counter, he glanced out the window above the sink. "There's that car again."

"What car?" She tugged open the kitchen curtains to peer out into the dusk.

"I saw it the night I got here. You expecting company?"

"No." A strange car was backing out of the parking area between the cottages. The driver wore mirrored sunglasses and his gray hair blew in the breeze from his open window. She flew out the door just in time to see the small car race down the lane in a cloud of dust and black exhaust, gravel spitting from the rear tires.

A shiver passed through her as she watched the speeding car fishtail when it took the corner.

What the hell? No way could it be Frank or Millie Law, the neighbors who'd opened up just a week ago.

Besides, they drove a brand new Prius. Frank had been showing it to her just the other day when she'd walked over to say hello. This was a beat-up, old wreck.

Back inside, Henry was washing plates and clattering silverware in a sink full of soapy water, even though she had a perfectly usable dishwasher.

Sophie took up a tea towel, prepared to dry. "Okay, that was weird."

"What?" Henry flipped on the hot water, rinsed the suds off a couple of forks, and dropped them in the drain basket.

"Oh, nothing." Sophie dried the forks and put them in the drawer. "Probably some idiot tourist got lost. But he spun out and tossed gravel all over the flowers I just planted." For some reason, another chill suddenly passed through her. Sophie went back to the screen door to secure the hook. "Did you say you saw it once before?"

"Yeah." He was focused on scrubbing brie off a plate, his gray hair flopping into his eyes.

She stopped, her hand hovering over a clean plate. "Are you sure it's the same one?"

"Yes. I'm sure." He leaned one hip against the counter and turned to face her, his hands still immersed in the steamy water. "That ancient, beat-up Honda is hard to miss. All that black smoke—it needs an oil change." He handed her another plate. "I'm guessing this is unusual? You don't get a lot of traffic back here?"

"Oh, we get people driving by to check out the cottages or trying to find a way down to the beach, but generally, it's pretty quiet, especially this early in the summer." She dried the plate and put it away. For some reason she couldn't put her finger on, the car bugged her. "There's nothing for sale down here right now though."

"This is really worrying you, isn't it?" Henry stared down at her, his blue eyes darkening with concern. For one inane moment and apropos of nothing at all, Julie's voice echoed in her head, *Nerds can be sexy.*

He *was* a pretty nice-looking guy, even with a couple of days of stubble shadowing his cheeks and his gray hair curling over his collar and falling into his eyes. Oh, he was showing his age and if he'd ever had six-pack abs, they had since softened into a comfortable belly, but Henry Dugan sure looked good up to his elbows in soapy water.

A tingle went through her as warmth flooded her core. What was it about a man doing housework that was kind of a turn-on? Dammit, Julie might be right. She probably did need sex, but not with her best client. Not with a good friend.

No, not with Henry.

CHAPTER 4

"Worrying?" Sophie shook her head as she realized that she was staring at Henry and had lost the thread of the conversation. She really needed to stay in the moment. "Well, maybe a little. What if someone's casing our places? There have been break-ins before. I just wish I'd caught the license plate." Sophie finished drying the dishes and hung the damp towel over the oven door handle. "I guess if they ever come back, I'll try to get it."

Henry pulled the plug from the sink and sprayed away the excess suds and then grinned. "Do you have a Scrabble game up here?" He dried his hands on a paper towel and tossed it in the trashcan by the door.

"I do."

"Well, get it out." He gave her shoulder a gentle shove and turned her in the direction of the living room. "Let's see if all those months of practice with your grandfather will serve you against…" He pointed to himself with both index fingers. "Yes, ladies and gentlemen, the 1983 San Jose State University Scrabble *champion*." Dancing around her like a boxer preparing for a fight, he jabbed his fists upward in a winning gesture. "Whoo hoo!"

His antics made her smile. Not only was he making a sincere effort at taking her mind off the car, obviously he also remembered what she'd told him about the endless Scrabble games she'd played with Papa Leo. She'd always known Henry was a nice person, but tonight, without even trying he was endearing himself even more and she wasn't sure how she felt about that.

"That wine's kinda gotten to you, hasn't it?" she said, heading to the cupboard by the fireplace to dig out the Scrabble game.

"It's good." He nodded. "Is there more?"

"There's another bottle in the fridge." Once again, her mind wandered back to Julie's suggestion that she have a hot summer fling, but was Henry in that context a good idea? What would that make them? Friends with benefits? Did that even work? Or was that one way to completely wreck a perfectly good friendship as well as destroy the working relationship she and Henry shared?

Perhaps she better set Jules to work on finding a single guy for her to experiment on—maybe one of Charlie's colleagues from the hospital. A few years ago, Carrie had complained about Julie's matchmaking with Charlie's golfing buddies. Why not turn Jules loose? But on the other hand, Henry was already here and single and a known quantity and… god, she missed sex. It had been almost a year.

"I'd better wait on the wine. I think I'm going to need my wits about me for this." He plopped into a chair and rubbed his palms together. "Set us up. You're about to see the word master at work."

They settled down at the kitchen table, the game and a battered dictionary between them. As they started to play, Sophie debated letting Henry keep his championship status—he seemed so proud of the title—but the tiles kept coming up in her favor. She beat him soundly in the first round. He took the second round by the skin of his teeth, then gulped a huge glass of water before demanding a tiebreaker. He didn't go for blood, but he played thoughtfully, taking several minutes each turn to form his word and consider his strategy.

At one point, Sophie couldn't resist teasing him. She got up and grabbed the rooster-shaped egg timer from the stove. "Three minutes, my friend," she declared as she set the dial.

"Whose rule is that?" Henry leaned back and crossed his arms over his chest. "This isn't tournament play. What's your rush?" He focused in on his tray of letters again. "You got a hot date later or something?"

"You're too freakin' slow, pal," she grumbled, but grinned at him so he'd know she was kidding. "I could take a nap, check my email, and jog up the beach and back in the time it takes you to make one move." She was thoroughly enjoying the evening, but found it odd that he didn't seem anxious to get back to his writing. He'd been pretty much locked up in his cottage since he'd arrived, and she assumed he'd been on a writing binge. It might be that he just needed a break. She wasn't a writer, so she had no idea how the creative process worked. As an editor, her job came later.

Henry dumped the wooden tiles back into the velvet drawstring bag and shook it at her with a grin. "Okay, this one is for the big win. You ready?"

"I've been ready all night, dude." Sophie chuckled. "Where's this amazing Scrabble guru you keep talking about? Have you used up all your high-point vocabulary over there writing your novel?"

Henry simply gazed at her over the top of his glasses, one brow quirked. "Just draw your letters, okay?"

Sophie reached into the bag just as someone coughed and rattled the hook on the screen door in the utility room.

"Hey in there!" a raspy voice called.

"Who in the world...?" She dropped the bag on the table. It was almost ten o'clock and she didn't recognize the shadowy female figure standing there, a cigarette glowing between her fingers. She hit a switch as she entered the tiny utility room.

Yellow light flooded the back stoop, revealing a tall, plump woman, dressed in frayed jeans and a sweatshirt. Long hair cut in 1970s Farrah-style layers hung past her shoulders. The unnatural coal black color made a stark contrast against her faded Purdue University hoodie. Green eyes were outlined thickly in kohl. Dark red lipstick bled over her lip line. She appeared to be in her late sixties.

"Yes?" Sophie asked, wary enough to leave the hook latched.

"Hey, kid." The acrid scent of tobacco wafted through the screen. "Guess who?"

The hair on the back of Sophie's neck rose. Her spine stiffened and she felt, rather than saw, Henry move closer. "I'm sorry." She thought she recognized the woman, but she couldn't quite place the face. "Do I know you?"

"Damn right, you know me, Miss Sophie Marie." Taking a deep drag on the cigarette, the woman blew the smoke out the corner of her mouth, over her shoulder.

Henry drew nearer, stepping behind Sophie in the small utility room. "Can we help you?" he asked, putting a hand on her shoulder.

"Who the hell are you?" The woman squinted through cigarette smoke and the screen.

Sophie's tension grew as his fingers tightened on her shoulder. With a gasp, she fell back slightly against him and put one hand to her mouth. "Oh, my God. Eva..." Twisting halfway, she gripped his arm. "Henry, it's Eva. It's my... my mother."

"Well, shit, I was kinda hopin' you'd call me Mama." Eva tugged on the door handle. "Let me in, will ya? The moths out here are the size of frickin' dump trucks."

Henry gave Sophie a questioning look. Trembling, she nodded, so he reached around her to unlatch the hook on the screen door.

Eva yanked it open and stalked past them, her dirty flip-flops slapping on the hardwood floor. Pausing in the kitchen long enough to run some water on her cigarette, she dropped it in the sink. Then she stopped by the bar, gazing all around.

"He made a few changes in the last forty-five years." She ran ferocious-looking maroon nails along the granite surface of the countertop. Wandering out into the screened porch, she made a swift tour through the rest of the cottage, peeking into the two bedrooms and the bathroom as she came back down the short hallway. "Took down my Hendrix and Joplin posters, the old bastard." Her grin displayed nicotine-yellowed teeth that seriously needed the services of a dentist. "Probably had a hell of beach fire with all my stuff."

Sophie stayed in the kitchen, holding onto the counter across from the bar for support. Close beside her, Henry wrapped a bracing arm around her shoulders. She sank against him as Eva plunked down on one of the barstools and pulled a crumpled pack of cigarettes out of the battered canvas purse she had slung over her shoulder.

"So did he ever install central air?" She shook out a cigarette and then rummaged through her bag before tossing the purse on the granite counter in disgust. "Shit. Dale must have copped my Bic again. Got a light?"

Sophie was speechless. A trickle of sweat ran down her ribcage, and yet she felt chilled. Her heart pounded. If Henry hadn't been standing next her, practically holding her up, she was sure she would have fainted dead away.

This...woman—who was now a lifetime past the beauty in the picture from Papa Leo's wall—this disgusting, unkempt person was her mother. She was here. Right here. After forty-five years. *Okay, breathe... just breathe.*

Focused on the frayed hood of her mother's sweatshirt, she took several deep breaths.

Eva crossed her legs and gazed expectantly at them, cigarette poised in front of her lips.

"We don't smoke in here," Henry said, rubbing one hand between Sophie's shoulder blades. The comforting gesture told her that he recalled the night a couple of years when she'd shared the story of her mother. She leaned into the contact as he murmured, "Courage. You can do this."

"Of course you don't." The unlit cigarette hit the counter as Eva rolled her eyes. "I always had to go down to the beach for a smoke."

"No," Sophie blurted.

Henry and Eva both started.

"No what, kid?" Eva asked.

"No central air." Breathing had become difficult again. Sophie pulled air in through her nostrils, trying to remember her yoga instructor's words.

In through the nose, out through the mouth. In through the nose... Okay, not really working.

Henry's warm hand on her shoulder was helping, though, so she pressed back against him.

"Oh. Well, that doesn't surprise me—cheap sonuvabitch. Summer I was pregnant with you, it was hotter than the hinges of hell up here. I sweat my ass off in that little room back there." Eva cocked her head toward the bedrooms. "I stayed here until you were born in the fall. September... or October... well anyway, they just wanted to get me outta Podunk, Indiana before all his buds at school and church found out I was knocked up. Mama and I came up the first of May that year, and he showed up when school ended. He wouldn't even let me finish out my sophomore year. Bastard. I missed spring formal."

"September." Sophie straightened up and crossed the kitchen. Tearing off a paper towel, she gingerly picked up the wet, lipstick-stained cigarette butt, wrapped it, and dropped it in the trashcan under the sink. Then she looked Eva straight in the eyes. "I was born September twenty-second."

She's got Papa Leo's green eyes. Like me. Oh god, I've got her eyes.

She dug her teeth into her lower lip to keep it from trembling.

"Yeah, all I remember is it was hot as hell." Eva drummed her long nails on the granite.

"What are you doing here?" Hands curled into fists at her sides, Sophie stood ramrod straight.

Eva gave her a sly smile. "I'm here to get reacquainted with my daughter. I realize it may be a little late to play the mom card, but I—"

"A little late? I'm forty-five years old." Sophie interrupted, inwardly cursing the tremor in her voice. "Excuse me, but again, *why* are you here?" Her blood pressure was rising, her stomach roiling, but at least she was able to speak. All the warm feelings that had been building earlier as she and Henry had shared supper and played Scrabble were gone, replaced by the nauseating premonition that Eva's presence here could mean nothing good.

"I told you, I'm here to get to know my kid." She returned Sophie's hard stare.

"You're about forty-five years too late."

Eva released a frustrated breath. "Look, missy, you can bag the Leopold-T.-Russo attitude, okay? I had enough of that holier-than-thou bullshit when I lived with him. Now, I came up here to try and make friends. But I'm still your mother and I ain't gonna put up with any crap from you, got it?"

"You were never my mother," Sophie replied, her tone as cold as ice. "Sorry, not interested. Go back to Georgia or Florida or wherever it is you currently reside."

"Florida," Eva said, picking up the cigarette again and tapping it on the granite. "We got us a nice little mobile in Venice, 'bout three miles from the beach."

"I couldn't care less." Sophie shoved her hands into the pockets of her jeans. It was the only way she was going to keep from slugging the smug woman lounging on her bar stool. She longed for Papa Leo's wisdom.

What would he do now? Welcome her home as a prodigal? Or turn her away?

Papa Leo would never have turned his own daughter away. But on the other hand, this repulsive creature wasn't the girl he'd lost all those years ago. Was she? Besides, all Sophie's instincts were telling her to beware of her long-lost mother turning up on the doorstep. Those instincts rarely failed her.

Glancing over at Henry, who leaned casually against the counter, she could see all his senses were on point. She took courage from the fact that he was ready to respond at the merest signal from her.

A knock at the back door broke the tense atmosphere. Eva jumped up. "That's probably Dale. He dropped me off while he made a beer run. I didn't know if you had any beer here—can't party on the beach without brewskies." She ran past them to the door, throwing it wide open. "Hey, baby, get in here and see where I grew up."

A scruffy grey-haired man yanked off a pair of mirrored sunglasses. *Why the hell was he wearing sunglasses at night?* His eyes were washed-out silvery grey, lost in the pouchy red flesh of his face as he blinked coming into the brightly lit kitchen.

Another chill passed through Sophie.

Dear God, the guy from the car earlier. She was sure it was him driving. *Had* they been following her? Casing the place?

Her eyes widened as her heart rose to her throat. This wasn't the mother-and-child reunion she'd fantasized about as a little girl —this was disturbing and frightening. She'd never been so confused, yet she was furious at Eva's high-handed manner. She threw Henry a helpless glance.

Toss me a line here, my friend.

Without a moment's hesitation, he stepped in front of the sleazy pair as Dale set the twelve-pack of bottles on the counter by the sink. "Folks." He blocked their path back into the cottage. "It's late and I think it's fair to say this has been... an unexpected turn of events."

"Who in the hell are you?" Eva's voice rose. She peered around Henry's broad body at Sophie. "Who is this clown?"

"I'm Henry Dugan. I'm a friend of Sophie's."

"Great. Move your ass, Henry Dugan." Eva glared up at him while Dale stood meek as a lamb behind her, one hand protecting the beer. She turned her head and said over her shoulder, "Go get the bags out of the car, Dale."

"Bags?" Sophie jerked to attention.

"Yeah, all our stuff's in the car," Eva said, glaring back at Dale. "We'll crash in my old room. We won't bother you two any."

"No." Holding up one hand, Sophie repeated, "No, no, no. You're not staying here. No way."

"Then open the other cottage up for us," Eva replied, belligerence emanating from her like heat from an oven.

"No, it's rented." Sophie moved over to stand next to Henry, almost toe to toe with her mother. With deadly quiet, she found her calm adult voice at last. "Eva, you have no right to come into my home and act as if you belong here. What did you expect to happen tonight? You abandon me when I'm three months old, disappear for years, skip your own mother's funeral, ignore all my calls about Papa Leo being sick, and then miss his funeral, too."

She ticked the list off on her fingers as she enumerated. "And *now* you show up? What's going on in your head?"

"We're outta money," Dale spoke up from behind Eva's back. "We don't got nowhere else to stay."

"Jeezus, Dale." Eva turned on him, her black hair flying around her face. "Didja have to say that?"

Henry leaned away from Eva's whirling hair, as he met Sophie's eyes. Then he pulled his phone out of the pocket of his shorts. "What's the name of that motel I passed down by the farm stand?" he asked, fingers poised over the screen.

"The Hillside?" Sophie's eyes filled with grateful tears, and she put a hand on his back, absorbing some of his confidence with the touch. "Yes, yes. Ask for Joe Pryor, he's the night manager."

"Little Joey Pryor's runnin' the motel now?" Eva's eyes flitted nervously from Henry to Sophie, but she was still cocky. "Is it still as much of a dump as it was when his old man ran it?"

Henry found the number and dialed, keeping his position as guard in the middle of the kitchen. Then he handed his phone to Sophie. Eva and Dale eyed him with suspicion while Sophie spoke to the Joey at the Hillside and made arrangements for them.

"Okay, you've got a room for the night." Without even trying to hide her sigh of relief, she handed the phone back to Henry. "Now go, and tomorrow morning, get on your way back to Florida."

"We ain't done, little girl," Eva sneered as Dale grabbed the beer and headed for the door.

"You're right, we're not done," Sophie replied, glad to be sounding much cooler than she felt. She picked up Eva's purse and handed it to her. "There won't be any done for you and me because we aren't ever getting started." She pointed to the door. "Go."

CHAPTER 5

Eva stared at her for a long moment. Sophie returned the cold look, searching her mother's green eyes for some trace of maternal feeling. Finally, the older woman broke the contact, spun around, and left.

"Evie, did you ask her about the treasure?" Dale had the screen door open and his half-whispered question came into the kitchen loud and clear.

"Christ, Dale, will ya shut the hell up?" Eva snarled, close on his heels. Then they were gone, the screen door slapping shut behind them.

Sophie ran to the door and hooked it, watching them climb awkwardly into a little low convertible parked across the road from the cottage. "Oh, my God!"

"What is it?" Henry hurried to the door to peer out into the darkness over her head.

"Oh shit, I don't believe this." Unhooking the door, she raced out, watching the red taillights disappear in a cloud of dust from the dry gravel lane. "She stole it! That bitch stole it! Shit. Shit. Shit." She stormed back to the stoop, pulling her cell phone out of her pocket.

"Soph?" He craned his neck, peering down the road. "Hey! Wait up!" He followed her into the kitchen. "Is that a vintage Mercedes roadster driving away?"

Furiously scrolling through contact numbers, she nodded and glanced out the window. "Noah?" She gripped her cell phone with both hands. "It's me, Sophie. No, no, I'm okay, but could you run out to your barn and check to see if Papa Leo's car is there?" Glancing up at Henry, she listened. "No, go take a peek, I'll wait." She drew in a frustrated breath. "Noah, I'm pretty sure I'm watching it drive away right now—please go look, okay?"

Henry reached in the fridge, grabbed the bottle of wine, and popped it pretty handily for a guy with limited corkscrew experience. He began opening cupboards, obviously searching for clean glasses. She pointed and he stretched over her to get to the cabinet above her head. Breathing in the warm male scent of him, she didn't even bother to move out of his way. Right then she seriously needed some distraction—she couldn't remember ever being so furious. Thinking about the possibilities with Henry was the only thing keeping her from screaming like a banshee.

If only they could rewind to right before Eva knocked on the door, she'd still be kicking the hot nerd's ass at Scrabble and getting to know him better... maybe a lot better.

Goddamn her.

Henry wished he could hear both sides of Sophie's conversation. He filled the two glasses and handed one to Sophie. She chugged it down like a beer, probably not even tasting it. Her grandfather was probably turning over in his grave. He remembered from one of their many phone conversations that Papa Leo had known and loved wine.

Henry poured more into her glass. "Do you want to tell me

what the hell's going on here? Should we call the cops?" He leaned against the counter, tapping one foot as his impatience and curiosity grew, but she shook her head, focused on her phone call.

"Hang on." She signaled with one hand as she paced in front of the kitchen sink. "Yeah? They cut the lock? Are you kidding me?" Listening silently for a couple of minutes, she let out a long frustrated breath. "Aw, crap. I know that car. No. No, that's okay. Don't call the sheriff. I'll take care of it myself." A moment's pause and then, "No, really. I know where it is. It'll be okay. Yeah, thanks, Noah. I'll call you tomorrow." With a grimace, she tapped the phone off and set it, none too gently, on the counter.

Another long deep sigh from Sophie, and Henry had used up the last of his tolerance. He took her arm and led her to the screened porch, grabbing her glass of wine as they passed the bar.

"Sit," he ordered.

Flopping onto the wicker sofa, she pulled the band from her hair and ran her fingers through the thick mass. With a wan smile, she accepted the glass.

"Okay, what the hell just happened?" He sat next to her. "I feel like I've walked into some bizarre film noir, but I missed the first twenty minutes."

"You know, Henry, if you're a smart guy—and I really think you are a smart guy—you'll get on the Web right now and book a flight back to San Jose." When she took a gulp of wine, her hand shook, and then all of a sudden, she was trembling uncontrollably. "Or–or at least, you should g–go back to the Sandpiper and h–hole up there and w–write."

"Frankly, I'm not feeling very smart right now, so how about you fill me in?" Henry caught her unsteady glass and set it on the trunk in front of the sofa. "You told me once your grandparents raised you because your mother abandoned you as a baby. Apparently your mom decided it was time to make an appearance."

"A–apparently." Sophie's teeth started to chatter and she crossed her arms over her middle.

"God, Soph, hang on." Reaching behind her for the afghan that was tossed over the back of the sofa, he wrapped her up. Then he put his arms around her and hugged her close, rubbing her arm, trying desperately to warm her shivering body with his own.

"S–sorry." Tears glistened in her eyes. "T–too much... dr–drama."

Frightened, he peered into her strained white face. He'd never dealt with anyone who was in shock before.

What the hell do you do for that? Brandy? Whiskey?

Pressing his lips against her hair, he continued the brisk rubdown. "Did Leo have anything stronger than wine around here?"

"B–below the bar."

"Hold tight. I'm going to find something to warm you up." Henry rose and snugged the blanket around her. Less than a minute later, he returned with a bottle of Jameson and two stubby glasses.

Thank God old Leo Russo knew good Irish whiskey as well as wine.

"Here." Pouring a generous measure, he handed it to her. "Drink this... slowly this time."

Accepting the glass, she sipped the amber liquid while Henry poured another even more generous glass for himself and paced the screened porch for a few minutes. "Okay, so that vintage Mercedes is your grandfather's car and she just helped herself to it? And who's Noah?"

"Yup, she took it." Sophie nodded and drank. "F–from Noah's b–barn. He's an old friend of Papa Leo's. Owns...owns the m–marina in town." The trembling was subsiding and she seemed to be relaxing. "It was them in the driveway earlier tonight. N–Noah said they left their old car in place of the Mercedes."

"Not the scabby brown Honda?" Henry frowned as she nodded. "Huh. Well, that solves that mystery. Do you think Dale hotwired the Benz?"

"No, he didn't have to. The keys were on a hook in the barn, but they did break the padlock on the barn door." Calmer now, she stretched out on the sofa and rolled her neck, her face contorted. "Noah said they covered their car with the Mercedes tarp and even replaced the keys with the keys to the Honda. Obviously, she inherited Papa Leo's sense of irony, eh?"

"What are we going to do?" Henry sat back down, and almost automatically lifted her chilled bare feet, and rested them in his lap. The gesture felt oddly familiar in spite of its intimacy, and she didn't pull away.

Rather, she gazed at him over the glass of whiskey. "*We? Really?* You don't want to be involved in this."

"Come on, Soph. Do you seriously think I'd leave you here alone with those two on the loose?" Henry chuckled. "Besides this has way too much story potential. I gotta see how it plays out."

"I hadn't planned on *my* life being *your* summer entertainment. You need to write." Clearly, Sophie's equilibrium had returned. She took another sip of whiskey, set her glass down, and ran her fingers through her hair before she laid her head on the arm of the settee and closed her eyes.

Henry massaged warmth back into her feet as he listened to the waves wash up on the shore far below, grateful she appeared to be calmer. What a bizarre night. He'd been presented with a couple of surprises about his friend and colleague. First, she wasn't the little wren of a librarian he'd expected. Her dark hair and curvaceous body were the opposite of the type of woman he was normally drawn to—case in point, Kristie, the ex-wife from hell, who was a tiny blonde bombshell. Second, although he already knew that Sophie was charming and intelligent and fun to talk to, he saw that she was also strong-minded and able to handle herself. Case in point again, her confrontation with her mother. He shook his head.

Eva Russo. Whew.

Now *there* was a woman who was an entire novel unto herself. *Holy shit...* She could turn into a fascinating character, but unfortunately, there was no place in the current book for her. He itched to reach into his pocket for his notebook and pen, but this wasn't the time.

Finally, the awkwardness he'd been feeling since he'd arrived was gone. By the time they'd finished their meal, the warm, bantering friendship he and Sophie had always shared in their phone calls and emails had returned. He was... comfortable, and that was the biggest surprise of all. Henry was never *comfortable* with women, although he'd spent most of the forty years since adolescence trying to prove otherwise. He always pursued relationships where he could be the bigger, stronger, and yes, the more intelligent partner. He didn't need Freud to point out that he chose ditzy younger chicks to compensate for being a giant geek all through school. It was Psych 101. When GeekSpeak Press took off and women started paying attention to him, well, that was Psych 102 wherein the nerd makes good and suddenly becomes very appealing to the head cheerleader. He knew why he made terrible relationship choices, he just didn't know how to stop himself.

Abruptly, Sophie popped straight up. "Did Dale say something about a treasure?"

"I believe he did. As they were going out the door, I heard him say, 'did you ask her about the treasure?' What treasure?"

"I have no idea." Sophie settled back on the sofa while Henry resumed gently rubbing her feet, letting his fingers work their way up from her instep to her ankle.

"You've never heard anything about a treasure?"

"Nope, never." Her head fell back against the cushion. "Well, I mean there are always stories around here of people diving on old wrecks in the lake and pulling stuff up. But Nonna and Papa Leo didn't dive that I know of. He never talked about finding a treasure."

"Maybe this goes further back than your lifetime." She had the softest skin he'd ever touched, even her feet were soft and god, those painted toenails. He was such a sucker for painted toenails, but only when they were tasteful. Kristie's toes were always neon yellow or blue or god forbid, lime green. The red on Sophie's toes was definitely... Sophie gazed at him from under her lashes obviously waiting for him to explain his cryptic remark.

Focus, Dugan.

"Um... I just mean, maybe Eva knows something you don't," he said, rubbing her ankle and then sliding slowly up her leg.

"I guess that's possible. But I can't imagine that Papa Leo had any secrets from me." Eyes narrowing, she pursed her lips. "Hmm. We could talk to Noah. He might have some ideas." She blinked, then let her lids drop closed. "But not tonight... I can't think anymore. I'll think about it tomorrow." Goose bumps rose on her calf under his kneading fingers. "Lord, Dugan, you have magical hands, has anyone ever told you that?"

One hand drifted higher to just below her knee, but he stopped himself before patting her brusquely and setting her feet aside to stand up. "Come on, Scarlett O'Hara, you're exhausted. I'm going back and try to get some work done. Lock up behind me, okay?"

Sophie rose and followed him to the door. When he turned, the look of confusion in her eyes nearly did him in.

"Henry—" She seemed so forlorn and something else. Something in her expression that he couldn't define, but it made him want to take her in his arms, stay with her, protect her...

No, better get out now. "You've got my number handy, right?"

"I'll put you on speed dial." The look was gone, replaced with a wry smile as she held up her cell phone.

He chucked her under the chin. "Lock up."

CHAPTER 6

"I'm glad you wanted to come to breakfast." Sophie greeted Henry as she opened the screen porch door and offered a wide welcoming gesture. "How'd you sleep?"

"Great after I wrote for a couple of hours." Henry gave her a lopsided smile as they headed for the kitchen. "Confession? I've been blocked. Haven't written a word since I got here, not even in my journal. But last night, I actually wrote and man, it felt... amazing."

"You've been *blocked*?" His unabashed honesty as well as his frank gaze stopped her dead in her tracks. "Really? Oh, Henry, I'm so sorry! Was coming here a bad idea?"

"Coming here was a fantastic idea." He grinned, and that grin made butterflies flutter in her belly.

He looked darn good in a navy polo shirt and jeans with his feet shoved into worn leather sandals and his hair soft and brushed back off his forehead. She'd put extra effort into herself today when she'd chosen crisp white capris and a red-and-white-striped boat-neck top. A bit of makeup set off her green eyes and the new haircut she'd gotten made her feel sassy. She hoped he would notice, but mostly, she was going to need all the confidence she could muster if she intended to repossess the Mercedes.

She was glad he'd slept, but she sure hadn't. She'd spent the night stewing—involved in a game of mental and emotional volleyball that had started even before Eva showed up and was still going on in her head this morning. Those bouncing thoughts were the reason she'd texted him to join her for breakfast. The easy, comfortable rapport they'd always shared was in full force last night, but the vulnerability she'd shown after Eva's visit and his unselfconscious, rather intimate response unnerved her. She might need sex, but she sure didn't want another man in her life right now, despite the tingles his hands on her feet sent through her.

He had to have sensed the pull between them—it was out there. Hell, he even looked like he wanted to kiss her when he left last night, and she would've let him, dammit. Maybe it would be fun. But pursuing a friends-with-benefits discussion with Henry was going to have to wait. This morning, she needed to get her car back. Breakfast was her attempt to restore some equilibrium to their relationship.

"I've got coffee and bagels and fruit and yogurt."

Their eyes met and held for a moment before he shook his head and plopped into a chair at the table. "I can't tell you how much I'm looking forward to something besides Cheerios for breakfast." He seemed to relax as he accepted a mug of steaming coffee from her and smeared a toasted bagel with cream cheese. "I should've done more shopping I guess, but I just couldn't get motivated to cook. This morning, I'm starving."

Their feet touched under the table as they ate fruit and bagels with cream cheese and jam. Sophie watched Henry devour the first bagel and then get up and pop another one into the toaster. She couldn't help it—a glow warmed her heart at how perfectly at ease he was here.

He glanced back over his broad shoulder. "You want another one?" The package dangled from his fingers.

"I'm good, thanks. I'm going to have some yogurt and more berries."

He sat back down with the hot bagel. "Okay. What are we going to do about Eva?"

"We?" Heat suffused her cheeks when she realized how she sounded. Her gaze dropped to her plate. "I mean, I appreciate your thinking you want to help me out, but honestly, I meant what I said last night. You don't have to get involved in this. I'll handle it." She gave him a smile. "Last night... last night was so much fun and I hope we can... um... well, you know, do it again, but—"

"Stay out of your personal life?" He dropped the bagel on the plate in front of him. His furrowed brow and closed expression told her he was hurt.

"That's not what I'm saying."

"Sounds like it to me." With a quick frustrated swipe, he smeared more cream cheese on the toasted bagel.

"You're the one who said you needed peace and solitude."

"But aren't we friends?" Henry's eyes shot navy sparks. "Helping you with Eva is part of being a friend."

After hesitating for a few seconds, Sophie nodded. "Okay. Thanks." Should she confess her fear that allowing him into the new chaos of her mother's sudden appearance in her life felt rather like a relationship to her? This was deeply personal, and she didn't want to fall for Henry. As kind as he was, it would be so easy.

Suddenly, sitting across the breakfast table from him was way too cozy. Maybe it was a mistake to invite him over. How was he reading the gesture? For all her bravado overnight as she'd tossed and turned and considered a friends-with-benefits deal with him, she had no experience with casual sex. Even if Jules was convinced that was exactly what she needed this summer. But was it? Besides who was Jules to talk? She fell in love with the first man she had sex with after her husband died, and they were currently in a very serious relationship.

"Good." Henry picked up the bagel and took a big bite. They ate in silence for a few minutes before he asked hesitantly, "How old was Eva when she left?"

"Sixteen." Sophie's response was clipped. "Too bad for her, she never made it to Woodstock, which was her plan, according to Papa Leo, when she was about to deliver me. She didn't miss Altamont, though. She left when I was three months old—most likely in a VW microbus with peace symbols and rainbows painted on it."

"She was a *hippie*?"

"She wanted to be." Sophie snorted a laugh. "Eva was born almost too late to pull it off. I'm sure she lied about her age when she got to California."

"A flower child, huh?" Henry teased, clearly attempting to lighten the mood. "'Turn on, tune in, drop out'?"

"Well, not too far out." Sophie rolled her eyes. "She made sure Papa Leo and Nonna knew where to send the checks."

"Tell me about this Noah guy."

"He and Papa Leo were friends long before my time, but from what I understand, Papa Leo invested in Noah's marina. He was a boat mechanic after high school and when the previous owner wanted to sell, Noah came to Papa for help to buy the old guy out. He's a few years older than Eva."

"Sounds like your Papa Leo was a very generous man."

"He was." The pang in Sophie's heart wasn't as sharp as usual. Maybe she was finally healing. "Here's my plan, tell me what you think." Setting her chin on her palm, she gave him a shy smile. "If you'll go with me, we can go to Noah's and pick up the

Honda. If I can stand to get into it, I'll drive it to the Hillside while you follow me in the Jeep. We'll drop it off, rescue the Mercedes, and bring it back here with us. Hopefully this operation will require no more contact with Eva and Dale than it takes to get keys from them."

"Okay," Henry mumbled around a mouthful of bagel before he swallowed. "And because I'm such a good friend, *I'll* drive the Honda, so your delicate sensibilities won't be offended by whatever might be growing in it."

His wink and crooked smile sent a rush of heat to her core. *Goddammit!* She may as well bow to the inevitable. She was a horny old broad, and Henry Dugan was here, probably hers for the taking. How did this happen? If she didn't know better, she'd swear Julie had set this whole thing up to get her laid. *Grrrr.* "You *are* a good friend, thank you."

They ate in silence for a few minutes with Henry getting up to refill both their coffee cups, handing her the carton of half-and-half as though they'd been sharing breakfast together for years. Tension was building inside Sophie at the thought of confronting Eva. Anxiety tightened the muscles of her shoulders and neck. Her mind tumbled back to the night before and Eva's disturbing appearance.

"Hey?" she said. "What *do* you think Dale meant last night about a treasure?"

"Dunno. What do you think?"

"Why would Eva think there's a treasure?" She mentally sifted through the memories stored up from all the years of living with her grandparents. "Papa Leo never mentioned anything like that to me. Truly. Although, you know... There are lots of stories about shipwrecks up here. Somewhere around here, there's a map..." With a snap of her fingers, she slid out of her chair.

Padding barefoot into the living room, she rooted around in

the built-in cabinets and drawers on either side of the big stone fireplace. "Ah, here we go." She carried a large rolled piece of paper to the table. "Look at this. It's a map of most of the wrecks in Lake Michigan—there are literally hundreds of them in the Great Lakes." Unrolling the map, she set the bowl of fruit on one end and the pitcher of orange juice on the other.

Henry shoved his plate aside and peered at the diagram of Lake Michigan. There were dozens of red and black dots marked at various longitudes and latitudes. "These are all shipwrecks?" He traced the dots with his finger, following them down the coastline.

"Yup, and also planes that went down." Sophie pointed to Willow Bay on the map. "A ship called the Westmorland went down in the 1850s right near here. In fact, shipwrecks are actually a tourist attraction up here. You can go on diving expeditions to see some of the wrecks." She plunked down into her chair. "Come to think of it, Papa Leo was fascinated by shipwreck history. He has a shelf full of books about them over there. He volunteered every summer as a docent at Willow Point lighthouse. Loved to tell tourists about the shipwrecks and the lighthouse."

"But you say he didn't dive on the wrecks?"

"Not that I know of... unless like you say, maybe when he was younger." The old map started curling up on one unweighted corner. She smoothed it absently, trying to remember if her grandfather had ever mentioned diving to her. "Noah would know. We should ask him."

"Come on." Henry stood and started stacking dishes. "Let's clean up and get going. We'll rescue the Mercedes and then maybe we can go by Noah's and talk to him about the whole treasure thing, okay?"

"But you need to write... I don't want to keep you from your work."

"Trust me, I'm writing." Henry was at the sink, rinsing bowls and plates before drying his hands on a tea towel. "We should probably do the car thing early, before Eva and Dale have a chance to get up and get going. Let's roll, okay?"

"So now what? Are we just going to stand here in the parking lot until they wake up and come out?" Henry looked down into Sophie's face as she leaned against the door of her car, arms crossed, staring moodily at the Mercedes parked in front of Room 17 at the Hillside Motel.

Eva had been wrong about the Hillside—it was a very clean, homey motel with long low buildings, well-kept flowerbeds, and shady trees. Henry had no doubt that she and Dale had spent a comfortable night here.

His gaze followed Sophie's to the Mercedes roadster, a red 190 SL with a black soft top that appeared to be an early 1960s-era automobile. He'd be able to tell when he saw the front of it. His father was an antique car buff and had taken Henry and his brothers to car shows all over the Bay area and central coast. He'd picked up enough knowledge to know this was a valuable classic car.

How the hell did a college history professor afford a ride like this? Back in the sixties, it would have been pricey, but today, in good condition, a collector would probably pay upwards of seventy grand for it and consider it a deal. From here, the car looked mint. "Soph?"

Taking a deep breath, she straightened up. "Okay, let's do it." She strode toward the car, peering in, no doubt checking to see if Eva had left the keys in it. But it was locked up tight, so Sophie knocked briskly on the door. No answer. Then she pounded with a fist. "Eva? Wake up."

A moment later, a scantily clad Eva yanked the door open. "What the hell...?" She squinted in the morning sun. "Oh, it's you. Hang on." She disappeared for a minute before shoving the door wider with her hip as she tied a faded cotton robe around her plump middle. "What time is it?" she asked with an exaggerated yawn.

Sophie ignored the question and dangled the Honda keys from one finger. "I brought your car back. May I have the keys to the Mercedes, please?"

"No. It's mine." Eva rubbed her face, weathered with lines and creases in her leathery skin that made her seem much older than her sixty-one years. It was obvious to Henry that she'd lived hard.

"How do you figure that?" Sophie folded her arms under her breasts and glared at Eva.

"He told me I could have it when I graduated. I'm here to pick up my property, that's all."

"Really? Last night, you said you came to get to know your daughter," Henry observed from his position behind Sophie. Eva glared at him.

"Doesn't matter what Papa Leo told you forty-five years ago," Sophie replied through gritted teeth. She glanced back at Henry.

He leaned against the front of the Mercedes, his thumbs hooked in the pockets of his jeans, and hoped he looked matter-of-fact enough Eva would realize they meant business.

"The car belongs to me," Sophie insisted. "Papa Leo left it to me in his will. If you want to contest the will, I'll give you the name of his attorney. In the meantime, give me the keys and we'll be on our way."

Dale suddenly appeared behind Eva, clad only in a faded pair of striped boxers, his gaunt chest practically concave and covered in gray hair, his eyes heavy with sleep. "What's up?"

"They want the car."

Dale stared groggily and then blinked and hauled Eva inside. "Hang on," he said and shut the door in their faces.

"That's interesting," Henry said as Sophie backed up and stood next to him. He could feel her trembling. "What do you suppose he's up to?"

"Who knows?" She tugged her hair into a ponytail and then released it in a gesture he already recognized as her stress reliever. "Thanks for coming with me."

He smiled down at her. "I wouldn't have missed it. It's probably just a technicality, but I'm betting she never graduated from high school, so you have that going for you, too." He winked as the knob on the door turned.

"Okay," Eva said as she opened the door. "See that restaurant over there?" She jabbed a finger toward a retro steel building across the street that reminded Henry of an old diner. "We'll meet you there in fifteen minutes." She started to shut the door.

Sophie put her hand on it. "Eva, wait."

But Eva slammed the door so fast if Sophie hadn't pulled her hand back, it would have snapped closed on her fingers.

"Crap." She turned to Henry. "Crap. Crap."

"Come on," he said, inclining his head toward the cars. "We'll park the Honda so close beside the Mercedes they won't be able to get the door open and then we'll back your car in the same way on the other side." Feeling pretty clever, he grinned down at her, sauntered to the front of the little sports car, and lifted the hood. "Here, I can fix it so they can't start it."

Using the Honda's ignition key and a clean tissue Sophie produced from her pocket, he removed a battery cable, then dropped the hood with a bang. Sophie moved her Jeep close beside the Mercedes, while Henry parked the Honda within six inches of the driver's door.

Henry had to admit this was getting more and more fascinating. It could turn out to be a hell of a story. Once again, he wished he dared pull out little black memo book he always carried, but it would've been tacky to start taking notes in front of Sophie. However, he allowed the writer to kick in, already building characters in his head as they walked across the road to wait for Eva and Dale.

CHAPTER 7

Twenty endless minutes later, Eva and Dale wandered into the diner and plunked down in the booth across from Henry and Sophie. Eva had tied her hair up and applied the same heavy black eyeliner she'd worn the night before. She wore a short skirt and a tank top, revealing her considerable cleavage. Sophie drew her lips into a grim line when Henry's eyes widened as Eva leaned over to tap the table in front of them.

"Okay, kid." Stale tobacco odor wafted on Eva's words. "Here's the deal."

"I'm not dealing with you." The slow burn was returning. Sophie blew out a frustrated breath. "Give me my car keys or I call the cops."

"Will ya just listen for a second?" Eva's voice was still gravelly. "Dale, go get us some coffee."

"Eva, no—" A touch on her leg stopped Sophie's protest.

"Soph, hang on," Henry said. "Why don't we listen to what she has to say?"

"Henry…" What the hell was he thinking? She just wanted to get as far away from them as fast as she could.

He put his arm over the back of the booth and tugged her closer on the seat. "Let's see what she wants. It'll be okay," he whispered, his lips close to her ear. Louder he said, "What's the deal, Eva?"

"Is this guy your fiancé or boyfriend or what?" Eva groped in her purse, pulling out a new pack of cigarettes.

"Just talk, will you?" Sophie jerked her head toward the sign above the door. "There's no smoking in here."

"Shit." Dropping the unopened pack back in her bag, Eva twisted in her seat. "Where the hell's Dale with my coffee?"

"Eva..."

"Okay, okay. First off, I already talked to that sonuvabitch lawyer down in Indiana." Her dark red lip curled. "He told me that except for the five large he sent me, you got everything, right down to the last of roll of toilet paper and the old bastard's big baggy boxer shorts."

Insides roiling, Sophie struggled to remain passive as Eva grabbed a mug from Dale, who'd appeared at the table with coffee and donuts on a tray.

Three creamers and two sugars later, she took a long sip and then continued. "We may have had our trouble, but he always took care of me, kid. Whenever I needed cash, he sent it. So how I figure it is... well... he didn't ever disown me, so I think I deserve some of the estate."

"Oh, you do, do you?" Sophie folded her hands in front of her, feeling rather proud of the fact that she hadn't yet come across the table at her mother. But Eva was seriously pushing her luck.

"Yes, I do." Eva sounded bold, but her gaze flitted back and forth from Sophie to Henry, clearly avoiding eye contact.

"So what? You want me to give you the car?"

"Um... maybe—" She glared at Dale, who'd elbowed her, none too gently, in the side. "Goddammit, Dale!"

"If not the car, then what?" Henry asked, while Sophie gave him a hard stare, simmering at his presumption. Was he going to try to make a deal with these two? Surely he wasn't trying to get her to agree to give them anything.

"Did the old man ever talk to you about a treasure?" Leaning across the table, Dale gave the question a behind-the-hand, sly kind of read.

Eva let out a sigh of disgust.

He glared at her. "Well, hell, Evie, you're going all the way 'round Robin Hood's barn with this thing. Why not just come out and ask her?"

"No." Sophie squared her shoulders and set her jaw.

"That's why, you asshole." Eva punched Dale on the arm before she turned back to her daughter. "Did it ever occur to you, little miss princess, that Leo Russo lived way beyond the pay grade of a college history professor?" When Sophie only stared impassively, Eva enumerated, waving her talons. "He drove fancy cars, had a library full of first edition books, and drank expensive wine. He never had a mortgage payment, either up here or back home. He and Mom went on hotshot vacations to New York and Hawaii and all over frickin' Europe, and Mom never worked a day in her life." She took another long pull of coffee.

Sophie swallowed hard, wishing she had ordered a cup of coffee, just so she'd have something to wrap her hands around to keep them from trembling. What bullshit that her mother turned her stomach inside out. She was the one with right on her side, not Eva. She glanced down at her fingers, which were beginning to hurt from gripping them so tightly.

"I know for a fact his parents didn't have no dough—they sank everything they ever had into those ratty cottages. And Mom was an orphan."

"Why don't you at least use his name once in a while?" Sophie couldn't resist baiting her mother. Somehow it made her feel calmer and she unclenched her hands and dropped them into her lap.

"Listen to me, missy." One maroon nail jabbed the air in front of Sophie's nose. "That old bastard—" Her jaw snapped shut as Sophie scooted across the seat, preparing to leave. "Okay, okay. Just stay here for a minute."

"Where's this going, Eva?" Sophie shifted back into the seat, moving closer to Henry.

Eva didn't even trying to hide her scorn. "*Father* donated thousands to restoring that moldy old lighthouse. Spent every summer of my teenage years up here workin' his ass off at that godforsaken place. Go look. His name is listed as one of their primary donors... and if you don't believe me, ask Noah Dixon. Hell, he wouldn't be in business today if it wasn't for the shot of cash Dad gave him when old man Brown sold out."

All three of them jumped when Eva whacked her fist on the table. "Where did the money come from?" The question came out in a sneer, as she slanted in. "Where did all the goddammed money come from? Not from teaching in a tiny college in Podunk, Indiana, I can guaran-frickin'-tee you that!"

With a grimace, Sophie looked up at Henry, who was watching her, one brow raised. Dale took a big bite out of a donut, and powdered sugar snowed down all over the table in front of him. Sighing, Eva pulled a handful of napkins out of the holder on the table and threw them at him.

"Where do *you* think the money came from?" Henry asked the question when Sophie didn't.

"Treasure!" Dale said around a mouthful of donut. "Ouch! Dammit, Evie!" He rubbed his arm where Eva had punched him again. "What the fuck?"

"Okay...here's what I think." Vinyl creaked as Eva settled back into the booth with a sideways frown at Dale. "He found something—a treasure—and hid it. Used it slow so no one would know he had it." The look of triumph in her mother's eyes sent a chill down Sophie's spine. "Kid, he dove on wrecks all the time when I was a little girl. Later, he paid Noah to go with him. He was always draggin' stuff home from those dives. Old dishes, pieces of metal, crap mostly. Where do you think all that shit in the cottages came from? All those pieces of pottery and the bottles and stuff?"

"I guess I thought he picked it all up on the beach. You know how stuff washes ashore after a storm." Sophie gave an irritated sigh. "It's always been there. I never thought about it."

"Maybe you better get curious." Eyes alight, Eva dug in her purse. "Once he gave me an old coin he found. Look." She pulled out her wallet, brought out a worn copper coin, and set it on the table. "He found this when he was diving up by South Manitou the summer I was twelve."

Henry picked up the coin, holding it to the light for Sophie to see. It was larger than a modern-day penny and so worn you could barely see the shape of a woman's head. The only writing left on the front was United States of America and the first two numbers of a year in the 1800s. The words One Cent showed faintly on the back. He handed it to Sophie, who glanced at it before she set it back on the table.

"Eva, there's no treasure," Sophie said. "Okay, he found a coin. What of it? Papa Leo never mentioned a treasure to me. Not once."

"I think he had some source of income besides his teaching money," Eva declared before taking a big bite of jelly donut, catching the jelly with her tongue as it dripped out.

"No. He did not." Sophie frowned as she watched her mother eat. "Now, the facts are my grandfather didn't leave you anything in his will and I'm not giving you that car. I think we're done here." She held out her hand. "The keys, please."

"What am I supposed to do?" Eva whined after a long

moment's stare-down with her daughter. "I don't even have enough money to make it back to Florida."

Sophie sat still for a minute and then pulled her wallet out of her purse. Yanking several bills from one zippered pocket, she tossed them on the table. "Here, this is all the cash I have on me. Take it, give me the keys to the Mercedes, and get the hell out of my life."

"There's over two hundred bucks there!" Dale reached for it, but Eva grabbed it first.

"Two hundred and seventy-five dollars, to be exact." It was the emergency money she kept in her wallet when she traveled— thank god she hadn't removed it yet. It was a small price to pay to get Eva and creepy Dale out of her life. With that, Sophie slid across the seat and stood up. Henry was close behind her. "Consider it the final payment from your father." She held out her hand. "The keys?"

Casting a sidelong glance at Eva, Dale dropped the Mercedes keys into her palm.

Sophie laid the keys to the Honda on the table. "Goodbye, Eva."

Henry hurried to catch up with Sophie as she marched away from the diner. He could practically see the steam coming out of her ears, but damn, was she ever magnificent in there. Kept her cool and walked out on the best exit line ever, a simple *goodbye*. Perfect. Elegant. Right to the point. He hadn't needed to say a word as he followed her out of the diner. He had no idea where this story was headed, but he was definitely making notes as soon as he got into whichever vehicle he was driving home. Secretly, he hoped she'd toss him the Mercedes keys, but either car was fine.

Unexpectedly, she stopped dead in the middle of the motel parking lot, and he nearly smacked into her as he composed narrative in his head. Her hands fisted at her sides as her shoulders shook, and when she dropped her head, her hair fell forward on her neck. "God, Sophie!" Henry steadied himself with his hands on her back. "Are you okay?"

Her breathing was uneven and when she lifted her head, her cheeks were bright red. Tears shimmered in her eyes. "I cannot believe her." The words came out a choked sob.

"Awww, Soph." Without a second thought, Henry pulled her into his arms, one hand on her waist, the other holding her head. "I'm so sorry."

"That was my mother, Henry. My *mother*!" She cried quietly into his shirt while he continued to rub her back.

Unsure of what the appropriate comforting words would be best, he simply held her and let her cry out what had to be a maelstrom of emotion. As she wept, he tried to figure out why Sophie's catharsis seemed so different from Kristie's drama-laden hysteria. What made one woman's tears touch his heart while another's only made him want to flee far and fast? He stroked her back and pressed his lips to her forehead.

"I–I keep thinking, w–what would Papa Leo do, you know?" She sniffled and rubbed her cheek on his shoulder.

He lifted her chin. "When he died, you told me he left her some cash in his will, right?"

She blinked and nodded, licking at the tears that dripped down her cheek and onto her lips.

"Then I think he already did whatever he would do in this situation, don't you?" It was a long shot, an answer way outside the emotionality of the situation, but he hoped the logic would appeal to her. "Not to take anything away from your own personal charm, my friend, but I'm fairly sure money's her motive for turning up out of the blue."

"I guess." She rested her forehead on his chest. For that brief instant, her hair brushed his chin, and he caught a subtle scent of flowers and... peaches? Did they make peach-scented shampoo? "I mean, obviously, I know that's why she's here. It's just disheartening as hell to realize *she's* all the family I have left in the world."

"I imagine it is, Soph, but cliché as it is to say, you can't choose your relatives."

"Ain't it the truth?" When she stepped back, he released her reluctantly, then reached into his pocket, pulled out a clean white handkerchief, and pressed it into her hand.

She unfolded it partway and looked up at him, one brow arched. "A cotton handkerchief. Really? Who carries handkerchiefs anymore? What is this—1954?" The twinkle in her green eyes assured him she was only teasing.

"Go ahead, make fun." He held up both hands. "I realize my brothers and I are probably the only males on the planet under the age of eighty who carry handkerchiefs, but it was ingrained in us at a young age. Grandma Dugan still irons all of them every Tuesday—and she still expects us to have a clean one at a moment's notice, so we do."

Relieved that the tears were disappearing, he winked at her, stooped over an imaginary cane, and rasped in a shaky voice, "And by the way, girlie, can I interest you in a peppermint? I have some here in my pocket—they might have a little lint on them..."

"You're more than a little crazy, you know that?" Sophie giggled through her tears, wiped her eyes carefully, and even blew her nose. "Thank you." She tucked the square of cotton into her pocket. "I'll wash this and get it back to you, ASAP. But I probably won't iron it."

"Hey, you'd better or I'll sic Grandma Dugan on you."

"Thanks for letting me cry on your shoulder, Henry."

"Anytime, Soph. Anytime." He patted her shoulder and then

extended one hand toward the cars in front of them. "Okay, which car do you want me to drive home?"

To his delight, she didn't even hesitate before she tossed him the keys to the Mercedes. "Have fun." Without so much as a backward glance toward the diner, she straightened her shoulders and marched to the Jeep.

CHAPTER 8

"This place is huge." Henry drew several deep lungsful of air, slowed his pace and let Sophie get ahead as they stepped up on the wooden docks of Dixon's Marina, which did take up a good piece of the north end of Willow Bay. He casually perused the harbor as he caught his breath—no sense in letting her see how out of shape he was. The trip up the beach wasn't as far as it sounded when Sophie first suggested walking to town, but he *was* a tiny bit winded. He seriously needed to get more exercise. His plans to jog on the beach every morning while he was in Michigan somehow got derailed with the frustration of writer's block.

"Noah and Margie have owned it ever since I can remember." Sophie glanced over her shoulder, then stopped while he caught up to her. "When I was a teenager, I used to work at the bait shop now and then, selling night crawlers, bee moths, and minnows." She gave him a grin. "Kept me in movies and milkshakes and lip gloss. There aren't many boats here now, but they get a lot of summer boaters stopping for a night or two, especially when the yacht races are going on. Chicago Yacht Club has a big race from Chicago to Mackinac Island every year in July."

"No kidding? I'll bet that's cool." Henry's breathing had evened out, thank god, so he no longer sounded like a wheezy old fart. *Jesus!* If she noticed, she graciously didn't mention it.

"Yeah, it is. The Mac's been going on for over a hundred years. Noah's marina is a port in a storm if the yachts have to hunker down during bad weather, but otherwise, they sail all day and all night for over three hundred miles." Her love of the area was written all over her face. Willow Bay certainly suited her.

He followed her up to an old Dutch Colonial house perched at the top of the hill. The view from the wide porch was spectacular, and he pulled his notebook out of the pocket of his jeans to jot down a few notes about the race and his impressions of the harbor as she pulled open the screen door and called in.

"Eva's back again, eh? And she's still looking for a treasure." Noah Dixon shook his head as he dropped down next to his wife in the wicker swing on his own front porch. "She's a piece o' work, isn't she?"

Sophie sat in the big wicker rocker, and Henry settled on the settee next to her, already feeling at home with the Dixons. Wiry, bewhiskered Noah and his tall, rail-thin wife Margie had welcomed him like an old friend when Sophie made introductions. Margie laid a tray of cookies and lemonade on the low table between them, and smiling slyly, mentioned that she had something stronger to tip into the ice-cold beverage if he was interested. Taking his cue from Sophie, Henry declined and reached for a cookie.

"Understatement of the year." Margie rolled her eyes and elbowed her husband gently in the ribs. "She was younger than us, but she chased after Noah every summer from the time she was in junior high and—"

"I'm sure that's got nothin' to do with what our girl's here to talk about, Margie," Noah interrupted. "This isn't the first time she's been up here, Soph. She's showed up several times over the years. Last time was right after Leo died. When she couldn't get into the Firefly, she came over here looking for a spare key."

"Why didn't you tell me about this?"

Noah shrugged. "I didn't want to worry you with it. You had enough on your plate getting things settled in Indiana. I just sent her on her way. The times before, I called Leo and he wired money for me to give her."

"I can't believe this." Sophie's scowled. "Is she crazy, Noah? Is there a treasure?"

Noah sat silent for a few minutes, sipping lemonade while Sophie stared at him. Henry could almost see the wheels turning in the older man's head.

"Well, there was... something... maybe... I don't know for sure," Noah hedged with a quick glance at Henry before he leaned forward, his hands clasped between his knees. "As far back as the fifties, my dad and Leo dove on wrecks all along here. Brought up all kinds of crap. In the early sixties, once I got to be about fifteen and learned to use the scuba equipment, they let me dive with them sometimes. That was before Dad died. A lot of the stuff we brought up is in the glass cases at the lighthouse. Some of it's up in the Maritime Museum at Sleeping Bear. But a good bit of it ended up in the trash." He shook his head. "Mostly 'cause that's what it was—nothin' but trash."

"Eva showed us a coin that she said Papa Leo gave her," Sophie said. "It was just an old copper one-cent piece. Historic, maybe, but not particularly valuable. Is that why she thinks there's a treasure?"

"Maybe. Dunno for sure." Noah stared out over the docks, clearly lost in thought.

Henry followed his gaze. The afternoon sun lying low in the

sky painted the horizon all shades of red and orange. He was dying to ask Noah how much Sophie's grandfather had invested to help him make the marina the very successful enterprise it was today. He tried to think of a diplomatic way to phrase the question when Noah spoke again.

"Okay. I think he *did* find something. I'm damned if I know what it is... or was, but his lifestyle sorta changed a couple of years before you were born, 'bout the time Eva got to be a teenager. Not big changes, but noticeable ones if you knew him. He bought nicer cars and took Gina on fancy vacations. That was Sophie's grandma," he explained in an aside to Henry. "Then they started having problems with Eva. Leo and Gina tried everything, but she just wouldn't stay on the porch, you know what I mean? Summers, she ran around with the bad kids, always smoking, drinking, breaking into locked-up cottages to party. God, she was a wild child."

He shook his head before focusing his gaze on Sophie. "Anyway, after you were born and Eva ran off, Leo stopped diving. I think it was because he and Gina had to look after you."

"Papa Leo never talked to me about diving. Never." Sophie's teeth worried her lower lip. "I mean, he told me stories about people finding shipwrecks in the lake. I loved hearing him do his spiel down at the lighthouse—he was great at it. But he never said a word about diving himself."

The swing creaked as Margie and Noah rocked silently for a moment. "He never mentioned anything?" Margie asked. "Not even before he passed?"

Sophie lifted her hair off her neck, holding it atop her head for a moment before letting it fall over her shoulders again. She shook her head slowly and then looked at Henry, almost as if she needed some kind of validation. Was she remembering something that might be significant? He nodded and she continued, hesitantly, "There was one time he tried to tell me something. It seemed really urgent, but he started coughing and he couldn't talk. I gave him his meds to calm him down and he went to sleep. He never spoke again. He—" She swallowed hard and Henry, without even considering what the Dixons might make of his gesture, put his hand over hers on the arm of the chair. She laced her fingers with his. "He died that night."

By the time they left the marina, an exhausted and confused Sophie only wanted to get home. It took all her concentration to walk and not leave Henry lagging behind. The pointless conversation with the Dixons replayed in her mind. Noah hadn't had any more idea of what Eva was talking about than Sophie, but he did set her to wondering about Papa Leo's finances.

She'd grown up in a modest house close to campus, nothing fancy, but Papa Leo had always driven very nice cars, including the Mercedes. He'd paid for her college education all the way through grad school—she'd never had to take out a student loan. But she'd had jobs from the time she turned sixteen and covered her own personal expenses by working for minimum wage throughout her school years. They did take expensive vacations to Europe and Hawaii and other exotic locales. Sophie's childhood had been full of rich and exciting experiences, both in the U.S. and abroad.

It never occurred to her to ask Papa Leo about his finances. When he got sick and she moved into the house to help him, he added her to his bank accounts and gave her power of attorney. After Tom left and she'd moved back home with Papa Leo, she used her own money to pay the household expenses because she worried that she would need her grandfather's money for his care.

"You're awfully quiet." Henry observed as they reached the beach steps up to the cottages. "What are you thinking about?"

"Papa Leo and money." Sophie gave him a smile. They'd walked more leisurely this time, giving her a chance to let the knot in her stomach unravel just a bit, plus it seemed easier for Henry. Even though he'd tried not to show that the he'd been a little bit winded earlier, she'd noticed and it kind of surprised her. Hadn't he mentioned being a jogger back in San Jose? Maybe he hadn't done any running since he'd been here.

"What about his money?" Henry stopped at the bottom of the steps and she wondered if he was dreading the climb.

She turned to him in the circle of light from the sodium vapor lamp next to the stairs. "His will was straightforward, no surprises. I'd been handling his finances for a couple of years, so I knew what to expect. When I was growing up, we didn't live an extravagant life, even though we did do a lot of traveling, but—" She paused, unsure how to continue without sounding like a spoiled child. "I never thought about where the money came from. Should I have? I mean, even when I saw the size of his pension checks, I didn't stop to consider how he could afford expensive wine and cars and trips. He bought me a brand new car when I graduated from high school and another one when I got my Masters. I have a chest full of very nice jewelry that was Nonna's as well as some pieces he gave me for birthdays and Christmas."

"Why would you wonder? If things had always been that way, I mean?"

Henry had asked a reasonable question, but Sophie's mind raced through years of expensive gifts, luxurious vacations, and the fact that, thanks to Papa Leo, she'd left college and graduate school without a dime's worth of debt. He often helped out friends and colleagues, and yes, Eva was right—he had given a lot of money to the lighthouse restoration. She couldn't recall ever being concerned for one moment about money. Papa Leo's remarkable generosity had even continued after she was an adult and on her own.

Henry touched her arm. "Maybe he was simply a good money manager or there was money from his parents that you never knew about. They did own these two cottages, isn't that what Eva said? They've got to be worth a fortune in today's real estate market and —" His cheeks reddened slightly. "God, I'm sorry. I don't expect you to reveal details about your finances, Sophie. I'm just trying to figure out what Eva…I mean…why she thinks…"

"Henry, don't be silly. We're friends. I don't have anything to hide from you. These cottages are worth quite a bit. According to the will, this property's worth about a million and half. It's not cash in the bank, but he talked often of how they were our 'security.' That was the word he used. He'd never have risked them in any way." Sophie's heart sank as she realized how easily she'd taken her grandfather and her life for granted. Did he know how much she loved him? How much she appreciated all he'd done for her? "What kind of spoiled brat doesn't ask questions? What if my whole adult life, I should've been asking how he was doing all that stuff—even how he paid the taxes up here—instead of just accepting everything as if I was entitled to it?"

"What?" Henry's brow furrowed as he peered at her in the twilight. "You were entitled. For all intents and purposes, he was your father. Even though I never knew him, I guarantee he knew how much you appreciated him. Hell, you cared for him through his entire illness."

Sophie nodded. "Let's go inside and open a bottle of wine, okay?" She sighed as they climbed the stairs with Henry now vigorously in the lead. She had to chuckle, wondering whether it was the idea of wine that drove him or that he was trying to prove to himself that he could do it without stopping.

They passed through the patio and checked the Mercedes on

the way to the Firefly, making sure it was still secure. Henry had found a tool in the trunk that locked the steering wheel, so once they were certain that the unfamiliar key on the car's key ring did indeed go to the anti-theft device, they had installed it. No way was Eva taking the car again. He took her key, unlocked the door to the cottage, and led the way through the kitchen, turning on lights as he went. Stopping short when he approached the granite bar, he let out a groan. "Aw, shit."

"What?" Sophie crowded behind him, then gasped as her heart leapt to her throat.

The living room was completely torn apart. Bookshelves had been emptied onto the floor, cupboards were open and the contents strewn around the room. Papa Leo's big oak desk had been thoroughly searched, the wing chair was overturned, and the sofa cushions carelessly tossed aside. The blanket chest on the screened porch yawned wide, beach towels pulled out of it, and the door to the patio was ajar.

"Goddamn you, Eva!" Sophie cried and scooted around the end of the bar.

"No, wait." Grasping her arm, Henry tugged her back. "Don't mess with anything. We need to call the police." He pushed her through the kitchen toward the back door. "We don't know for sure it was Eva."

"Oh, come on." She stopped in the utility room, staring at him in the glow of the porch light. "Who else would it be? Of course, it was Eva. And that weasel she's traveling with."

Pulling his cell from his pocket, Henry dialed 911. "We don't know that for sure. It could've been anyone, and they might still be in there." He spoke to the dispatcher, giving details and the address. Promising they'd wait by the road for an officer to arrive, he took her hand and led her outside.

Sophie sat down on the bench by the stoop, laying her head against the cottage's rear wall. "My God, she'll stop at nothing, will she? I should've given her the damn car. Maybe she would've just left and—" Her voice choked and she swallowed hard, determined not to shed a single tear over her mother.

Henry sat beside her and put an arm around her. "Don't." Stroking her arm, he leaned down to peer intently into her brimming eyes. "Even if you'd given her the car, she'd probably still be hanging around. She's on a mission."

Sophie relaxed into the warm circle of his embrace, again feeling grateful to have him with her. "What if the stuff she believes is true and there really is a treasure? How could Papa Leo have kept a secret like that?"

"I think we better find out what's real before Eva and Dale take apart the entire town," he replied with a smile. "We'll figure it out. I promise."

For a moment, his face hovered so close, she was sure he was going to press his lips to hers. Frankly, she'd have welcomed not only the distraction of his kiss, but also the opportunity to see if there was anything to the attraction that seemed to be sparking between them now and again. His eyes darkened another hue as he gazed at her and she lifted her face, waiting... ready.

Henry blinked and then gave her shoulders a squeeze, cleared his throat, and pulled out his damned notebook as a siren wailed in the distance.

CHAPTER 9

"How about we think about all this in the morning, Miss Scarlett?" Henry gave the question a Rhett Butler reading as he stood with his hands on hips, watching Sophie sweep sand and broken shells into a dustpan.

The sheriff had come and gone, and the two of them were back in the living room, surveying a mess that blew his mind. She'd said nothing was missing as far as she could tell, but how could she even begin to know? Someone had gone through the entire cottage, dumping drawers, pulling open cupboards, and tossing bedcovers. They'd even emptied the medicine cabinet in the bathroom. The only room they hadn't destroyed was the kitchen.

Sophie sighed as Henry reached around her to flip the light switch.

"My place is still in one piece," he said. "Come on."

He turned her around, gave her a gentle push, and herded her out through the screened porch and across the patio.

"I wonder why she didn't tear up this place," she mused as he unlocked the door of his cottage. "I mean, why couldn't he have hidden something in here just as easily as he might have in the Firefly?"

"Probably figures he wouldn't have hidden anything valuable in a rental unit." He frowned as she peered out the window into the dark night. Clearly still nervous, eyes red-rimmed and shoulders sagging, she looked ready to drop.

"Okay, it's bedtime for you, milady." With one hand on her back, he walked her slowly to the guest bedroom. Thank god he'd cleaned up when he got home last night. But, shit—he'd tossed all his laundry on the guest room floor, and there was his guitar and a mountain of papers on the bed, which as far as he knew had no sheets on it. Now what?

Oh what the hell? He passed the guest room and guided her into his bedroom, grateful the sheets were clean and the bed was made—mostly.

At the door, she turned to him. "I'm so sorry you got dragged into this crap."

"Do you hear me complaining?" He gave her a smile before digging through his drawer and pulling out a San Jose State jersey. "This actually has the makings of a great mystery novel. That's why I'm taking copious notes." He hoped the gentle teasing would help her relax enough to go to sleep.

"I'm lost, Henry." Sitting on the edge of the bed, she slipped out of her sandals. "What if I never even knew who Papa Leo really was? Right now he feels like... like a stranger."

"Stop. That's crazy talk." The mattress dipped as he sat down beside her. "Whatever's going on, we'll figure it out... but in the morning. Come on, get some sleep."

"I want to brush my teeth and wash my face first." Shoulders slumped, she padded to the bathroom.

He heard her rummaging in the linen closet for the spare toothbrushes, towels, and other toilet articles kept there for renters. Dropping back, legs dangling over the side, his mind whirled with the events of the past twelve hours.

Poor Sophie must be reeling.

She'd barely had enough time to deal with Eva's unexpected appearance before the shit truly hit the fan. Between the confrontation at the diner and the break-in, the day had suddenly turned into a bad TV movie.

Water rushed in the bathroom as Henry stared at the ceiling fan spinning lazily overhead. Something felt... off. The sheriff figured the intruders had pried the latch on the screened porch door. Easy enough to do with a screwdriver, and Sophie hadn't locked the French doors out of the living room. There was no need if the screened porch was locked. His teeth tugged his lower lip as he tried to capture the elusive notion that disturbed him.

Sophie told the sheriff she believed her mother had vandalized the cottage, even gave them a description of the old Honda and both Dale and Eva. But why would those two trash the cottage? Even if they had broken in, wouldn't they have simply gone through Leo's stuff, looking for whatever it was Eva believed her father had hidden? Snooping made sense, but why would they leave such dramatic evidence they'd been there?

The pair was greedy and probably had no compunction about stealing, but Henry didn't get the feeling Eva Russo would've destroyed the place where she'd grown up. It felt... out of character.

But how the hell did he know shit from caviar about Eva Russo's character? She certainly hadn't demonstrated any of the charming, well-brought-up characteristics of her daughter. It was his gut reaction—he couldn't explain it. Eva was an intriguing woman. Not in the same way Sophie was intriguing, of course, but something about that aura of false bravado and toughness made him think perhaps there was more to her journey to Michigan than money.

His thoughts shifted back to the mess across the patio. The trashed cottage seemed almost like... His mind refused to even think the word. One clenched fist smacked the mattress.

Okay, a warning. Christ in heaven. It seemed like a warning. But from whom?

Sighing, he sat up and pulled his shirt over his head. He'd been reading one too many mysteries, or maybe it was just that his imagination had suddenly gone into high gear. A good thing for the writer, not so great for the friend who was only trying to help.

He exchanged places with Sophie, closing the bathroom door to give her some privacy getting ready for sleep. He dawdled in the bathroom, half-hoping she'd be asleep by the time he got out. Confused and yes, a little wary of the new feelings he'd been having for his editor, he didn't need any more motivation to take her in his arms. Besides, tonight wasn't the time for exploring the growing attraction between them.

However, when he opened the bathroom door, she'd changed into the oversized shirt and was perched on the edge on the bed.

She hopped up. "Um, sorry I'm still here. I forgot to get some sheets for the guest room. They're in there." She gave a nod toward the bathroom as she cleared her throat. "I don't want to kick you out of your bed." Color suffused her cheeks and she gazed at her feet, the ceiling, everywhere but at him.

Henry heaved a huge sigh. "The guest room bed is covered in my stuff and honestly, I'm too tired to clear it off and make it up. This is a big bed, we can share it."

"I–I don't know—" Sophie stuttered. All the boldness she'd demonstrated earlier had disappeared. Now she just seemed tired and frightened and as confused as he felt.

"Look, Soph, I think you know I'm attracted to you and I think it might be mutual."

She met his gaze over the wide expanse of the bed and simply nodded, her teeth worrying her lower lip.

"But this just isn't the time. It's been a long day. You're exhausted and I'm tired. I'm not going to jump you, I promise." He tossed his clothes into the chair under the window and clad only in knit boxers, yanked the covers back. "Just get in bed and let's get some sleep, okay?" Frustration made him sound gruffer than he intended.

When her face crumpled and she wrapped her arms around her waist, he backpedaled. "Here, let's do Clark Gable and Claudette Colbert."

"What?" She swung her hair back off her face in a gesture eerily reminiscent of her mother.

Henry grabbed a few pillows from the stack at the top of the bed and placed them in a line down the center of the mattress. "Your bed." He waved his arm over the side closest to her. "Mine." He hopped in and pulled the covers over himself and gave her grin and a raised brow.

With a giggle, she slipped into bed. "I thought he hung up blankets."

"Cripes, everybody's a critic. I'm improvising." He rolled over, turned out the light, and punched his own pillow into a more comfortable position. It was going to be a long night.

"Hey, Clark?" Sophie's voice was soft and tremulous in the darkness.

"Yeah?"

"Thank you." Her whispered words were muffled by a huge yawn.

Henry grinned and closed his eyes. "You're welcome, Claudette. Goodnight."

CHAPTER 10

Henry awoke with a start, not certain what had jolted him out of a deep sleep. Lying very still, he listened, unsure of what he was straining to hear. In one of those surreal moments when reality and dreams seem to collide, his fuzzy mind tried to grasp something solid.

Turning his head on the pillow, he glanced at Sophie curled up next to him, dead to the world. The clock was the only light in the room, and the numbers showed five thirty a.m. There it was—a little clicking sound. It stopped and then started again... tap, tap, tap.

A light flashed on the ceiling of the bedroom. He sat straight up and threw his legs over the side of the bed. Grabbing his jeans and t-shirt off the nearby chair, he jerked them on as he crept to the door.

Through the open window came rustling sounds in the garden below and a whispered, "Fuck!"

Adrenaline pumping, he scurried down the hall, keeping his tread as quiet as he could.

When he got to the living room, he saw two shadowy figures outside, one coming around the house wielding a small flashlight, the other bent over the latch on the screened porch door. The motion light at the top of the beach stairs illuminated the patio enough that he recognized Dale's pale hair.

With a disgusted, "Goddammit," Henry opened the French doors and flipped on the ceiling fixture.

Eva jumped back with a squeal as the porch was suddenly bathed in light.

Henry slipped the latch and held the door wide. "What the hell are you two doing? Back for a go at my place?"

"Jeezus! You scared the crap outta me." She stood on the patio, a metal nail file clutched in her hand.

"For God's sake, be quiet." Henry jerked his head toward the interior of the cottage. "Sophie's finally asleep."

The two of them stared wide-eyed at him, appearing for all the world like a couple of guilty teenagers sneaking in after curfew. Eva shoved Dale and he almost dropped the flashlight. "Goddammit, Dale. I told you not to go wandering around. You woke him up."

"I was trying to find an open window." Dale shined the beam in her face.

"Turn off that friggin' light." With a scowl, she turned back to Henry, who was lounging in the open door of the porch, arms crossed over his chest. "We gotta talk."

"About what?" Henry kept his voice low, hoping against hope he could handle this situation before Sophie woke up. The last thing she needed right now was another encounter with her mother.

"My daughter." She stuck the nail file in her canvas bag and sidled closer.

"Well, this should be interesting." He moved aside and with a nod, invited them into the porch. But he pulled the French doors closed before he sat down in a wicker chair, resting one ankle on the other knee and giving them what he hoped was an inflexible stare.

They parked themselves on the settee across from him. Eva dug in her bag and pulled out a pack of cigarettes, but after a glance at Henry, dropped them back in.

"What about Sophie?" he asked coolly.

"Wait, what did you mean by 'back for a go at my place'?" Her eyes narrowed as her teeth nibbled at the ragged rim of lipstick on her lower lip.

"Come on, Eva," Henry scoffed. "We know you trashed Sophie's cottage. Didn't find what you were looking for?"

"What the hell are you talking about?" Her voice rose in indignation. She seemed honestly puzzled. "We haven't been anywhere near that place since we were in there with you guys last night."

He raised one brow and gazed at her without commenting.

"I didn't trash the Firefly."

"Who did?"

"How the hell should I know?"

"Then why were you trying to break in here?"

Eva scowled. "We needed a place to crash. Old man Pryor wouldn't give us our room back at the motel 'cause he said we stunk it up with cigarettes. Threatened to charge me for cleaning it too, the old bastard."

"Yeah," Dale added, "we were gonna sleep in the car, but it got too friggin' cold, so we came over here. We didn't see no strange cars around. It was all dark. We figured she'd lied about it being rented."

"*I'm* renting it. The silver Prius parked out back is my rental car."

"Oh," Dale shrugged. "I thought it was hers. You know, like a second car. The lawyer said she moved up here."

"Well, hell!" Eva exclaimed. "I thought you two were asleep over at the Firefly. Together. Sure seemed like you were an item." She fidgeted with the handle of her purse. "So her place got trashed?"

Henry ignored her question, still not completely convinced that Eva and Dale weren't the culprits. But he was willing to give them the benefit of the doubt long enough to find out what she had to say about Sophie. "You said we needed to talk about Sophie?"

"Yeah, well..." She clasped her hands in her lap so tight the knuckles were white. "I don't wanna leave without settling things with her. You gotta talk to her and..." She raised her eyes to Henry's. "... and make her see that he wasn't as perfect as she believes. She needs to hear my side of things 'cause we're all each other's got now. We're family."

"Family?" A voice from the French doors made them all jump. "That's rich coming from you, Eva."

～

Sophie, all wrapped up in a quilt, interrupted their early morning gathering. Trembling more from sheer anger than from the morning chill, she strode out onto the porch. "What the hell are you two doing here?"

Henry crossed the painted wood floor in three swift steps and caught her by the shoulders. "Easy," he murmured next to her ear. "They just showed up a couple of minutes ago."

Furious, she glared at him. "Why would you let them in, Henry?"

"We're just talking, okay? Come on." Grip tightening on her upper arm, he led her to a chair and pushed her gently down into it. Eva and Dale remained uncharacteristically close-mouthed as Henry settled into the seat next to Sophie's. "Eva says they didn't trash the Firefly."

Eva's kohl-rimmed eyes welled with tears. "Honest, kid. We had nothin' to do with it."

"Whatever." Sophie's lip curled in a sneer. "What's going on here? Why aren't these two on their way back to Florida?"

She turned toward Henry, trying to shut out the sight of her mother weeping on the settee across the porch. Rage seethed deep inside her. Diluting it with any sympathy for Eva's distress seemed like a bad idea.

"W–we didn't t–trash the Firefly," Eva stuttered in between loud sniffs.

"Really?" With a glance over her shoulder, Sophie gave a disbelieving snort as she folded her arms under her breasts and shifted her attention back to Henry. "What's going on? You're just collecting material here, aren't you? Where's your little note-book?" She was close to exploding. Kicking all three of them down the beach stairs sounded really appealing.

"Listen." Placing one hand on her knee, which was peeking out of the quilt, he leaned closer. "I don't think they *were* respon-sible. Eva was as shocked as we were when I accused her."

"Yeah, well, Eva's a hell of an actress."

"I don't think she did it." With a quick squeeze, he released her leg to grab a tissue box from the table between them and toss it to Eva.

Honking loudly, she blew her nose. "I only want to talk to you, Sophie. That's all. You're my daughter."

"It doesn't matter what you want." Sophie's stomach churned. Her hard gaze focused on Eva's tear-stained face, where mascara ran in black rivulets down her cheeks.

Do not feel sorry for her.

With a shake of her head, she continued, deliberately callous. "So you just figured you could erase forty-five years of nothing simply by showing up here? I'm not stupid, Eva. You're looking for money."

Eva only sniffed as she wiped her face with another tissue. Scraping off a layer of make-up made the lines around her eyes even more evident. She looked old and exhausted.

Sophie couldn't help the pity that edged along the well of her anger. What kind of life had her mother led all these years? A headache began to throb at the base of her neck as she twisted in her chair to meet Henry's eyes.

Would life ever be normal again?

"Okay, Dugan, why do you believe her?"

"Just my gut. It's rarely wrong."

His unruffled demeanor irritated the hell out of her. At oh-dark-thirty in the morning, she was in no mood to play twenty questions with her mother and her sleazy boyfriend. "I need more. How'd they end up back here?"

"They got kicked out of the motel."

"Why?" She was almost afraid to ask.

"Smoking in the room."

"Of course."

"Will you two stop talking about us like we're not even here?" Eva whined with another big honk into a tissue. "We were tryin' to find a place to sleep 'cause old Matt Pryor kicked us out."

"Too cold to sleep in the car." Dale added a long shiver to his two cents.

"Swear to God we didn't trash the Firefly." Two fingers in the air like a child making a vow, Eva defended herself. "We don't know anything about that."

"I told you I'd rented this place." Sophie was weakening and she hated herself for it, so she straightened up in the chair, striving for a more commanding presence. It was a little hard swathed in miles of antique quilt.

"We thought all the cars were yours," Dale pointed out. "And we was only lookin' for a warm bed."

"How about this?" Henry gave her a smile that she read as

work with me here. "Let's give Eva and Dale the benefit of the doubt for a few hours. Let them catch some shut-eye in the spare room here while you and I go over to the Firefly, have some breakfast, and start cleaning up."

A grateful smile from Eva grated on Sophie's already raw nerves, however technically this was Henry's place. He'd paid her for the whole summer way back in April and there was nothing in the rental contract that kept him from having guests.

Where was he going with this?

It was impossible to tell what was in his mind from his deadpan expression. Why on earth would he invite Eva and Dale to use his spare room? Did he know something she didn't? Well, she certainly wasn't going to find out anything at all unless she got him alone.

Oh hell, maybe there was no harm in letting them get a few hours of sleep.

At least she'd know where they were and what they were up to. With a short nod to him, she rose from her chair. "Okay. They can sleep here. But this isn't a damn hotel, you two, so don't get comfortable. Oh, and—" She held out her palm to her mother. "—the cigarettes, please. No, on second thought, just hand over your purse."

"Jeezus." Pulling herself up from the settee, Eva tossed the canvas bag on the chair behind Sophie. "I just had a déjà vu moment. For a second, I'd a sworn you were Leo."

"I'll take that as a compliment." Shouldering the bag, Sophie headed for the door. "Use the guest room. Sheets and towels in the linen closet. Henry, you can clear the bed off for them, and I recommend you collect up any stuff you value and bring it over to the Firefly." Quilt dragging the floor, she swept out of the cottage.

S plashing milk into a bowl of granola, Sophie barely looked up as Henry ambled into her cottage, tugging his wheeled duffel behind him, his guitar slung over one shoulder and the messenger bag over the other. Papers and a red folder sticking out of the bag showed evidence of how quickly he'd packed up and left the Sandpiper to its new, but very *temporary*, residents. Skirting a pile of books, sofa cushions, and broken jars of shells, he came to a halt by the table.

"Coffee's hot." She concentrated on adding blueberries to her cereal.

He dropped the bag on the bar, put the guitar on the floor, and released his hold on the duffel. "You're all dressed. That was fast work." Helping himself to coffee, he got a bowl out of the cupboard.

She eyed him as he settled into the chair across from her, leisurely adding cream to his coffee, slicing a banana over his granola, and pouring a glass of orange juice.

"I'm not going back to sleep." She kept her voice cool. "I just want to get this mess cleaned up."

Remarkably, the kitchen had been left untouched and it took only a few minutes to reload the medicine cabinet, so she'd showered, found clean shorts and a t-shirt in the pile of clothing in the bedroom, and French-braided her damp hair.

"You even got a shower," he observed after gulping the entire glass of juice.

"Yup."

"I'll get one after we're done cleaning up."

"Whatever."

They ate in strained silence for a few moments until at last he sat back in his chair. "Okay, you're pissed."

"Pissed?" Sophie glared at him. "Try furious. Or how about *invaded*?" Milk splattered on the table as she shoved her bowl aside. "What the hell are you thinking? Haven't you heard anything I've said about her? Did you check out completely during our charming little confrontations here and at the diner?"

"Sophie—"

"The woman's a loon. I want no part of her." Pushing her chair back, she strode to the sink. "She stole my car and... and look what she did to my house!"

A damp dishrag hit the table in front of him. With a sigh, he reached around and grabbed her by the wrist. "Sit. Please?" The chair at the end of the table scooted as he pushed it out with his foot. He pointed. "Sit down and listen."

Scowling, she sat. "Okay, I'm listening."

"With an open mind please."

"Just talk, Dugan."

"I honestly don't believe they trashed your cottage."

"Why? And don't tell me about your gut again. I need to hear from a source other than your intestines."

"Think about it for a minute. Why would she vandalize this house?" A broad gesture took in the entire the mess. "It doesn't make sense."

"Maybe to get back at me. Or because she hated Papa Leo so much."

"If that were the case, she'd have torn it up when she was here after your grandfather died. Or even one of the times she came up while he was still alive." He quirked one brow. He was making sense, dammit. "I think she's here because she's looking for something, but I don't think she did this."

"Well, then who did... this?" Sophie's sweeping gesture imitated his.

Where was he going with this crazy defense of Eva? Confusion and irritation struggled in her head and she hoped it was evident on her face. She was still angry, but sitting there across from her, he looked so concerned, so... intrigued, and fuck all, kinda handsome. Why couldn't they simply turn back the clock? Henry was a prime candidate for her hot summer fling, and given that Julie hadn't come up with anyone else for her yet, she would much rather be practicing her seduction techniques on him instead of dealing with Eva's reign of terror.

However, the chaos surrounding them was definitely not at all sexy. She sighed. "She even destroyed the photo albums. That really sucks."

Henry took her hand. "She has no reason to destroy photo albums or smash jars of shells. Now, I wouldn't put it past her to break in and do a search of the place. She may be sneaky, but she's not stupid. She wouldn't leave evidence of having been here. I honestly don't think this is her handiwork."

"Whose is it?"

"I'm working on that." He ate the last bite of granola and then tipped the bowl and finished off the milk with a loud slurp and a grin. She could tell he was trying to jolly her.

"Charming." But she couldn't help returning his smile. Rolling her eyes with a little giggle, she tossed him a napkin from the basket on the counter behind her. "Who would search the place so carelessly and leave it in such a mess?"

A new voice startled them both. "It's a warning. You got somethin' somebody wants." Dale sauntered in, stepping carefully over the debris. "I couldn't sleep," he added. "Can I have some coffee? Please?"

A jerk of her head indicated the coffeemaker and mug rack on the counter, and Henry scooted the sugar and cream across the table. Dale's grey-blond hair stuck up in tufts, his silvery eyes were bloodshot and shadowed with purple. Sophie cast a curious eye at Henry as their uninvited guest filled a mug and took a long pull before he plopped into a seat at the table.

"What do you mean a warning?" she asked. "What could I possibly have here that would make someone do this?"

"That's what we gotta figure out, I guess." He stretched and tilted his chair back on two legs, resting dirty sneakers on the pedestal of the round oak table.

"We?" Henry said it before Sophie had a chance. She threw him a grateful smile.

"Look, I figure we can work together on this or we can work separate, but one way or 'nother, we gotta find out who the hell trashed your place and why." Dale dropped back onto all four chair legs. "Personally, I think it has something to do with Eva's old man."

"We're listening," Henry replied with a guarded glance at her.

"Mind if I have some cereal?" Dale stared hungrily at their empty bowls, so with an exasperated sigh, Sophie got up and brought him a bowl and a spoon. Filling the bowl almost to the top, he added a handful of blueberries and a splash of milk.

His granola crunching was the only sound in the kitchen for a couple of minutes as he emptied the bowl. Finally, she couldn't stand it anymore. "Who? Who do you think did this?"

"I dunno, but I think it's about that treasure."

"What do you mean?" Sophie demanded. "You think somebody is looking for this imaginary treasure besides you two?"

"Dunno. Could be."

CHAPTER 11

After swallowing another gulp of coffee, Dale had clammed up and fled back to the Sandpiper. Too confused to even question him before he walked out, Sophie didn't stop him from leaving. Rather, she found the aspirin bottle, swallowed a couple, and got to work cleaning up.

Taking broad swipes at the sand-and-shell-covered hardwood floor in the living room, she scowled. Then she leaned against her broom handle and watched Henry stack books back into the bookshelves by the stone fireplace. "A treasure? Seriously? A *treasure*?" One brow raised, she gazed at him.

"How many times are you going to say that?" He grinned, dropping several heavy volumes on the table.

"As many times as it takes for me to get back to reality. Does he seriously think we're going to start *treasure hunting* with him and Eva? " She stabbed the air with fake quotes and rolled her eyes.

"Soph, I still don't think Dale and Eva did this." One dirty hand indicated the disarray that was slowly getting cleared away. "Frankly, I wasn't going to mention my own theory, but now that Dale's opened that particular can of worms—"

"Oh, come on." Tossing the broom aside, Sophie grabbed some books from the floor, shoving them in with the others with more force than was necessary. "Do *you* think there's a treasure hidden in here somewhere? And even if there was, who do you think is hunting for it?"

He pulled out a chair, plopped down, and raked his fingers through his hair. "I think someone was in here looking for... God knows what. They didn't find it, so they trashed the place. Probably in a fit of pique, but—"

"Pique?" She snorted a laugh. "Really? That's your word for the tornado that hit my house? A fit of *pique*?"

"Probably because they were royally pissed," Henry amended. "But maybe they also wanted to leave you... us... a message."

"And the message is?" She wasn't at all sure she wanted to hear this.

"How about, 'you've got something we want'?" His interpretation was as interesting as it was frightening.

She expelled a quick breath, then rubbed her face, probably smearing the streaks of dirt that she was sure had landed there in the throes of cleanup. "This is just crazy. Who, Henry? And what do they—assuming there is a *they*—think is here? As far as I can tell they didn't take anything. All my jewelry's still here, the TV, the rest of the electronics, my laptop and Kindle."

"That's what we're going to have to try to figure out."

"I don't even know where to begin." A chill formed in the pit of her stomach as she went back to sweeping and dumping dust pans full of sand into the trash can. Somehow, believing her mother vandalized the house seemed easier than wrapping her brain around unknown thugs breaking in. It was too much of a coincidence. Papa Leo's long-lost daughter had returned and suddenly his beloved cottage filled with years of personal treasures was a mess.

Worst of all, Papa Leo wasn't here. She had no idea how to

handle this weird turn of events without him. "Henry, I'm getting scared."

"I know." He extended a hand. When she accepted it, he surprised the hell out of her by tugging her down onto his lap. After wiping his dirty hands on his jeans, he touched her cheek with one finger. "But I'm here. I'm not going to let anything happen to you."

"You didn't sign up for this kind of drama, Dugan." She perched delicately, feeling the sharp points of his knees against the backs of her thighs. He had kind of skinny legs, what if she was too heavy? But he didn't act like she was too heavy. In fact, he pulled her closer.

Oh, what the hell?

With a sigh, she relaxed into the haven of Henry Dugan's warm embrace, linking her arms around his broad shoulders. "Let's just let the sheriff handle it. Maybe he'll end up hauling Dale and Eva away to jail, and we can go down to the beach and take the first swim of the season. What do you think?"

"When the going gets tough, the tough go swimming?" Henry's eyes twinkled and Sophie's heart leaped to life. Why hadn't she noticed before how blue they were? They were blue like the sea. Like an October sky. Like sapphires ... Like... Gazing at him, she ran out of appropriate similes.

"Hey?" He brushed one thumb over her chin and brought her back to the moment. Neither of them said a word. She touched his beard. He tilted his head and found her lips. Then he was kissing her and she was kissing him back. He pulled her closer, and she opened her mouth to his, deepening the contact.

The warm pressure of Henry's mouth on hers kindled a response that set her pulse hammering. She'd never been kissed like that before. All she wanted was to keep the contact, his mouth on hers, his hands on her body—it was so incredibly right. She increased the pressure of her mouth, pressing herself against him, while the thought, *this is Henry, it's Henry,* kept going around in her addled brain. When at last, he lifted his lips, her one clear thought shocked her right down to her socks.

Thank God, it's finally Henry.

His eyes were dark blue and questioning, and he looked exactly how she felt, a little bewildered and wary. But he didn't move back or take his hands off her. They were both breathless.

Sophie closed her eyes, tipping her head back for second, trying hard to get her brain back in gear. Then she met his eyes again. Not a single word had passed between them yet. He watched her, his expression full of wonder and so much tenderness that she wanted to crawl inside his heart and stay there forever. "Henry..." Words failed her.

His glasses were askew on his face, so she took them off and laid them on the table. He nuzzled her neck, letting his lips travel from her ear to that sensitive spot just under her chin.

Tilting her head, Sophie leaned into his touch as his hand roamed under the faded t-shirt to find her bare skin. Whoa boy, apparently, cooking up the seduction of Henry Dugan wasn't going to be necessary. He was doing just fine on his own.

When he finally spoke, his words were completely unexpected. "Soph, I really don't think anyone's interested in hurting you, but you must have something they want." Muffled against her collarbone, the tremor in his voice was the only indication that they weren't simply sitting across the table from one another having this conversation. "It's an adventure. A mystery to solve."

How could be making out with her, while simultaneously thinking about their mystery? He was an enigma. Sophie gave a mental shrug and went with it, teasing, "Don't you get enough of that writing your novel?" His attempts to ease her mind weren't really working all that well, but curiosity began to override her fear as she sat safe in Henry's arms. Hadn't Papa Leo once told her great adventures were ahead? Yes, when he was so sick. It was after they'd had the private duty nurse argument for the hundredth time, and he was still trying to convince her to move out and live her own life.

Was that a foreshadowing? Or could he have meant it literally? Was that what he tried to tell her the night he died? About some treasure?

"But the question is..." Henry paused for another long, deep kiss before he continued. "...who are they and what do they want?"

"That's two questions. Mmm..." A little moan escaped her lips as his hand found her lace-covered breast, sending a rush of sensation through her. "Think they're looking for a map to a sunken treasure maybe? Nah, that's a little too Nancy... mm... Drew, don't you think? Oh, Dugan, your hands are—" But suddenly, she grasped his hand and sat up straight, practically falling off his lap in the process. "Oh, my god."

"What?" He tipped forward as she stood up with his hand still caught under her t-shirt. Pulling it out, he regained his balance and gave her a puzzled stare.

"There's a bunch of boxes, a couple of old trunks, and a wooden file cabinet in the attic of the Sandpiper. I haven't been up there since I was a kid, but I remember seeing that stuff." Her heart pounded a faster rhythm. "Maybe there really is a treasure map."

His breathing was uneven. "Neatly filed under *T* for treasure or *M* for map?"

"Why couldn't it be that easy?"

"Because it never is." He flopped back in the chair and blew the hair off his forehead. "Trust me, I know about these things. I'm a writer."

"It could happen. Papa Leo was unnaturally organized."

"What about the attic here?"

"This cottage doesn't have an attic because of the vaulted ceilings." A careless wave of her hand dismissed the notion. Her mind was filled with foggy memories. A rainy day exploring the upper regions of the Sandpiper. She, Papa Leo, and Nonna opening trunks and boxes up in the dingy attic.

"Okay, obviously the idea of a treasure hunt entices you more than my charms at the moment, so we need a plan." He dug in his messenger bag for a notebook and pen.

"It's not that you're not enticing, honest..." Sophie reached out to stroke an errant piece of hair off his forehead. She thought he was teasing, but she planted a quick kiss on his lips just in case.

The kiss earned her a killer grin. "You get a pass for now. I'm deeply hurt, however my curiosity is piqued too." He found a clean page in the spiral notebook. "After we get this place back in order, we'll check out the attic next door. We also need to hit the library in town and... um... museums. Do I remember Noah saying something about a maritime museum?"

"Yup, it's up at Sleeping Bear." She was getting a kick out his attempts to organize their little mystery. The computer geek in him outlined a plan and made a quick list.

"And there are the newspaper archives." He scribbled on his list. "We'll check for any kind of news story about something valuable being found in a wreck in the lake."

"Oh, God, tons of stuff's been brought up from wrecks." Sophie stacked cereal bowls and carried them to the sink as Henry wrote. "Some big find makes the paper at least once a summer."

"That's probably true, but..." Tapping his pen on the note-book, he chewed his lower lip. "If he found something big, why didn't he tell you of all people?"

Shutting off the water, she dried her hands slowly as she walked back to the table. "I don't know."

"We'll check the Web. Google to see if there were any finds in the lake in the early sixties." He glanced back over his shoulder, his brow furrowing. "You okay?"

"Yeah, just thinking. If he found a treasure all those years ago, why did he keep it a secret?"

He shrugged. "Maybe he didn't want to share it."

"No." She tossed the dishtowel on the countertop. "He was the most generous, kindhearted man in the world. Wherever his money came from, he shared it. He donated tons of money to restoring the lighthouse, Eva's right about that. And Papa Leo tithed—more than tithed—to the church back home and the one up here. He gave money to anyone who asked for help."

"Okay." He'd turned his notebook sideways and was drawing what looked to be a timeline or a chart of some kind. "Maybe he didn't want a lot of publicity."

"Nope. He wasn't a bit shy. A news story about a big find on a wreck would've been right up his alley. There should be a scrapbook full of clippings and pictures somewhere if he'd found a treasure. He would've told me the story dozens of times, in excruciating detail. Secretive just doesn't fit—he'd have been sharing it with the whole town. The entire state."

"Maybe he didn't want anyone else to know he had it. Maybe it wasn't from a wreck at all. Maybe it was from some other source or—" Henry's eyes bored a hole into her.

"Are you thinking Papa Leo was involved in something illegal?" Sophie bristled.

"I didn't say that."

"Do you think it was like drug money or stolen or something?" Her voice squeaked on the question that came out way more hostile than she intended.

"I didn't say that, either."

"Then what are you saying?" Fear manifested as antagonism in her tone as she paced the room, wringing the tea towel in her hands.

"I'm not saying anything at all. I'm just trying to lay out all the possibilities," he replied. "Brainstorming. We're working blind here. We still have practically no information."

"Well, he wouldn't have done anything illegal. Never. Not in a million years, so take that off the table. It's not who he was." She strode back to the kitchen and washed her hands. And then for reasons she didn't comprehend, she washed them again. Her mind was going a million miles an hour, in a thousand directions.

Where did Papa Leo get all the money he'd spent so freely her whole life? She ransacked her memory for any kind of clue, trying to remember some story or event that might tell them what was happening, but her mind was a complete blank. Bile rose in her throat and she leaned over the sink, trying hard not to lose it.

"Hey. Hey, now." Henry appeared behind her, his hands on her shoulders. He turned her to him, and she buried her face in his worn t-shirt. Tears threatened as he enfolded her in his arms, rocking her gently, one hand holding her head close to his chest. "It's okay. It's gonna be okay."

"Sorry." Swallowing, she fought back the tears. "I'm sorry. I didn't mean to be so defensive." She rubbed her face on his shirt, inhaling the male scent of him. He was big and warm and safe. "I don't think I could bear finding out Papa Leo was involved in something... awful."

"I know." His hands smoothed up and down her back as she wrapped her arms around his waist.

"Can't we forget this?" Tipping her head back, she gazed into his face. "Please? Let's just go take a swim, okay?"

〜

Henry's heart lurched at the fear in her eyes. "I don't think we can forget it." He touched his forehead to hers. "We need to find out what's going on before—" He stopped, unwilling to finish, given the thoughts racing through his brain.

"Before what?" The words came out in a shaky whisper that made him want to flinch.

"Before our whole summer is ruined and I get nothing at all written," he teased, reaching for her towel and using it to wipe away the tears that had mixed with dirt on her face. "You look like a kid making mud pies, Russo."

He hadn't meant to frighten her, but his own uneasiness nagged at him and he'd foolishly voiced his thoughts without thinking how she might react. From what she'd told him, her grandfather being involved in some illegal activity certainly did seem unlikely. On the other hand, Eva's arrival in Willow Bay appeared to have set something odd, even sinister, in motion.

Sophie sniffed back tears, which in turn became sniffing the air. Her nose wrinkled and she peered around him. Easing out of his arms, she stepped gingerly past the piles of books and broken glass and shells on the living room floor through to the screened porch.

"Crap," she said. "Eva's awake. And Dale must've grabbed her bag when he left here—she's smoking out on the patio."

"At least she's on the patio, not in the house." Almost unwilling to bring up anything else that might upset her again, Henry began in as neutral a tone as he could muster. "You know..."

But when Sophie glanced back over her shoulder, her green eyes narrowed. "What?"

"She may be a valuable source of information."

Her spine stiffened and her jaw set, a posture that had already become familiar to him. Clearly she was preparing for an argument about Eva staying around even ten minutes longer.

He had to talk fast, and he had to be convincing. "She was raised here, too and—" Holding up one hand to stop her from interrupting, he made his best point. "And she was here when Papa Leo was diving."

"Nooo." With a little shake of her head and stomp of her foot, she stretched out the word like a headstrong kid.

"To quote Michael Corleone, my dear editor, 'keep your friends close and your enemies closer.' I think that's not bad advice as far as Eva and Dale are concerned."

She assessed him silently.

He could almost see the wheels turning in her head, so he gave her an encouraging smile.

Finally, she sighed. "So, what they say is true? All wisdom can indeed be found in *The Godfather* movies?"

"Absolutely." He winked and gave her an even bigger smile as she headed out to talk to her mother.

CHAPTER 12

O n her way out the door, Sophie grabbed a large mussel shell, one of the few that hadn't been smashed by the vandals, and carried it to the beach steps where Eva sat smoking. "Here, use this."

Her mother accepted the makeshift ashtray and flicked the long ash of her cigarette into it before taking another deep drag. "Goddamn things'll kill ya, kid. Don't ever start."

"I'm forty-five. I'm fairly sure I won't start smoking this late in the game." She eased around Eva, then plopped down beside her on the second-to-the-top wooden step, keeping enough distance between them that their shoulders didn't touch. Her sneakered foot brushed at the sand that invariably coated the steps as the silence between them expanded.

Another puff or two and Eva finally spoke, "So... I saw the trash can. Is it really that bad? Did they tear stuff up?"

"They smashed some things and tore through all the cupboards and Papa Leo's desk," she replied, staring straight ahead.

"Did they take anything?"

"Not so far as I can tell." Sophie released a deep breath. The lake sparkled in the noon sun, and she ached for the days when she and Papa Leo would get up early, grab the metal detector, and hit the beach to search for treasures. Truth was she missed her grandfather more than she had since January. Right now, she was longing for his wisdom, his calm, his perspective.

And some answers only he could provide.

"He had a ton of shit in there." Eva extinguished the spent cigarette in the opal center of the shell. "How would you even know if something was missing?"

"The fact that they destroyed things leads me to believe they didn't find what they were looking for. They didn't take anything they could sell, like the TV or the DVD player or my computer."

"Shit. Are you kidding me? They didn't take your computer? That fancy laptop you had on Dad's desk?" Squinting, Eva swung her head around to stare at her.

The sunlight emphasized the harsh wrinkles at her mother's temples and the little vertical lines above her lips that testified to years of smoking. But gazing into her green eyes was like looking in a mirror. Looking at her mother in the daylight and without all the heavy makeup, Sophie could still see vestiges of the attractive young woman Eva had once been. What had gone wrong when her mother was a girl? What made her take the path she'd chosen? How could she and Eva see Papa Leo so very differently?

Henry might be right.

Eva had earlier history with her father than Sophie did—maybe she knew something that would help them. Clearly, she paid attention. How else would she remember the new laptop sitting on the desk in the Firefly from the short time she was in there? "Eva, why are you really here?" She laid one hand on her mother's leathery arm. "The truth... please?"

With a glance at Sophie's hand resting on her arm, her mother set aside the shell and leaned back against the top step, propping her elbows behind her and stretching her long legs out. She'd removed the dark polish from her toes. Now they were bright coral, as were her fingernails.

When the hell had she found time to do that?

Eva sat staring silently out across Lake Michigan and the long moment of reticence bugged Sophie. Was she concocting another wild story or debating the value of actually telling the truth?

"Dale and I want to buy a horse farm down home—west of Ocala. It's forty acres, a couple of beat-up barns, and a farmhouse that barely has running water. The fences are a wreck and the pastures need to be reseeded, but it'd be a start for us. He's been a groom his whole life, so he knows horses, particularly racehorses. Frankly, I was going to ask the old—" She took a breath. "I was going to ask Dad for down payment money."

Sophie didn't say anything, but simply gazed at her mother.

"When I got your message he was sick... well, I guess I figured there'd be time," Eva went on, her eyes downcast. "Then Dale got into a mess with some guys over a gambling debt, and we had to lay low for a little while. We split so fast I left my cell charging in the trailer and when we got back, there was your voicemail that he'd... died." The word came out on a little gruff choking sound.

Sophie's eyes narrowed. Was Eva really crying or was this another Oscar-worthy performance like the one she'd given earlier? Her mother swiped away a tear with the back of her hand. If it was fake, it was pretty darn convincing.

Damn, damn, damn. I have no idea whether she's lying or telling me the truth.

"So that was when? January or February?" she asked. "Where've you been since then?"

"Earning the bread to get back up here." Eva sniffed. "I'm a cocktail waitress at the track. Pretty good tips when the ponies are running."

Grasping at the one part of the story that worried her most, Sophie asked, "Dale's got a gambling problem?"

Her mother heaved an exaggerated sigh. "He swears he's got it under control. He hasn't bet on a horse since February. He's been picking up grooming gigs at the tracks around Florida, but—"

"But you thought you'd come up here and see if I'd just hand over my inheritance," Sophie finished for her.

"I figured there'd be a buttload of money and you might spare some for your long-lost mama." Eva squirmed on the step, leaning her arms on her knees as though avoiding Sophie's hard stare.

"You figured wrong on both counts."

"What happened to all the money?" The question came out rather quietly, with none of the belligerence Eva had shown that first night.

"All the money?" Long tendrils of hair had escaped her braid and Sophie shoved them behind her ears. "There was a little insurance. Some savings that paid for the funeral. These cottages and the house down home. That's it, Eva."

"That car alone's worth eighty grand, kid. I looked it up online at the library." Some of the old Eva avarice had returned, causing Sophie to shake her head in frustration.

"Fine." She scowled at her mother. "Take the car," she said through gritted teeth. "Take the damn thing. Sell it, crash it, or drive to South America. I don't give a shit. Just go away." Popping up from the step, she turned, but Eva grabbed her wrist.

"No wait. Wait." She patted the step next to her. "Sit down here. Please."

Sophie hesitated, then dropped back down with a weary sigh. "What?"

"You know I'm right, don't you? You know there's more.

That's why you're so willing to let me have the Mercedes, isn't it? You and that geeky dude found the treasure, didn't you?"

Sophie silently counted to ten. Ignoring the question, she asked one herself instead. "Why does Dale think there's someone after this... treasure?"

Eva's eyes slid away as she suddenly became very interested in the hem of her ratty bathrobe. "When did he say that?"

"This morning when he came by for breakfast."

"Hell, who knows?" She barked a laugh and tossed her black hair back. "Dale's got a great imagination. He's been watchin' too many cop shows."

"How long have you... been with Dale?"

"Couple of years." Pulling the packet of cigarettes out of her pocket, she lit up, inhaling smoke into her lungs, held it, and then released it.

Silence yawned between them long enough that she realized her mother wasn't going to give her any more information without being pressed. If Eva and Dale were up to something, she sure wasn't tipping her hand. A loud gurgle rose from the vicinity of her mother's stomach, so Sophie stood and brushed off the back of her shorts.

"You want something to eat?" she asked. "They left my kitchen alone, so you can make yourself some breakfast... well, lunch."

"Let me get dressed first." Eva tapped the flame from the barely smoked cigarette, then extinguished it against the mussel shell and tucked it back into the pack.

Sophie watched, fighting the urge to roll her eyes.

"What?" Eva quirked one penciled-on brow. "These things are freakin' expensive." She set the shell carefully on a big rock next to the steps and got up. "Dale and I'll come over and help you clean up the mess."

"How'd it go?" Henry peered at her over the top of his glasses, which had slipped down as he'd worked on his laptop. He pushed them up on his nose, returning to the screen.

"I don't know. She's still convinced I'm hiding a fortune from her." Sophie sighed, dropped into a chair across the table, and reached for his spiral pad and pen. "What are you looking for?"

"Just doing a search on shipwrecks here in Lake Michigan." He bookmarked the page he'd been reading and closed the computer. "Is it possible the only *treasure* here are these cottages?"

"It's possible, I guess. But she really believes there's something more."

"Well, unless we can get her to tell us what she knows, we have nothing to go on." Henry rested his chin in his palm and watched Sophie doodle cubes across the top of a sheet of lined paper. She put a letter inside each one, but they were random. Then she drew another set of cubes and reset the same letters, this time spelling out the word *shipwreck.*

A couple of years ago, he'd read an article about doodles and what they meant—why some people drew squares while others scribbled triangles or spirals or even stick figures. Apparently, what you doodled said something about your mood or personality. Until he read the article, he'd always drawn chains while figuring out a knotty problem. But when he read that chains indicated feeling trapped in a situation or relationship, it hit a little too close to home. After that, he made a conscious effort to only draw circles or spirals or even arrows—a sign that you were ambitious and motivated, although consciously choosing your doodles probably defeated the psychology of the study.

Henry tried to remember what cubes meant. Was it that you had the ability to see all sides of a situation? That made sense and fit what he knew of Sophie. He watched her fingers, the nails neatly manicured but plain, not painted, and let his mind wander farther afield. Sophie was as different from Kristie—and yes, all the others who'd occupied his heart and his wallet over the years —as lead was from cotton. He wanted to explore the growing pull between them, talk about those earlier kisses and touches that had begun and then ended so quickly his head spun. Was she inter-ested in him in that way? He wanted to take his cues from her... but the memory of those fingers touching his beard and toying with the hair hanging over his collar sent a spasm of yearning through him. Remembering Sophie's soft, round behind nestled on his lap caused him to shift uncomfortably in his chair, and the need to confess his attraction to her became overwhelming.

"Hey?" Sophie tapped his arm with the pen. "Do you think?"

Oh, shit, had she asked him a question? He blinked. "What?"

She blew out a frustrated breath. "Where *are* you?"

"I'm here, sorry." Heat crept up his neck. "I... I drift some-times. Used to piss off my ex-wife."

"It's okay, Henry." She chuckled. "I do it, too."

He straightened, then reached across the table to take her hand. "Sophie, can we talk about... about what happened earlier?"

She gave him a little mysterious smile. "You mean, the kissing?"

"Yeah."

"I liked it."

"So did I." He felt his face growing hot. Suddenly, he was back in high school, working up the nerve to ask the prom queen for a date. How did one take a relationship that had always been colleagues and friends to another level? His adult experience with women was pretty much limited to young, bold girls who simply grabbed what they wanted. All he'd had to do was flash his credit card and the rest took care of itself. This one was on him. He took a deep breath. "I'm... I'm attracted to you."

"I'm attracted to you too. I think you've probably figured that out." Sophie's expression didn't hold a hint of guile.

Confused and aroused, Henry nodded, trying not to overthink where she was headed with that declaration.

"So what's wrong with simply having some fun together this summer? No expectations? No commitments?" A little shrug of her shoulders, a slight shake of her head, and a dark tendril of hair slipped out of the elastic band holding it in place. When she reached back to pull it loose, the mass spilled over her shoulders.

His gut lurched.

Just have some fun? Was she serious?

This was an unexpected side of a woman he thought he knew well. "Friends with benefits?" he asked, trying to lighten the atmosphere, but his voice sounded hoarse.

"Sure. Why not?" She sat composed, her eyes wide. Her tongue ran over her lips.

"Can we do that?" Henry asked quietly, even though his knees shook and his palms were sweating. "Can *you* do that?"

How could she sit there cool as a cucumber?

"I'd love to give it a try." Rising from the chair, she slipped around the end of the table.

"No, don't." Holding up both hands, he leaned away. "Don't. We need to think about what we're doing here first."

"Why?" She moved closer to him. "How 'bout we try not thinking at all?" A few more steps and they were only inches apart. "But I guess if you're not sure..." One hand on his chin, she ran her thumb over his lips.

With that, he lost the tiny grip he had on his self-control. Groaning, he stood up and pulled her into his arms. She melted against him, kissing him hungrily, opening her lips to his. His restless hands moved over her back, finding the hem of her shirt and then touching soft skin.

"You're killing me here, Russo," he murmured against her lips. "God, you're irresistible." He took her lips again, his tongue plunged into her mouth.

When Sophie moaned into the kiss, he ran his hand up her spine, relishing the silky feel of her curls between his fingers. Her hands were driving him insane—lightly, she traced the muscles of his shoulders and fire followed each touch. He got bold and brought his other hand around, but she arched against his palm, so he slid his fingers under her bra to cup her breast. As his thumb brushed her nipple, sanity rose to the surface for a brief moment. Dear god, they were really doing this. He wasn't sure what astonished him more, the fact that he'd actually said the words *friends with benefits* or that *she'd* acted on them.

One more devastating kiss and it no longer mattered. Dancing her hands down his ribcage, she reached under his shirt to touch the skin of his back. She explored around the low-riding waistband of his jeans and he cringed a little. He forgot he wasn't wearing a belt, and in another moment of clarity, he wished he'd opted to run on the beach instead of sitting on the sofa guzzling beer. But her touches told him she didn't mind that he didn't have rock-hard abs. Resting her fingers lightly on the snap above his zipper, she went up on tiptoe to taste his tongue.

His hands traveled down to caress the curve of her hip and pull her closer to him, close enough he hoped, for her to feel the effect the kiss was having on him. His erection pressed into her stomach and she moved her lips to touch his beard, his stubble-rough cheek, his ear, while he dropped tiny kisses across her chin and down her neck. His pulse pounded in his ears as he shoved the oversized t-shirt off her shoulder to nibble the flesh there. Sliding her hand into the waist of his jeans, her fingers followed the arrow of hair below his navel and his heart nearly stopped.

"Ahem." Someone behind them cleared their throat loudly.

Sophie jumped back and when she yanked her hands out of his jeans, her ring scratched his belly. Henry dropped his hands and shoved her behind him, blinking in confusion at Dale and Eva, who stood smirking amidst the mess in the living room.

For once, Eva refrained from making a smart-ass remark. "Um, we're here to help clean up."

Henry tugged his t-shirt down over his fast-fading woody and glanced back over his shoulder to see a beet-red Sophie managing to put herself back together. She gave him a chagrined smile before stepping around him.

"Okay," she said with only the slightest tremor in her voice. "Let's get busy."

CHAPTER 13

Dusk had cast long shadows across the patio before Sophie noticed her mother was turning a little gray. An uneasy truce had settled over the cottages as Eva and Dale pitched in to help clean up the mess at the Firefly. The two of them worked like Trojans, with vigor equal to Henry and Sophie's, but now, with her arms full of cushions, Eva's breath came raspy and shallow. Sophie took the pillows from her and arranged them on the wicker settee on the screened porch.

"Sit down, Eva. Take a break." She jerked her head toward the sofa. "You look exhausted. I'm going to start some supper."

"I'm okay, kid, don't worry about me." Eva flopped on the cushions anyway, yanking the hair band from her ponytail and massaging her head. Then she repeated for what seemed like the hundredth time, "Jeezus, they really did a job in here."

Order had mostly been restored. Henry and Dale were putting the last of the books away after they'd flipped through every volume in the cottage. That particular search had been Dale's bright idea.

"Hell, you see it in movies all the time," he'd declared as he'd begun rifling books that were already shelved. "Old geezers leave cash or a map or some kind of clue in between the pages of a book."

Now, as he and Henry put the last of the books on the shelves, Henry almost reverently fondled a leather-bound copy of Hemingway's *To Have and Have Not*. "Another first edition! And it's autographed and dated." He held it up. "Nineteen forty. That's not very long after it was published."

"Hemingway was pretty familiar with this area, you know." That tidbit came from Eva, who was lounging on the sofa, long legs crossed, eyes closed. "His family spent summers near Petoskey. It's where he learned to fish and hunt. A lot of the Nick Adams stories came from his own experiences up here. His first novella*, Torrents of Spring*, was set in Petoskey."

Sophie gaped at her mother as Henry and Dale, obviously also shocked, stared at her in silence.

Eva opened one eye, then frowned. "What? You think 'cause I only got a GED that I'm a complete illiterate?"

"But... but how do you...?" Sophie tried to find a way to ask without sounding patronizing or insulting.

"What the hell do you think I did the entire summer I was pregnant with you?" Eva scowled at the three of them. "I laid around like a beached whale and read every goddamn book in this place, that's what." She closed her eyes again with a small smile that Sophie found both annoying and endearing. Her mother was creeping into her good graces, and she wasn't entirely sure she was pleased about that.

Henry tossed Sophie a grin. She rolled her eyes as she pulled plastic wrap off a package of chicken and plopped the pieces into a baking dish. A quick brush of olive oil and then she sprinkled garlic powder, basil, and salt and pepper generously. With a twist of the oven knob, she started it preheating as he wandered into the kitchen, grabbed her by the hand and pulled her into the utility porch.

"Hey, wanna take a shower with me?" he whispered, slipping his arms around her and touching his tongue to the sensitive skin just behind her ear.

"Are you sure showering together is allowed in this non-relationship?" She wrapped her arms around his neck. "Particularly before we've even been to bed together?"

"Perfectly fine, I checked the handbook." He nuzzled her neck, kissing and nibbling. "Page six, under Benefits." His mouth found hers as his hands slid down her back to cup her bottom and tug her closer.

Sophie leaned into the kiss, opening her lips to his seeking tongue, basking in the pure pleasure of his caresses. Several long kisses later, she reluctantly pulled away from his embrace. "Let's get supper over and get those two back over to the Sandpiper so we can explore that handbook together."

"Sounds like a plan to me." Henry dropped one final kiss on her lips. "So you're going to let them stay another night?"

"Oh hell, I guess so." She shrugged, but when Henry grinned, she shook a finger at him. "Just don't get all 'I told you so,' okay? I still don't trust either of them any further than I can throw them. But at least I'll know where they are and what they're up to."

"Hey, wait! Could that be it?" Dale called suddenly from his perch. "Could the treasure be all these books? They gotta be valuable."

"No, the books came after," Eva responded in a tired voice.

Sophie hurried into the kitchen. "After what?" She leaned over the granite bar to peer at her mother.

"After he found the treasure," Eva said, putting one hand over her eyes when Henry snapped on the ceiling fan light against the encroaching dusk. "Ugh, too bright."

Henry turned the dimmer to lower the light, then plopped down at the table and grabbed his notebook and pen. "Okay, conference time." He patted the seat next to his. "Soph, sit down and let's try to get this story on paper before the chicken gets done. Dale, Eva, come join us, huh?"

Dale scuttled down the ladder and dropped into the chair across from Henry as Eva, emitting a jaw-cracking yawn, rose slowly from the sofa and pulled out the chair opposite Sophie. Folding her hands in front of her on the table, she stared at Henry, who returned her gaze.

"Talk," he said after it became clear to Sophie that Eva wasn't going to say anything without some prodding. "Tell us exactly why you think there's a treasure. We're listening... and with open minds. Right, Soph?" He gave her a sideways glance.

"Yes." She tried very hard to sound as if she meant it. Although she still doubted there was a treasure, she couldn't wait to hear whatever Henry might pull out of Eva. Her mother had proven to be a bit more interesting than she'd originally thought. Plus, learning anything at all about Papa Leo was bound to be intriguing.

Eva stared down at her fingernails, her teeth nibbling her lower lip. Dale patted her hand. "Come on, babe. Give it up. You tell your part, I'll tell mine."

Sophie's mind reeled. *Her* part? *His* part? What part could Dale possibly play in this little scenario? He had nothing whatsoever to do with Papa Leo or Willow Bay.

Did he?

"Okay, so here's what I know for sure," Eva began, the words hesitant as she linked her fingers with Dale's on the table. Her grip on his was so tight, her knuckles were white.

Sophie glanced over at Henry with a little frown, but he reached under the table to put his hand on her knee. Just that small touch comforted her enough to encourage Eva with a nod.

"When I was a kid, Dad dove every summer, all summer long. He brought a ton of crap up from the bottom of that lake—broken dishes, old pieces of metal and wood." She snorted a laugh. "Even a trunk full of moldy old clothes that mama wouldn't let him bring into the cottage. God, that thing stunk to high heaven when we opened it down on the beach. He found some old coins like the one I showed you. He gave me that one as a good luck piece. Told me to always carry it with me. That it would... it would be like he was with me... keeping me safe." She swallowed hard and her eyes closed for a moment. "Shit." Eva's eyes brimmed with tears.

Sophie crossed her arms under her breasts and straightened her shoulders, resolving not to get pulled into any kind of fake sentimentality. She caught Henry's eye, but he simply reached back for the napkin holder on the counter and set it in front of Eva.

Wiping her eyes, Eva continued. "Then when I was about twelve or thirteen, things changed."

"How?" Henry asked, pen poised over his pad of paper.

"Dad got... like... secretive. It was right after a dive he did in early June. He went down after this giant storm. The biggest damn storm to hit the Great Lakes in years and years. I remember the beach was covered with all kinds of trash and Mama wouldn't let me go down there barefoot. We spent days picking stuff up."

Sophie pictured it in her head as Eva spoke. So many times she and her grandparents had cleaned up detritus that had accumulated on the beach after a storm. Logs, boards with rusty nails, pieces of metal. She remembered one time, a section of a small plane's wing appeared on the beach after waves had been huge. She and Papa Leo had scoured the library trying to find out what planes had gone down in their area, hoping to figure out some history on it. They finally ended up taking it to the recycle—with no markings to identify it, it was only another hunk of metal the lake had given up.

"What do you mean he got secretive?" Henry probed.

"He spent hours at the museum and the library, and if I asked about what he was doing, he was... I don't know, gruff. And after that summer, he stopped diving."

"Noah said he stopped diving when I was born," Sophie said, relaxing her posture to lean her elbows on the table.

"Noah went in the Navy the year I was thirteen, right after he graduated high school. As far as he knew Dad was still diving, but he actually stopped after that summer," Eva corrected. "I remember because I was furious that Dad wouldn't let me go out with him, but after that storm, he only went down a couple more times. He stopped bringing home stuff he found." She frowned. "That was another weird thing. He always had things to show us, even it was just broken dishes or a chunk of wood. But that also ended after the storm."

"Okay, interesting. But how does it all this lead up to a lost treasure?" Henry drummed the pen on the table.

"You think I'm nuts, don't you?" Eva squinted at him, but although he gave her that dear, sweet smile that certainly worked its magic on Sophie, her mother seemed immune. "Laugh all you want, hotshot, but I'm telling you, things changed."

"Again, how?"

"Dad went to Toronto before we went back to Indiana that year." Eva fidgeted with the damp napkin, folding it into different shapes.

"Was that odd?" Henry asked with a quick glance at Sophie.

"He went up there *alone* and he never did that. He always took us with him when he traveled. He was gone about three days and he and Mom spent a lot of time whispering in the bedroom." Eva tossed the napkin on the table. "People think their kids don't notice stuff, but I knew something was different.

"Then a few months later, he bought the Mercedes. Just came home with it one day. Thanksgiving, we burned the mortgages on these cottages and the house in Indiana." She snickered. "Big ceremony—I remember it because they let me have a sip of champagne."

"So?" Sophie stood up to check on the chicken baking in the oven. "He made a good salary teaching and managed his money well. Maybe they just decided to finally live a little." Opening the refrigerator, she grabbed a bag of romaine lettuce hearts and set it on the counter.

"Trust me, kid, he didn't make *that* good a living. Not a Mercedes Benz kind of living. College history teacher, remember? Jeezus, I'm starving." Eva rose too, washed her hands, and hauled a huge wooden bowl out of the cupboard below the bar. "Do you have red potatoes? I make a mean garlic mashed. I can show you how."

Sophie blinked and nodded her head numbly as Eva tore lettuce with practiced efficiency.

"Well...get the potatoes scrubbed and don't peel 'em." Eva tossed over her shoulder. "We can have it ready when the chicken's done if you chop 'em up small." She turned and rummaged in the refrigerator, pulling out a cucumber, green pepper, celery, and a bag of shredded carrots. "Ah ha! I love carrots in a salad. Oh and you need fresh garlic and butter for the potatoes. And Parmesan."

"Okay, I've got all that." Sophie went to the little utility room and brought back a small bag of red potatoes and began scrubbing them at the kitchen sink.

How surreal is this? I'm cooking supper with my mother.

"Anyway, those things were only the beginning." Eva went on with her story as she sliced and chopped cucumber, fresh green pepper, scallions, and celery with the ease of a professional chef. "They went to Italy on his spring break, he started buying expensive wines and new appliances and redoing the house and the cottages. It was out of character."

"Seriously?" Sophie turned around, a potato in one hand,

paring knife in the other. "Money was never an issue when I was growing up. He did whatever he wanted. Even helped out others when they needed it." She was ransacking her memory of life with Papa Leo and Nonna when she was a kid, but couldn't remember a time when they'd had financial troubles.

"Yeah, *after* the treasure. When I lived with him, he was tight as a tick," Eva said. "Always squeezed a nickel twice before he'd spend it and constantly went on and on about saving for college and needing money for retirement. Blah. Blah. Blah. Not that he wasn't charitable before. He was. But even that changed after the storm."

"What do you mean?" Henry was taking notes as Eva talked, but he stopped to watch the two of them preparing supper together, and his mouth quirked a little as if he found the whole scenario more than ironic.

Once again, Sophie found herself wishing they were alone so she could kiss the half-smirk off his handsome face.

"He stopped giving so much to charity?" he asked.

"No. Hell, no. He got crazy generous. Gave tons to his church, the alumni association, a homeless shelter, and the lighthouse renovation up here. I mean like thousands—I know this for a fact because his name is up on a plaque there as a member of, I don't know... the big donors club or something."

"This is why you suspect they found a treasure? Because he started spending money?" Sophie dumped the colander of diced potatoes into a pan, covered them with water, and put them on to boil. She began peeling garlic cloves at her mother's instruction.

"Not just money, a *lot* of money." Eva sliced a tomato, adding the red wedges to the salad with a flourish. "Okay Dale, your turn."

CHAPTER 14

Henry turned his attention to the older man sitting across from him. Dale's connection to Sophie's grandfather's treasure—if a treasure actually existed—was bound to be intriguing. Eva's story was interesting, even compelling in its own way, but not hardcore proof of anything.

Dale sat with his chin in his palm, watching the two women cooking. He seemed older than Eva, but it was hard to tell because years of rough living had clearly taken their toll. His eyes were lined and bloodshot, his skin sallow. His dirty-blond hair was streaked with gray, and when he spoke, he had the gravelly voice of a hard drinker. His age could have been anywhere between sixty and seventy-five.

Eva plunked back down next to him. "Tell 'em about your grandpa, babe."

"Well, my grandpa, Richard Case... that's my name by the way, Dale Richard Case. I don't think we ever were properly introduced." He extended his hand to Henry.

With a glance over his shoulder at Sophie, Henry shook it. "Nice to meet you."

"Anyhoo, back in the Depression, my grandpa was a numbers

runner. You know what that is?" He quirked a brow at Henry before glancing up at Sophie.

"Weren't they the guys who collected gambling money for organized crime?" she asked, drying her hands on a tea towel and coming over to stand behind Henry. She almost knocked him out of his chair with the odor of garlic on her hands.

"Sheesh, Soph," he said, wrinkling his nose and leaning away from her. "Did you lie down and roll in that garlic?"

"Hey, I'm making *your* supper, Dugan." Swatting him with the towel, she returned to the sink and flipped the faucet handle to rewash her stinky fingers.

"Do you have a stainless steel knife?" Eva asked.

"Um…yes." Henry heard the caution in Sophie's tone.

"Rub your fingers on it, then wash 'em. It'll get that garlic smell off."

"Really?" Sophie stroked her fingers over the wide blade of a stainless cleaver she pulled from a magnetic rack above the stove. Henry couldn't help grinning when she sniffed her fingers after washing them and then said in amazement, "It worked!"

"Kid, I've been working in the restaurant and bar industry my whole adult life. I got a million little tricks like that." Eva leaned back in her chair. "Go on, Dale, tell 'em about your grandpa."

"Where'd I leave off? Oh yeah, numbers runners." He gave Sophie a nod. "You're right. That's basically what they did, but he also ran other kinds of… errands for the people he worked for."

"Who'd he run numbers for?" Henry asked.

"Have you ever heard of the Todaro family?"

Sophie, who was back in her chair at the table and no longer reeking of garlic, shook her head, but cold settled in the pit of Henry's stomach. If Dale was talking about Salvatore "Sonny" Todaro the Third, then Grandpa Case hung out with some pretty vicious criminals.

"He worked for Sonny Todaro?" Henry's voice cracked, and

Sophie's head whipped around. He knew she was staring at him, but he didn't look over. Rather he wrote furiously in his notebook.

"Not the one who makes the news today." Dale gave a short bark of a laugh. "He worked for the current Sonny's grandfather, the first Salvatore Todaro. But they called him Sonny, too, back then."

"Who are the Todaros?" Sophie asked. Her hands were clenched together on the table, her knuckles whitening with tension.

"Mob family," Henry said, trying to keep his tone matter-of-fact. "They ruled south Chicago with an iron fist in the nineteen twenties and thirties. Originally, they made their fortune from racketeering and bootlegging liquor, mainly wine and whiskey from Canada. Today, their bread and butter is casinos, with a little heroin and cocaine thrown in for pocket money. They moved their operation to Las Vegas sometime in the nineteen seventies."

"How do you know all this stuff?" Sophie unclenched her hands and flexed her fingers, but tension still showed in her expression.

"I read." Henry gave her a little wink, hoping to relax her enough to hear Dale out. He gave the older man a nod.

Dale continued his story. "Grandpa's last run for Todaro was in November, 1933. He picked up a package in Washington and carried it to Michigan where he gave it to Todaro's boat captain, who was supposed to deliver it to Chicago."

"*Supposed* to deliver it?" Henry tapped the pencil on the notebook page. "It never got delivered? What happened to it?"

"Nobody really knows for sure." Dale leaned back in his chair, clasping his hands behind his head. "My grandpa took his payoff and moved to Florida. Bought a little farm and started raising racehorses. Several months after he'd made the delivery, a couple of Todaro's goons found him in Florida. They questioned him." Dale paused and gazed at each of them in turn. "Beat the holy crap out of him, too."

Henry swallowed a frustrated breath as Dale seemed to want to let the drama build. Sophie tensed more and more as she sat on the edge of her seat, and even Eva's dark-rimmed eyes were getting bigger in anticipation, even though she had to have heard the story before.

Henry dropped the pencil and looked at Dale over the top of his glasses. "So what did they want?"

"They wanted to know what he'd done with the package."

"What kind of package was it?" Sophie burst out. "Why do you keep calling it that? Just tell us what was in it!"

"I'm gettin' to that, girly. Just chill, okay?" Dale clearly relished his captivated audience.

She tossed Henry an eye roll, and again, he reached under the table to pat her thigh. She caught his hand and laced her cold fingers with his. Since she was getting really nervous, he encouraged Dale with a curt, "Go on."

"Todaro's goons were convinced Grandpa had taken the contents, sold them, and used the money to buy the farm. They beat him up pretty good, but he swore on everything he owned that he'd delivered it to the boat like he'd promised he would."

"But it never got to Chicago? Is that what you're telling us?" Sophie's voice sounded strained. "How does that connect in any way with my grandfather?"

"Grandpa heard through some of his pals, who also worked for Todaro, that the boat never showed in Chicago, but as far as he knew, it wasn't ever reported sunk or lost. Todaro sure as hell wasn't going to report a boat full of bootleg liquor and stolen gold to the authorities at the time." Dale leaned his bony elbows on the table. "Then Evie told me the story of her dad maybe finding a treasure of some kind in the lake, and I remembered the story of Todaro's lost gold. The mob kept a close eye on grandpa for years. But of course they never caught him with anything because he didn't have it—he swore on his deathbed that he'd given it to the boat captain."

Henry drummed the pencil on the pad for a few seconds, perusing his notes. "You said stolen gold. What kind of gold? Where'd he get it?"

"According to my grandpa, he picked it up just outside of Washington, DC."

"What was it?" Sophie pulled her hand away from Henry's and crossed her arms over her belly.

Dale leaned in and dropped his voice to almost a whisper. "A leather pouch filled with ten brand new Double Eagle twenty-dollar gold pieces fresh from the U.S. Mint. My grandpa met a guard from the mint and hand-carried the coins back to Michigan. Apparently, the guard was on Todaro's payroll too. He lifted 'em from the stash Roosevelt had ordered melted down and sent to Ft. Knox. Hell, stories about missing coins made the news back then, and about every twenty years or so, one of those 1933 Double Eagles shows up at a coin auction."

"How do you know that?" Sophie rose and paced the kitchen.

"I've been following this story my whole life. Ever since my grandpa told me about it. At this point, those coins are damn near priceless. The last one I know about sold for just over seven million back in 2002—that's dollars, sweetcakes." Dale smacked his hand on the table. "Government gets plenty pissed when they sell, too. They're considered government property, so there's always a big stink about it."

"And you think Leo found Todaro's lost coins?" Henry asked, his eyes drilling into Dale's watery gray ones.

"I'm sure of it." Dale met his gaze head on. "If he knew anything at all about what he'd found, he'd never try to fence them all at once. He'd sell them gradual and to private collectors. I've researched and researched who owned the one that came up for sale back in the sixties, but I ain't been able to find a thing. It went for about two million."

"Frankly, Dale and I came up a couple of years ago, trying to scare up some evidence of what Dad found that summer." Eva hauled herself out of the chair and went to the cupboard to pull down plates and salad bowls. She set them on the table and then turned to Sophie, who was leaning on the bar, looking as if she'd been hit upside the head. "If the rest of those coins are hidden here somewhere, they're worth a lot of money. Millions."

"No, no. I can't believe that they're here." Sophie's braid swung as she shook her head vehemently. "Papa Leo loved history. He'd have known immediately how important those coins were. Do you really think he'd have kept something like that a secret? He would have never sold them to some private collector. He'd have turned them in. Announced it to the world and returned them to the government."

"Oh, honey, you are so young." Eva snorted a laugh as she put a loaf of rye bread and the butter dish on the table. "Your precious Papa Leo was no more immune to dollar signs than any other human being on the planet."

～

Sophie shifted restlessly in her bed. Between the drama of Eva and Dale's revelations at supper and the memory of Henry's kisses and touches, she wasn't going to get a wink of sleep. Sitting up, she flipped her pillow over and then curled up on her side. It'd been a disconcerting conversation that went on past dinner and the men cleaning up, which they'd grumbled about good-naturedly.

"It's only fair," Eva had said with a wink to her daughter. "We cooked, you guys wash up."

The fact that they all seemed so at home with one another

creeped Sophie out more than she cared to admit. Eva and Dale were next door at the Sandpiper, settling in like they belonged there, and in a move that had shocked her speechless, Henry had made himself at home in the guestroom across the hall from her. She heard him in there tapping the keys of his laptop.

Disappointment had swelled in her when he kissed her good-night and packed her off to her room like a child. Obviously, he was rethinking the benefits part of friends with benefits, although she was certain it wouldn't have taken much to convince him to join her for that co-ed shower they'd talked about earlier.

Maybe he had decided not to pursue a physical relationship, although he'd certainly been affectionate enough all day long. Perhaps the situation with her mother had become too disconcerting, and he was across the hall, talking himself out of a summer fling. Maybe he was even making reservations to fly back to California.

She'd had her opportunity.

You're irresistible. He'd said it twice.

Sophie tossed over on her back. She'd had her chance and now in all the chaos, it was gone. She was so restless she could hardly breathe. She wanted him, but dear God, things had gotten complicated fast. Now her mind was awash with a frustrating mixture of longing for Henry and confusion about Papa Leo and Eva. A tear leaked out of her eye and dampened the pillow under her cheek.

Cripes. Weeping over a guy? Unbelievable! All she needed was his letter sweater and a locked diary under her pillow, and this scene could play in any B movie from the sixties.

Hello, Gidget. Sheesh.

She closed her eyes and tried to let the sound of the breeze in the trees and the water on the shore far below lull her to sleep. A knock at her half-open door brought her bolt upright in bed. A hand pushed it the rest of the way and there was Henry, standing in the shadows.

"Can you sleep?" His voice was husky.

"No." She wasn't sure why she was whispering.

"Me, neither." Bathed in moonlight, he stood uncertainly, his hair tousled as though he'd been running his fingers through it.

When she hopped from the bed and crossed the room, he reached for her and kissed her hungrily. Finally, he raised his head. "I was writing and I got to a love scene. Funny thing was I couldn't stop thinking about you."

"So what am I?" She touched his cheek. "Research?"

"Oh, my friend, you are so much more than research." He reached behind her, closing the door. For a long moment, he gazed deep into her eyes in the dim glow from the safety light at the beach steps. "I don't want to be alone tonight. I want you."

Without another word, she took his hand and led him to her bed.

CHAPTER 15

Henry's heart pounded as he watched Sophie pull off her faded t-shirt. It damn near stopped when she turned around to face him clad only in lacy bikini panties. Her skin glowed golden tan in the moonlight except where her swimsuit had protected soft white flesh. Her breasts were round and firm, but not perky, her pink nipples hardening in the cool night air. Her belly wasn't flat, he couldn't count her ribs, and her strong thighs touched each other—she was beautifully, deliciously, imperfectly perfect. He sucked in a breath as she smiled at him—a shy smile that completely belied the bravado of pulling off her shirt almost as soon as he opened the bedroom door.

"Your turn," she whispered, closing the steps between them to help him tug off the polo. Sophie kissed his shoulder, running her tongue over the skin. When she pressed against him and rubbed her breasts on his bare chest, all the angst about his thickening waistline fled. He just wanted her... desperately.

Henry slid his hands over her back, loving the silky feel of her skin. He traced the path of her spine, then his lips found hers. They kissed, deep, hungry kisses, tongues meeting in a sensual duel. Tasting her lips only increased the urgency, the hot need to be inside her, to feel her legs wrapped around him. "Sophie..."

He wanted to explore every inch of her, from her neck to her toes and back up again, making intimate stops all along the way. Releasing her lips, he kissed his way down her neck. "Oh, God, Soph..." Repeating her name, the thought flitted through his mind that he should think of something more intelligent to say.

He was a writer for God's sake.

But his vocabulary had gone missing when she put her lips on his shoulder. All he wanted was to lose the rest of their clothes and fall into bed.

Hands trembling, Sophie unbuttoned his jeans and slid the zipper down, letting the back of her hand brush against the hard evidence of his desire. He couldn't believe *she* was being so brazen—it was the most erotic thing that had ever happened to him. Hunger flooded his body as she dropped her head back to grant him access to the soft skin of her throat. When she slipped her hands in the front of his tight knit boxers to briefly squeeze his erection, he nearly lost it.

He backed her toward the bed and when her legs hit the mattress, she fell back on the sheets. He hooked his fingers into the lace at the top of her panties and glided them down her legs, then let his hands skate back up her thighs. The sight of his demure little editor splayed across the bed for his pleasure made him want to moan out loud.

Wordlessly, he reached into his pocket. Dropping his jeans and boxers to the floor in one swift movement, he tossed a packet on the night table. When he turned back to Sophie, she reached for him. Clutching his shoulders, she pulled him down to her kisses. Their tongues danced and their hands were everywhere, exploring and stroking.

Henry cupped her breast, loving how she shivered when he brushed it with his thumb. Moving his mouth down, he took her nipple between his lips. The scent of her skin—flowers and musk —intoxicated him. "God, I want you." The words were muffled against her flesh. "I'll never get enough of you."

With a throaty hum, she thrust her fingers into his hair as his tongue teased first one pink nipple and then the other. His hand skimmed the soft skin of her stomach, moving over her hip to caress the muscles of her behind. She whimpered and arched into his hand. Pulling her closer, he pressed his erection into her belly. His fingers found the heat and wet between her legs.

Gasping, she raised her hips to his touch. His heart was about to burst.

"Henry, please..." she begged.

Reaching between them, she curled her fingers around his erection, tugging gently. She opened her legs. "Now..." With her other hand, she pulled his head up to gaze into his eyes. "I need you... now."

Henry reached out to grab a foil packet from the night table. In seconds, he was sheathed and sliding slowly into her heat as he stared into her wide emerald eyes. His eyes closed as she traced the muscles of his ribcage around to his back. He shuddered as her fingers gripped his hips.

A low groan escaped when she wrapped her legs around him and rose to meet his long teasing strokes. She surrounded him, tight and hot as they moved together in a perfect rhythm. Slipping one hand between them to find the nub of her desire, he thrust even faster, raining kisses on her throat, her neck, her ear while she buried her face in his shoulder.

On a sharp intake of breath, she cried out, "Henry, Henry, I... I..."

When her muscles spasmed around him, Henry let go too, pressing his lips into the warm hollow of her neck as he climaxed deep inside her.

Sophie lay with her head on Henry's chest, running her fingers idly over his naked stomach as her mind wandered back to Eva and Dale's revelations at supper. She couldn't help it.

Now, they were all steeped in a mystery, and Sophie had to come face to face with some difficult facts. Perhaps she didn't know Papa Leo as well as she'd thought. Maybe Eva knew him better.

"Hey, want to join me here?" Henry's voice took her out of her reverie while his fingers tracing up her bare spine sent a shiver of sensation through her.

She tipped her face up to kiss him. "I'm sorry. I'm here."

"What's on your mind?" His hand was on her rear end now, caressing her and making it very hard to think clearly.

She was still amazed at how his touch could take her right out of herself. She grasped his fingers to stop him for a moment. "I've been thinking."

"Yeah?"

"Papa Leo always drove nice cars. Not just the Mercedes. He bought a new car at least every couple of years, and when I graduated from high school and grad school, he bought me new cars, too, plus he paid for my education. Every dime."

"Okay... your point?"

"I mean expensive cars, Henry. Really expensive cars." She was reaching for something that seemed to keep eluding her. "How did they afford those cars? And my college and the vacations and paying off the mortgages? Papa Leo taught at a small college. Nonna never worked outside our home." She rose up on one elbow. "Dammit, I hate that Eva's right, but maybe she is."

"Nice cars don't prove anything." A frown furrowed his blond brow. "Maybe that's where their priorities were."

"Not Papa Leo, no. He wasn't in the least materialistic." She scooted closer to him, his hands on her were distracting as hell and the current line of thinking was making her tired. "Oh, I don't know what I'm going for here." Laying her head back on Henry's chest, she closed her eyes and inhaled the masculine scent of him. He smelled so wonderful.

"You want there to be a treasure, don't you?" He pressed a kiss against her forehead. "In spite of Eva showing up and Dale's stupid story about the mob, you're intrigued with the idea of finding a treasure."

"I don't know. Yeah. No. Well maybe, but not if it's going to get us hurt. It's kind of exciting, though, don't you think?"

When she gazed up at him, he grinned. "It has the makings of a great mystery or adventure novel, that's for sure." He pulled her closer to him, letting his hands roam over her skin again. "We have a lot of research to do, starting with the attic next door."

"There's a bunch of stuff up there. I remember several old trunks and boxes, plus some furniture. Maybe tomorrow—"

"Shhh..." His lips on hers interrupted what she was about to suggest. He kissed her, a light kiss that turned into a deep kiss and then another. His lips moved down to find the soft skin of her collarbone and then further down.

With a moan, she thrust her fingers into his thick hair and very quickly, the attic trunks, the books, Eva, and even the coins were all forgotten—replaced by that wonderful, mindless heat that only Henry could create.

CHAPTER 16

"Y ou slept." Sophie grinned at Henry as he wandered into the kitchen, looking sleepy-sexy in only a pair of khaki shorts and a t-shirt slung over one shoulder. Although incredulous, she also felt wonderful, if a tiny bit achy from the night they'd spent in her bed. This whole summer romance thing was definitely nothing to be scared of—so far, it was marvelous.

"No thanks to you, you wanton creature." Henry tugged her into his arms to kiss her thoroughly. "I do have to admit, last night was a record."

"Didn't I tell you we'd have fun, Dugan?" She ran a hand over his soft goatee and then his stubbly cheek. "However, if we plan to make this a regular thing, I am going to have to insist you shave sometime soon. Not the beard, I love it. But the rest? Look." She pulled open the neckline of her short robe to show him a rash on the top of her breasts. "This is not going to cut it."

"Oh, damn." He ran a finger over her reddened flesh. "Did I do that? I'm so sorry. I guess I should've shaved last night before I showed up at your bedroom door." Leaning down, he pressed his lips to the spot. "You drive me crazy, Russo. What can I say?" His hands slipped inside the robe. Cupping one breast, he let his thumb brush the peak. "I'm betting this isn't the only place I'll find it—why don't I just do a quick exam..."

A shiver coursed through her as he let his tongue travel from the top of her breast down to her nipple. Then he untied the robe.

"Henry." Inching back, she gave a quiet moan. The memory of the last time they'd come together in the wee hours of the morning, of him sliding into her, slow and sexy, made her reluctant to pull away too quickly. Making love with him had been more delicious than she'd ever imagined. A tiny voice niggled at the back of her mind, reminding her that it was purely sex with no strings and no obligations, but she ignored it. She'd wanted him and now, she had him. The how and why of it was immaterial. Right now, she only wanted to bask in the pleasure part.

"Hey, I've had—" He glanced up at the clock on the microwave. "—two and half hours of sleep. I'm good to go again." Pulling her back to him, grasping her backside, he proved it by pressing his pelvis against her.

Sophie sighed in mock despair and kissed him. "Let me go. You depraved writers are all alike. Sex, sex, nothing but sex. I've got coffee here, and I'm going to make breakfast. We need sustenance."

"You are my sustenance, Sophie-fair," Henry teased, nibbling her shoulder before she covered it back up and stepped back from his arms.

"*You* are so full of it." Giggling, she poured coffee into two thick mugs.

Dear God, I'm giggling. This man is driving me completely insane.

"We should probably eat, I guess." Accepting a mug of steaming coffee from her, he yanked on the t-shirt and sat. "I'd hate for Eva to come in and find us naked in bed together, all wizened and dehydrated. Besides, I'm starving."

Their laughter was interrupted by a knock at the door. Sophie glanced around to see Jules and Carrie peering through the sheer curtains.

"Oh, it's my friends." Sophie snugged her robe tighter and went to answer their insistent knocking.

"You didn't show up at the Grind again this morning, so we brought coffee and muffins to you," Jules announced, give the screen door a tug while Carrie held up a tray of coffee containers and a sack. "Unlock the door. Why are you still in your jammies?"

As soon as they walked into the kitchen, they stopped short, turned around, and grinned at Sophie.

"Oh." Carrie set the tray and bag on the counter. "Um, I think we see why you're still in your pjs." She extended her hand to Henry, who leaned back in his chair, looking sexy and sated in his shorts and t-shirt. "Hi, I'm Carrie Reilly."

"Henry Dugan." He rose and shook her hand before reaching for Jules's. "Nice to meet you."

"Hey, Henry." Jules didn't even try to hide her curiosity. "I'm Jules. You must be the writer slash nerd slash computer geek."

"Personally, I prefer *intellectual badass*, but yeah, you've got it just about right." With a grin, he raised both hands in a gesture of surrender.

"I like him already!" Jules gave him a high five.

"I've only got three coffees, but we brought half a dozen muffins. Perry had a BOGO today." Carrie, ever the perfect hostess, bustled around the kitchen, opening a cabinet to pull out a large plate for the muffins and gathering napkins and forks.

"That's okay, Carrie, we've already made coffee." Sophie offered Henry a rueful smile. "I'm going to go throw some clothes on. Try not to interrogate him while I'm gone, okay you two?"

Henry waved her off. "BOGO?" he asked, adding cream to his coffee and passing the carton to Carrie.

"Buy one, get one." Carrie explained. "He does that once a week, which is great because…"

Their friendly chatter followed Sophie down the hall. But she barely got the bedroom door closed before it opened again and Jules rushed in.

She held up a lipstick as she glanced over her shoulder. "Hey, Soph, here's that lipstick I was telling you about," she said loudly as she shut the door behind her.

"Well, that was subtle." Sophie reached for the tube, but Jules pocketed it before she could take it. With a frown for her friend, Sophie went to the closet.

"No time for subtle. I need details, missy. Come on, dish." Jules glanced at the unmade bed and waggled her brows. "You've totally got that well-laid look about you this morning."

"Do you think he doesn't know why you came back here?" Sophie pulled a black and white sleeveless top from the closet and put it together with her denim skirt, dressing hurriedly.

"I'm sure he does." Jules followed her to the bathroom, leaning against the doorjamb as Sophie splashed water on her face and moisturized. "I don't care. He's hot, by the way. Love the glasses, and that rumpled professorial thing totally works for him, but the name? *Henry?* Can we at least call him *Hank*?"

"Not if you expect him to answer." Sophie chuckled. "He hates 'Hank' with a passion. Apparently his ex-wife insisted on calling him that because she thought 'Henry' was too nerdy. He told me several years ago never, ever call him *Hank*." She tossed Jules a knowing grin. "*Henry* worked just fine last night."

"Tell me everything." Jules plopped down on the edge of the bathtub.

"I think you've pretty well figured it out."

"Was it fantastic?"

"He certainly knows his way around a female body." Sophie

dabbed on some blush, ran a brush through her hair, and brought the tresses up off her neck with a clip.

"Like that's nearly enough." Jules met her eyes in the mirror. "I need more."

"He blew my mind, okay?" Sophie grabbed a pair of silver earrings that happened to be on the sink and slipped them in, her mind filled with Henry and his intoxicating effect. "Fireworks lit up the heavens. The angels wept. It was amazing. He's amazing."

"You turkey. That's great!" Jules gave her butt a little swat. "I'm so glad for you. Nerds do try harder in the sack, baby. It's like they've got something to prove, thank god!"

"You know, Jules, I've been thinking. Maybe this was just another connection he and I needed to make. Over the years we've worked together, we've gotten close on so many other levels—colleagues, friends, confidants. I've always loved talking to him. He's intelligent and well-read and funny and sensitive and open." She shrugged as she knelt down to search under the bed for her sandals.

She was attracted to everything about Henry Dugan. Fact was, she'd been daydreaming—okay, fantasizing—about him for a long time. Maybe the sex was just a logical progression. She sat back on her heels and thought for a moment about other men she'd worked with since starting her freelance career. It was always just business. Not for one moment did she have the slightest interest in any of them outside of the work they offered.

Henry and this attraction was something very unique. She could easily over-think it, as was her inclination with anything that involved looking inside herself. But did it matter really why or how it happened? All that counted was that they were finally together, even if only for a short while.

"Sophie?" Jules's voice interrupted her lovely dreaming.

"Ah, here they are." She pulled the shoes out and rose, mystified at her friend's sober expression. "What?"

"Be careful." Jules touched her cheek.

"What's this?" Sophie asked. "Where's my 'go for the summer fling' cheerleader?"

Jules pulled her into a quick hug. "Big sister kicked in. I still think if you've got a chance at a little happiness this summer, you should go for it, but you're kinda vulnerable right now."

"Says my oh-so-experienced friend who's had... um... how many relationships in her life?"

"Two, smart ass." Jules rolled her eyes. "But I know you, so just watch your heart, okay?"

CHAPTER 17

Over muffins and coffee, Sophie and Henry filled her two friends in on Eva's arrival, the vandalism, and the treasure story.

"Tony never said a word about you having a break-in." Carrie scowled at the news. "Did they take anything valuable?"

"Tony?" Henry raised one brow before biting into his second muffin. "I thought the sheriff's name was Earl Something."

"Tony's a good friend of my husband, Will, and Carrie's husband, Liam," Jules explained. "He moved here after Carrie and Liam got married a few years ago. Earl made him a deputy sheriff after his other deputy moved to Detroit to join the police force there."

"Tony's the new deputy?" Sophie couldn't help her chortle of laughter. "My God, that's great! He's gonna scare the crap out of any kid he stops." She turned to Henry. "He's a big guy, like Paul Bunyan big. Brawny and tall and gruff-looking."

"But he's a sweetie," Carrie added. "He wouldn't hurt a fly."

"I thought he was painting houses," Sophie said. "And no, they didn't take anything. It was pure vandalism."

"He is painting houses." Jules got up and rummaged in the refrigerator, pulling out the butter dish. "I'm zapping this, okay?" She put it in the microwave and stood by as it softened. "This deputy thing is only a part-time gig. The town can't afford to pay him full-time."

"Liam? Liam Reilly?" Henry remarked, staring at Carrie. "Is your husband Liam Reilly the conductor?"

"He is." Carrie nodded.

"Holy cow! Soph, you didn't tell me you had celebrities living here." Henry's eyes widened. "I saw him conduct the Berkeley Symphony at Golden Gate Park last summer. They did his *Countdown to Paradise* music. It was just incredible. That's one of my favorite movies—mostly because of the music."

"Thanks, I'll tell him." Carrie gave him a big smile. "Frankly, he'll be thrilled to meet *you*. He has every book you ever wrote about digital music software. He and Will couldn't have built his studio in the basement without you."

"You're kidding. Wow." Henry flushed, clearly enjoying the turn the conversation had taken.

"Hey, how 'bout we set up a fan-boy moment for Henry and Liam later?" Jules interrupted, smearing butter on her muffin. "Can we get back to Sophie's situation?"

Sophie giggled before becoming serious again. "There's no situation, Jules. I've just got to find a way to get Eva back on the road to Florida. It may have to involve giving her Papa Leo's Mercedes."

"Don't you dare!" Carrie wiped her mouth and tossed her crumpled napkin on the table. "It was Leo's pride and joy. Besides, Liam will kill you if you give away that car. He's been salivating over it since the first time he saw it."

"Sounds to me like she wants way more than the car." Jules popped the last bite of muffin in her mouth and chewed before continuing. "Do you think there's a treasure?"

"That's what we're going to try to figure out," Sophie said with a glance at Henry.

"How can we help?" Carrie rose and started clearing off the table.

Thanks to Carrie's connections, they spent the rest of the morning in the basement archives of the newspaper offices, scouring old copies of the Willow Bay *Herald Journal*. The papers they were interested in hadn't gotten onto microfiche or been scanned into data files yet, so the work was tedious, and as it turned out, a fruitless search. There were plenty of stories of stuff found in the lake by divers all during the sixties, but no articles that mentioned Leo Russo or gold coins from the Depression era.

Dusty and grubby with newsprint, Sophie led Henry down to the bay to walk along the shore and catch a breath of fresh air.

He surveyed the area where they stood on the north breakwater, looking back into the bay. The jetty protected the entrance to the bay that the town of Willow Bay sat on. From the wall, the view displayed the town to the east or the lighthouses and Lake Michigan to the west. "Did I read in the brochure you have in the Sandpiper that this harbor is man-made?"

She stared out across the grey-blue water. "No, only the channel. The original opening to the bay was farther up, north of the current channel. They dredged this one in 1860-something, so the harbor would be a safe place for ships to escape from a storm before going north into Manitou Pass."

He tugged her into his arms, pulling her back against his broad chest to rest his chin on the top of her head. Grateful for the contact, she felt small and protected within the circle of his arms.

Despite her good intentions, Sophie had leaned on him over the past few days like she might have on—she forced herself to admit it—like she might have on a lover... or a husband. She hadn't meant to, but his warm, generous nature made it so easy, and besides, she had no clue how to be in a summer fling. Apparently neither did he if his investment in her current situation was any indicator.

Things were getting complicated on every front.

She shoved that worry aside and let herself relax into his embrace. "What's next?"

"Not sure. The attic, I guess. And the Internet. Let's walk out there." He released her, then took her hand and started down the concrete breakwater toward the lighthouse.

They strolled out to the point. Sophie stepped up a short metal ladder to sit on a small loading dock, tucking her legs under her. Henry stood beside her, leaning against the concrete platform. She placed on hand on his back.

"Dale told the loan sharks about the coins, didn't he?" She asked the question even though she knew the answer, hoping that if she said it out loud, maybe they could figure out what to do.

"Yeah, I suspect he did." He stretched his back as she rubbed right below his shoulders. He moved closer so his hip was against her leg and gave a satisfied little moan. Obviously, she'd found a place that needed rubbing, so she continued while he mused, "If so, I'm thinking the guys he owes are giving him some time to find them."

"Oh, God. That means they could be following him." Her heart sank, then her pulse began to pound. "It might've been them who trashed the Firefly." She chewed on her lower lip, all the while pressing her hand harder into the tense muscles of his back. "Maybe they were trying to find the coins."

He leaned over to grant her access lower on his back. "I guess it's possible they're following him. But, I'm starting to rethink my earlier assertion that Dale had nothing to do with the break-in."

"Why?"

"He was very convincing about the connection between his grandfather and Eva's treasure story. But don't you think it's a hell of a coincidence? They meet and then discover this incredible connection between her father and his grandfather? I don't think so."

"What are you saying?"

"I don't know... just thinking out loud. Heck, maybe the gambling debts are bullshit to scare you into giving them the coins, which then, of course, assumes the coins even actually exist and that your grandfather found them." He heaved a huge sigh. "Cripes. Too many what ifs."

"Let's assume for a second that they do exist. What if Dale's been searching for the coins too? I mean, for years?" She stopped rubbing and touched his shoulder with a trembling hand. Her heart rose in her throat. "What if he or his father or grandfather have been up here dozens of times, diving and somehow, they figured out Papa Leo found them? What if they've been following my family for years waiting for a chance to grab them? Or worse, what if the mob guys have been looking all these years? Maybe Dale's telling the truth about that."

"Sophie, who's the writer here?" Henry turned around and rested his hands on her legs. "I'm not worried about the mob. That's too far-fetched. Besides, I'm fairly certain that if eighty years ago, some bootlegger lost a boatload of liquor and gold in Lake Michigan, he would've gone after it right then. That's not to say that maybe the family hasn't searched for it since, particularly with the great new technology they have today, but I doubt they've been watching every diver who ever went down in the lake since nineteen thirty-something."

"I'm scared." Sophie clutched his hand. "Maybe we should talk to the sheriff again."

"We can do that if it'll make you feel better. Maybe he can find out something about Dale." He touched his forehead to hers. "It's going to be okay. I'm not going to let anything happen to you."

The promise in his eyes eased her mind a little, but the cold in the pit of her stomach remained. Her instinct was to pack up and leave—simply disappear and let Eva and Dale deal with their own drama—whatever it was. With a resolute sigh, she kissed him and ran her fingers along the sun-warmed skin on his arm.

After a moment of staring out at the lake, he grasped her hand and helped her off the platform. "Come on, let's hit it. We'll go talk to the sheriff and then get started in the attic." With one finger, he touched the end of her nose. "If we don't find at least one solid fact pretty soon, your imagination's going to go right off the dial. I need you sane, so we can figure this stuff out."

~

Sheriff Earl Gibson simply shook his head, reiterating that he had no evidence to arrest Eva and Dale. "Why didn't you mention any of this stuff when I came out to investigate the vandalizing of your cottage?"

Sophie squirmed in her chair at his exasperated tone. "I didn't know any of it then... well, I didn't know most of it."

"Where are your mother and her boyfriend? I know they're not staying at the Hillside anymore. Joey told me they kicked them out."

She'd glanced at Henry out of the corner of her eye. "They're staying in the other cottage."

"Seriously?" Earl sighed and raised one skeptical brow. "First you tell me you believe she destroyed the Firefly, but you have no evidence. Now, she's your houseguest? Wanna make that work for me?"

"Earl, listen. I came to you because I'm scared." Perched on the edge of her chair, Sophie popped up, pacing the small office in agitation. "I don't know what's going on. Eva and Dale show up out of the blue with this crazy story, my house gets trashed—"

Earl cut her off. "Frankly, when you told me you thought they did it, I didn't have any trouble believing you. Hell, I've known your mother since she was a wild kid and I was nothing more than a punk deputy. Hauled her butt back home on more than one occasion, summers she spent up here. More than once I told your grandpa to let her stew in jail for a few days. But he always came and bailed her out." Earl stood up too, his full height barely reaching the top of Sophie's head. "Now here you are, protecting her exactly like he did. So unless you're ready to offer me some real evidence against Eva or press charges, I got nothin'." Earl folded his arms over his chest and rocked back on his heels as he kept his focus on Sophie.

"I'm just letting you know I think something's suspicious about Dale, okay?" Sophie marched back to his desk, placing her fingertips on the scarred surface.

"Okay. Thanks for the information. Now if you've got a specific crime to report, tell me. Otherwise, I've got paperwork to finish."

They drove home in relative silence with Henry at the wheel and Sophie's tension growing the closer they got to the cottages. How lovely would it be to simply discover the coins tucked away in the attic along with a long explanation penned in Papa Leo's tidy script?

Right, like that's going to happen.

Summer had started out so well with beach walks, settling into her new life, and seducing Henry being her main focus—

until her mother showed up. Now, chaos reigned and she blamed Eva for all of it.

Damn the woman, why couldn't she have stayed in Florida and left me alone?

"Well that was a bust," she said finally. "He thinks we're both nuts."

"I was afraid that would happen, but at least we tried. And now the authorities know something's up, even if he's not sure whether to believe us." Henry pulled into the parking area behind the cottages, shut off the engine, and sat staring out the windshield for minute before he turned to her. "Let's take a peek up in the attic. Maybe there are some documents or a diary of your grandfather's... hell, I don't know... anything."

"Okay, can't hurt to check."

They grabbed a quick snack, changed clothes, and then hurried over to start hunting for clues upstairs at the Sandpiper. The Honda was parked behind the cottage—evidently Eva and Dale were home, but when Henry knocked, no one answered. He tried the screened porch door. It was unlocked, so they walked in with Sophie calling out to her mother.

"They must be down on the beach," she said when there was no response. "Come on, let's go up to the attic."

The entry to the attic opened from the hallway ceiling with a set of pull-down stairs. He unfolded the ladder, climbed up far enough to see into the low-ceilinged space, and then clambered back down. "Two things, the light's burned out, so we need a flashlight, and I'm going to have to lose about a foot off my height to even begin to fit in there. You'll have to go up."

Sophie retrieved a flashlight from the kitchen drawer, glancing around as she walked through the cottage. Her mother was surprisingly tidy. She'd expected piles of clothes, a sinkful of dirty coffee cups, and the telltale reek of cigarettes. But there were no clothes lying around, the bed was made, the kitchen was clean, and the fresh air proved Eva hadn't been smoking inside the house.

So she's not a slob, she's still a pain in the ass.

Henry stepped aside and spotted her as she climbed the steps with the flashlight. The attic was dusty and had an odor reminiscent of an old boathouse, kind of musty and damp, which was odd since it was always dry up under the eaves.

"I'll be damned!" she exclaimed as she scanned the beam of light around the open area.

"What? What is it?"

"I remembered this place being full of boxes and trunks and all kinds of furniture and old junk, but now there are only a couple of beat-up trunks and a few dusty boxes. No file cabinets, either." She shined the light around again. "Know what? It seems smaller."

"Smaller? When's the last time you were up there?"

"When I was a kid, like maybe twelve or thirteen."

"That's probably why. Everything is big when you're a kid."

Sophie glanced down at him with a frown. "When did Papa Leo clear the stuff out of here, I wonder? I've been with him every summer and I don't remember ever cleaning out the attic."

"He could've had someone else do it," Henry offered. "Maybe Noah."

"Maybe." She scowled at the boxes, but crawled in and started shoving them to the opening for him to carry downstairs and haul over to the screened porch at the Firefly.

They both had hold of an end of the larger trunk and were wrestling it across the patio when a scream broke the hazy midafternoon quiet. In unison, they dropped the chest, letting it fall to the flagstones with a dull thunk.

"Where did that come from?" he glanced around.

"The beach?" She turned toward the steps just as another scream rent the air.

"Nooooo..." A guttural, agonized cry echoed up from below the cottages.

"That's Eva!" Sophie scrambled down the wooden steps with Henry close on her heels.

CHAPTER 18

Sophie's mother lay sprawled on her back on the second landing, her hands covering her face as Dale stood over her, clenching and unclenching his fists.

"Eva, are you okay?" Sophie took the remaining steps two at a time. "Did you fall?"

"Help me—he hurt me." Eva's words garbled as she scooted on her behind over the rough wooden surface into the corner, practically falling into the sand below.

"Eva." Sophie crouched down and clutched at her mother's shoulder, trying to hold her on the landing. "What happened? You're bleeding."

"He punched me." Eva lifted her head and bumped it on the second board of the rail fence surrounded the landing, She uncovered her eye; the lid was cut and already starting to swell. She stared at the blood on her fingers. "Jesus Christ, look at all that blood." Sitting up and leaning against Sophie's bracing arm, she sobbed.

Sophie dug in her pocket, found a ragged paper towel, and handed it to her.

Henry stepped in front of Dale and shoved him back, grateful for the six or so inches he had on the older man. "What going on here?"

"You mean besides the fact that she's a stupid bitch?" Dale snarled, heading for the steps to the beach.

"Hang on." Henry blocked his path. "You're not going anywhere, man. Sophie, take Eva upstairs and call the sheriff."

"Dale, you bastard!" Eva wailed, mascara streaking her cheeks. She shunted Sophie aside and struggled to stand up. "Do something, Dugan. Kick his ass."

"Eva, go upstairs," Henry said over his shoulder as he kept a close eye on Dale. "Now."

Dale seemed to shrink as Henry towered over him. "Look, man, don't call the cops. It's just a little misunderstanding."

"A little misunderstanding?" Eva screeched.

Sophie helped her mother get to her feet. "Come on. Let's go upstairs and get you cleaned up."

Clutching Sophie's shoulder, Eva continued screaming. "You son of a bitch, you ripped my shirt." She held out her arm. The sleeve dangled by a few threads. She jerked away from Sophie's grasp, and with surprising agility, jumped, landing on her feet just behind Henry.

Dale ducked and Eva's open palm struck Henry right across the cheek.

"Dammit!" Henry grabbed her wrist to keep her from striking out again, holding her against his side with one hand while he latched onto Dale's arm with the other. "Cut it out, Eva."

Eva twisted in his grasp, trying desperately to reach Dale who'd dropped down a couple of steps, forcing Henry to balance on his toes on the platform.

"Eva!" With a disgusted sigh, Sophie marched over and took control of her mother. "Come on. Chill out."

Breathing heavily and glaring at Dale, Eva backed off enough that Henry could yank Dale back up on the landing. "Okay, sit." He shoved Dale onto the built-in bench. "Now, what the hell?"

"He took my cash. He went into my purse like a thief." Eva rubbed her cheek and smeared blood into her hair. "When I called him on it, he hit me."

"Called me on it?" Dale started to get up, but Henry pushed him back down again. "You came after me like goddammed wild-cat." His voice turned whiny. "She attacked me. I was just defending myself. Look!" He pointed to three long scratches on his cheek. "I wasn't goin' for your money, you bitch. I was lookin' for your lighter."

"I don't keep my lighter in my wallet, asshole." In spite of her tough talk, Eva's voice trembled.

"I don't care who started this, it's done." Sophie turned and sent her mother up the steps ahead of her before twirling around to point one trembling finger at Dale. "I want you out of here right now. Come on, Eva, let's get some ice for your eye."

She led Eva up the beach steps. The woman was inconsolable, alternately hiccupping and weeping as she stopped every few steps to spit another epithet at Dale.

"Eva, stop it." Sophie was proud of her tone that brooked no nonsense. "Pull yourself together."

Eva's eyes widened as she stared at her daughter before submitting to her urging and clambering up the stairs.

Henry sat on the railing, rubbing his burning cheek and glaring at Dale. He ran his fingers through his hair, pressing the thatch against his head, trying to get his thoughts together.

As he stared at Dale's skinny white legs sticking out of his faded shorts, it occurred to him that the summer had started getting very complicated. He hadn't signed up for this. If he wanted drama, he could've stayed in California. He'd been getting plenty of theatrics from his ex-wife. Sophie's suggestion from a few nights ago that he pack up and find a flight back to San Jose sounded pretty good about now.

As soon as the idea crossed his mind, he abandoned it. Taking off meant leaving Sophie. He glanced up at her shapely backside as she hustled Eva up the steps. No, he wasn't going to be leaving Sophie and not just because she'd been the best sex he'd ever had, although that was certainly true. She was also funny and intelligent and warm and... dammit, she needed him. Nobody had truly needed him in a very long time. That part felt good. Really good.

Besides, in spite of Dale and Eva being royal pains in the ass, he was invested in the whole mystery of what Papa Leo had found at the bottom of Lake Michigan. He had to see this thing through. Then he could figure out all these convoluted feelings he was having about his editor.

"Hey?" Dale's gravelly voice interrupted his musing. "Is she gonna call the cops?"

"I'm leaving that up to her." Henry scowled at him, noticing that the old man's bravado had shrunk considerably.

"Don't let her do that, okay?"

"Why not? Some reason you don't want the police to know you're here?"

"No." Dale's stringy hair flipped as he shook his head. "No. I just don't want to mess with the cops, okay?"

"Sophie wants you out of here, so let's go up and get your gear. I'm sure there's a bus out of town."

"I ain't takin' no bus." Dale bristled. "That car is mine, not hers."

"Okay, then get your stuff and get on the road." Henry had never played the tough guy before—it was empowering. Mild-mannered computer geeks rarely got to be heroes.

Dale's eyes narrowed and he chewed his lower lip, but he didn't move from the bench. "You don't wanna be stuck with that old bat, dude. She's taking that girl for a ride."

"I think you're both taking Sophie for a ride." Henry sighed and extended a hand toward the steps. "Get going, okay?"

"She's one hell of an actress, man," Dale insisted, settling back on the bench and crossing his arms over his chest, clearly ignoring Henry's orders to head back up to the cottages. "She wants that gold and she'll stop at nothing to get it."

"Dale, move your ass."

"Listen to me." Dale leaned forward, hands on his knobby knees. "If you help me, we can find that gold and get—"

"If *I* help *you*?" Henry was floored at the man's balls. "Seriously? I'm not going to help you do anything but leave."

"We're so close," Dale's eyes gleamed with avarice. "I know those coins have to be here. The old fart found them all those years ago, I'm sure of it. And by God, if they're here, then they're mine. Don't you see? It was my grandpa who picked them up from the mint. By rights, they're mine."

"By rights, anything that's salvaged from a shipwreck belongs to the person who finds it. Come on." Henry was getting itchy. He hated leaving Sophie alone with Eva for too long. "And if we're going to get technical, those coins belong to the United States government. They were never meant to be taken from the mint in the first place."

"All the more reason for us to find them." Dale finally rose. "If Eva gets her hands on 'em, Uncle Sam'll never see them again. We need to find them so we can turn them in."

Henry couldn't help rolling his eyes. "How very noble of you, Dale. Haul your bony ass up the stairs and start packing."

"Eva, sit still." Sophie dabbed at her mother's face, wincing at the deep cut beside her eye. Dale must have hit the woman exactly right. The thin skin of her temple had burst like an overripe peach. The wound was so jagged, Sophie wasn't even sure stitches were possible.

"Ouch." Eva jerked away. "Dammit, that hurts. What'd you put on that cotton ball?"

"It's just peroxide. We've got to clean it out." Sophie tossed the bloody cotton ball in the trash basket behind her before reaching for another piece. She raised her eyes to the heavens, silently thanking Papa Leo for keeping a box of disposable gloves in the first aid kit. She wasn't squeamish by nature, but touching Eva's bloody head was beyond distasteful. "Here, hold this on it and use some pressure. I think I've got some butterflies in the box of Band-Aids in the bathroom."

"Do I need stitches, do you think?"

"Stitches?" Dale's shrill voice coming from the screened porch stopped Sophie in her tracks. He shoved past Henry who tried to grab him, but instead ended up nearly tripping into the porch as all he grasped was air.

"Baby?" Dale rushed to Eva. "Oh, God, Evie. You look like Rocky after the big fight."

"Thanks to you, you bastard." Clearly Eva was giving him no quarter. "I thought you were on your way outta here."

"You don't want me to leave, do you?" Dale's tone turned syrupy.

Sophie gave Henry a long look over her shoulder before going into the bathroom to get the rest of the first aid supplies. The sounds of Dale crooning to Eva made her blood boil. Did he really think she'd take him back after he blackened her eye? Surely Eva had more self-respect.

"Get the fuck outta here, Dale," Eva shouted and immediately restored Sophie's faith in feminism and tough old broads. She stepped out of the bathroom and ran into Henry.

"Do you want to call the sheriff?" he asked, blocking her path with one hand against the bathroom doorjamb. "We can have him picked up. He'll be out of our hair."

"Let's see what happens." Sophie took his hand. They moved closer, but stayed in the shadows waiting for Eva's next move.

"Dugan," the older woman called. "What the fuck? I thought you were getting rid of him."

"Are we calling the sheriff?" Henry followed close on Sophie's heels as she scurried back into the kitchen just in time to catch Eva shoving Dale away, a look of disgust on her bruised face.

"Get out. Now," Sophie ordered.

"Aw, come on, Evie." Dale's crooning became whining. "There's no need for the cops. It was just a little argument."

"If you aren't out of my house in the next five minutes…" Sophie tossed the box of Band-Aids on the table, pulled her cell phone out of her pocket, and glared at Dale.

"Go." Eva pointed to the door. "We won't call the sheriff. Just go."

Dale let out a long frustrated breath, spun on his heel, and headed out through the kitchen. Henry shadowed him without a word, letting the screen door slam shut.

Tired, hungry, and longing for the shelter of Henry's arms, Sophie grabbed the Band-Aids and fished out a butterfly. "Hold still and let me get this thing dressed. Then you can lie down on the sofa with a bag of ice."

Eva was unusually subdued as Sophie applied antibiotic cream and two butterfly bandages to the cut. When she finished, she helped her mother to the bathroom, standing in the hallway outside as Eva did her business. Too exhausted to even think, she leaned against the wall and closed her eyes, wishing she could rewind back to the day she'd arrived in Willow Bay and start again sans drama.

The bathroom door opened and Sophie jerked upright. Apparently, Eva had washed her face while she was in there. Devoid of makeup she appeared haggard and worn. Determined not to feel sorry for her, Sophie made her mother as comfortable as she could on the sofa in the living room, but the sound of the Honda's engine revving set off another bout of tears and cursing.

Henry came in the back, hooking the screen door and securing the inner door. "He's gone."

"Hey, Dugan," Eva said between hiccups. "Look in the cupboard under the bar. I'm bettin' you'll find the old man's Jameson. Drag it out and pour us all a glass. Put mine on the rocks."

He quirked one brow at Sophie. "Drink?"

She nodded as she swept bandages and the bag of cotton balls into the first aid kit, sprayed the table with disinfecting cleaner, and wiped it down with paper towels. Only then did she yank off the latex gloves and accept the glass of whiskey Henry offered her.

"Thank you, Henry," she whispered, closing her eyes and leaning her head on his shoulder. "This is such an unholy mess. I'm so sorry."

He wrapped one arm around her and pressed a kiss to the top of her head. "Hey," he replied softly as he touched his forehead to hers. "Friends, remember?"

CHAPTER 19

"Jeez, she's still out there smoking." Sophie peered through the bedroom window at Eva slumped in a cushioned chaise, smoking cigarette after cigarette, the overflowing mussel shell ashtray balanced on her belly. A cloud of pale blue smoke surrounded her, the pungent odor wafting back to the cottage.

Past midnight, Sophie and Henry had finally retreated to the privacy of her warm bed after settling her mother in the guest room. They may as well not have bothered to make up that bed with fresh sheets. Eva lasted about ten minutes before she slipped out to the patio to smoke. When an hour had passed, Sophie gave up the idea that she could talk her back in and simply took her a blanket against the night breeze off the lake.

"Come back to bed," Henry said. "She'll come in when she's ready."

"Why do I even give a shit?" Clad only in panties and a tank top, she shivered as she dropped the voile curtain and padded back to perch on the edge of the mattress. "I mean, seriously, what's wrong with me? Why do I worry whether she's warm enough or if she's eaten supper or smokes too much?"

"Because you're a good person, Sophie." He hooked one arm around her waist to pull her to him. "And she's your mother."

"She's never been my mother." She allowed him to snuggle her close to his naked chest, enjoying the feel of his furred skin on her chilled body. Reaching down, she pulled the covers up before relaxing into his embrace.

"You know what I mean."

"I don't want to care about her."

"You can't help how you feel." His breath warmed her forehead as he yawned.

She pushed closer while his hand moved over her back, stroking and rubbing. In spite of all the drama of the last few hours, Henry's arms were still a safe haven. He'd been a rock, staying by her side every moment as protector and hero. How was she ever going to stand it when summer ended and he left?

Exhaustion crept over her. She really needed to go to sleep, but her mind refused to shut off. The scene from the beach steps replayed—was the fear in her mother's eyes real or were she and Dale playing abuser and victim to win Sophie's trust? If so, it was a damn convincing show. Dale was gone and it had taken the better part of an hour to calm Eva enough to get her to eat something.

They'd had to counteract the liquor and whatever she'd taken from the bottle she'd produced from her purse after Dale left. *Just a couple sleeping pills,* she'd told them as she shook two tablets into her palm and gulped them down with another glass of Jameson before either of them could stop her. At that point, Sophie had removed the whiskey bottle from the table and insisted that Eva try to eat a sandwich and drink some hot tea. It almost seemed as if she were the mother—an idea that pissed her off. Mothering the woman who had abandoned her was just plain wrong.

"I'm so confused right now, I have no idea what I feel." She yawned too and let her fingers trace the line of fine hair from Henry's chest to his navel. "I just want it all to go away. Everything."

"I know." His deep voice soothed her. "We'll figure it out. Tomorrow, we'll go through the stuff we found in the attic." He tipped her head back to drop a kiss on her lips. "Try to go to sleep, Soph."

"How can I when she's out there in the dark, practically an open invitation to that slimy bastard? What if he comes back?"

"I seriously doubt Dale's coming back tonight. Trust me, he's holed up somewhere planning his next move." Henry rolled them both to their sides and curled his body around hers. "You know you can't force her inside. She's an adult."

"Huh." She sniffed as she plumped her pillow and settled his arm over her ribs in a more comfortable position. "That's debatable."

~

Sunshine streamed in the window, casting a yellow-white glow over the papers Henry had spread out on the kitchen table. Sophie had finally fallen asleep sometime after he did. She was still snoozing, so at sunrise, he'd crept out of bed and left her to get some rest. When he walked by the spare room, Eva was passed out on top of the quilt, the bottle of Jameson tucked next to her pillow.

For a moment, he'd clutched, fearing the worst. But when he tiptoed in, she snuffled in her sleep and her breathing seemed even. Lifting the bottle from her loose grasp, he returned it to the cupboard under the bar before making a pot of strong coffee.

It didn't look like she'd drunk too much more of the liquor, and he almost couldn't blame her for wanting to numb her senses. A shudder went through him as he recalled the ugly scene down

on the beach steps. He'd noticed drops of blood on the stairs and
Eva had left bloody handprints on the bannister. There was an
outdoor shower at the top for people to wash sand off before
coming on to the patio. He could probably hook a hose up there to
spray down the banister and steps. The idea repulsed him but he
sure didn't want Sophie to have to clean it up. She'd dealt with
enough playing nurse. He ought to just hand Eva the hose and a
rag. That is, if she ever woke up.

Glancing down at his notes from the past few days, he realized he was working through this mystery the same way he
outlined one of his computer books. When he wrote on his novel,
it was strictly by the seat of his pants, but he was taking this information step-by-step. First Eva showing up and her wild story
about treasure, then the Firefly being vandalized, and finally Dale
and Eva's stories seeming to click. However, he was becoming
more and more convinced that Dale didn't just happen upon Eva
and the story about her father finding treasure. No doubt, Dale
and maybe even his father and grandfather before him had
searched for the coins. They probably knew who had been diving
along that part of the lake, maybe even kept track of local news
on finds. It was simply too much of a coincidence. He tapped his
pencil on the timeline he'd drawn on a legal pad before pulling
his laptop closer. Research. That was the immediate order of
business.

He began by searching for the 1933 Double Eagle coins and
got over ninety thousand hits. Picking carefully through the
choices, he discovered Dale's story about the coins was true. They
were never supposed to be circulated, but a handful had disappeared from the Mint. The government was not at all happy when
the coins began showing up at coin auctions or word got out that a
private collector had bought one, since Uncle Sam felt the coins
constituted stolen property. There was one that sold at auction in

the sixties to a private collector in London. But he couldn't find any information about where the auction house had gotten it.

Next, he looked for anything he could find about the Todaros in the Depression era. Again, the Internet served up plenty of hits, but nothing of a particularly personal nature. Salvatore "Sonny" Todaro was almost as famous as Al Capone, so the press at the time sensationalized his every move. Henry clicked through several websites about organized crime in the 1930s. According to history, Todaro was particularly ruthless, killing anyone who got in the way of his South Chicago empire built on illegal booze, drugs, and prostitution. He amassed a fortune during the Depression by selling liquor and wine he'd smuggled down from Canada.

Learning what a big part the Great Lakes had played in the bootleg liquor industry of the 1920s and 30s came as a surprise. Most of what he knew about smuggling involved the East coast and rum running from the Caribbean. He'd never thought about the five lakes being a pathway for bootleggers. One site showed a map of the lakes that marked several shipwrecks—surely some were boats that had gone down while loaded with booze from Canada. A chart listing the wrecks, their owners, and cargo accompanied the map. One actually showed that it carried whiskey, but the wreck was from 1893. Too early for their purposes.

Chin cupped in his palm, he let his other hand rest on the track pad as his focus drifted to Todaro. If the wily mobster was smuggling liquor from up north to Chicago, wouldn't he have had his own boat to do it? With all the information out there on the Internet, there ought to be some story about Todaro's boat sinking. A newspaper article, maybe. On the other hand, it was probably a good bet that even if the boat had gone down in the lake, Todaro wouldn't have reported it missing. It was full of illegal booze and, if Dale's story held up, stolen gold coins. Or maybe he *would* have reported it to collect the insurance money.

Dammit. Henry slammed his fist on the surface of his legal pad. Speculation was a waste of time. They needed hard facts. Just one piece of corroborating evidence would help. One thing that tied Todaro to a boat lost in Lake Michigan near Willow Bay and Leo Russo to whatever was on that boat.

Henry clicked on another site. This one had grainy black-and-white newspaper photographs from the twenties and thirties posted—the famous one of the St. Valentine's Day massacre, a shot of Capone with a couple of his henchmen, another of a Ford Model A full of bullet holes. Maybe, just maybe, there might be a photo of Todaro christening a boat.

Yeah, right. That's gonna happen. Because everything else has been so easy to figure out.

Tapping the track pad, he clicked through the pictures until one stopped him. A man sat at a leather banquette in a fancy restaurant mugging for the camera, his arms around two very young and beautiful women. Black, slicked-back hair, a pinstriped suit, and flashy rings on both hands gave the guy celebrity status, but the caption told him it was Sonny Todaro. When Henry magnified the photo, Todaro's eyes were what struck him. Despite the grin on his face, his eyes were cold and dark. Evil eyes. The eyes of a man who found pleasure in other people's pain.

"Who's that?"

A voice behind him caused him to jerk upright. He hadn't even realized he was leaning into the screen. He stroked his finger across the track pad to take the photo back to normal size.

"The original Sonny Todaro, circa 1930." Henry reached behind him to take Sophie's hand when she bent over his shoulder to peer at the photo. "Dale's grandfather's old boss."

"He looks... um... kinda sleazy. What'd you find out about

him? Anything?" She dropped a kiss on his cheek before turning away. "Want a warm-up?"

"Sure." He shut the laptop and rose to hand her his coffee mug. "I was waiting to eat. I figured I'd make you some of my famous Dugan Family French toast."

"Sounds wonderful."

"A big breakfast seemed like a good idea before we start going through the stuff from the attic." He rummaged in the drawer under the stove for the griddle while Sophie got bacon, eggs, and orange juice from the refrigerator.

She carried plates and silverware to the table, setting three places. "I checked on Eva, she's still out like a light, but at least she came in from the patio."

"Yeah, I retrieved the bottle of Jameson from her pillow when I got up." Henry gave her a wry smile. He doubted Eva would be joining them, but he didn't stop Sophie as she carefully placed forks on folded napkins. It seemed including Eva in meals had become second nature—odd how quickly that had happened. He didn't mention it to Sophie. In her current state, she probably wouldn't have received that observation well.

Rather, he put bacon to sizzling on one end of the griddle and then whipped eggs for French toast, adding half and half, cinnamon, vanilla, and a touch of nutmeg. "I found a little information, but the Todaros kept their private lives separate from the rest of their activities."

"Wouldn't you if you were involved in organized crime?" she asked, pouring juice into three glasses.

"Yeah, probably. Here's something interesting. Sonny was only half-Italian. One article said his mother was from a wealthy, influential Rhode Island family named Howe."

"No kidding? Do you think that's where he got the money to start his empire?"

Henry shook his head as he dredged thick slices of French

bread through his eggy concoction and placed them on the hot griddle. "Nope. The story's pretty sketchy, but according to stories Sonny told, the Howes disowned their daughter after she ran off with a poor Italian immigrant. Sonny grew up in poverty in Chicago. Mom took in laundry. Dad was a dockworker. The crime element started with him. He worked his way up through the ranks of a neighborhood gang and started his fortune with protection money. Tough kid, eh?"

"Wow. I wonder if he ever knew his rich grandparents at all," Sophie mused. "God, that smells heavenly, Dugan."

"It's the only thing I can make even halfway well." Henry tossed her a smile over his shoulder, all the while lifting the French toast gently to make sure it wasn't overbrowning. For reasons he couldn't explain, it pleased him to cook for her. It gave him a homey feeling, the two of them making breakfast together. There was something quite comfortable about sharing a kitchen with Sophie Russo.

The spatula clattered to the floor as a scary realization struck him full force. He wanted to be in love again and for the first time in his adult life, he wanted a woman who was his peer. He wanted Sophie. The one thing he'd sworn he wasn't going to do again for a very long time, and here it was—mere months after his divorce was final.

Son of a bitch.

All his big talk about this non-relationship, about only having a summer fling was just so much bullshit.

Nah. Maybe it was just the events of the past few days.

Hell, didn't people come together in lifeboats, but then after all the drama was over, they never saw one another again? That had to be it. He'd never been in a lifeboat situation, but this one kind of qualified. He retrieved the spatula and gave it a quick wash at the sink.

And the sex. The sex was pretty damn incredible. Maybe he

was confusing sex with love. That had always been his problem before actually. But he knew that wasn't it. The sex with Sophie *was* great, but it was great because he was involved, invested... and probably falling in love. *Oh, Jesus.* Is this what truly loving a woman was? Not a crazy, hormone-induced urgency but this... this calm, contented, warm desire to just do everyday things with her?

He got busy with the spatula, trying to focus on the golden slices instead of the scent of Sophie's soap as she brushed past him to fetch the syrup. He'd lost their conversation, so he jumped when she stopped behind him, nudging him with her shoulder.

"Do you think?" she asked.

"Think what?"

"Do you think Todaro knew the Howes?" Her lovely brow furrowed. "Are you listening?"

"Yeah. Just wandered off for a minute. Sorry. Um... no... I mean, I don't know." Heat flushed his face. He sounded like a freakin' idiot. "I mean, I only found that one mention of his mother's family. Nothing else." He exhaled a long breath that ruffled the hair hanging over his forehead and managed to meet her perplexed expression with a calm smile in spite of the spasm of emotion racing through him.

Nice work, Dugan. It's not like things here aren't squirrelly enough. Let's toss in some extra drama.

She sure as hell didn't need *that* at the moment. With a Herculean effort, he kept from grabbing her, kissing her stupid, and declaring he'd fallen head over heels. Instead, he gestured to the steaming French toast and crisp bacon.

"It's ready. Let's eat."

CHAPTER 20

"Let's start with these boxes."

Sophie set her coffee cup on the wicker table and pulled Papa Leo's Swiss Army knife out of her shorts pocket. Whatever had been bugging Henry while he was cooking had apparently resolved itself as they ate breakfast. He seemed cheerful and focused again, ready to dig into the stuff they'd dragged down from the attic.

Flipping the blade open, she ran it carefully along the strapping tape on the top of the box. Dust floated to the floor when she lifted the flaps. The box contained LPs, eight-track tapes, and a transistor radio.

"Look at this." With a grin at Henry, she held up the radio. "From the titles of the albums and tapes, I'm guessing this belongs to the woman passed out in my guest room."

"Jimi Hendrix. Janice Joplin. The Rolling Stones. The Byrds..." He recited the bands as he sifted through the box. "Yeah, I'd say these are Eva's." He dropped the tapes back in and brushed his hands together. "Actually, three of these boxes are labeled with her name."

"She was wrong. Papa Leo didn't have a beach fire with her

stuff." Sophie closed the box and set it and the other two aside.

"This one says *Photos*. Want to take a look?" Henry reached for the knife on the table.

"You think there'll be anything in there that'll help us?"

"Um... maybe." He slit the box open. "He might've taken pictures of the stuff he found when he dove."

"Pictures of the coins you think?" Anticipation surged through her as she reached for a stack of albums and loose photographs.

"Don't count on it." He took his own pile of pictures from the box.

Fifteen minutes later, it was obvious to Sophie that the box of photos dated at least two generations back, the most recent being a wedding photo of Papa Leo and Nonna taken in the early 1950s. Releasing a frustrated sigh, she packed the worn albums back in the box. "These must have belonged to Papa Leo's parents. They owned the cottages before he did."

"Did you know them?"

"No. They died before I was born. I think it was when Eva was little." She held up a sepia-toned photo in a worn leather folder. "This is them when they got married in Italy. They immigrated sometime before World War II and bought the old cottage that was here. Tore it down and built this one and then the other one. He was an autoworker, so they lived in Detroit, but came here every summer. Papa Leo was practically raised here."

Henry took the case, handling it with the same reverence he'd shown Papa Leo's first edition books.

Her lips curved into a smile at his gentle touch. Most men would have tossed it aside as old and not important to their search, but he lifted the photo to the light, studying it.

"You look like your great-grandmother," he said. "She was... beautiful."

"Thanks." Sophie leaned over to give him a little kiss, which turned into a longer kiss when he tugged her to him. His arms slid around her as their tongues touched and danced. The now-familiar heat flooded her insides at his touch, and she arched her back to push her behind into his exploring hands.

"You two have a room back there. Why don't you use it?" Eva's grumbling from the doorway startled them apart.

"You're up." Sophie couldn't believe how bad her mother looked.

Purple shadows smudged the bruised skin below her blood-shot eyes, chewed lipstick emphasized the vertical lines pleating her upper lip, and her robe gaped open, revealing tight shorts and an old t-shirt underneath. She'd lost her bandage at some point during the night and the cut on her temple was still swollen. One of the butterflies was falling off. The Jameson bottle dangled from her fingers.

"Barely." Eva coughed and shook back her stringy hair. "And not for long. What is all this crap anyway?" A sweep of her arm took in the boxes and trunks. "Hey—"

Sophie grabbed the whiskey as she brushed past. "You need coffee. Come on, I've got a pot going, and I'll make you some toast and eggs."

"No, thanks. Not hungry." Eva wandered out to the screened porch on legs so unsteady that Sophie cringed.

Henry reached out for her, but Eva shrugged his hand away.

"I'm okay. Is this my stuff?" She pulled the flaps on one of the boxes they'd set aside. "Holy shit, will you look at that? All my posters and books... and... and my hats." Plopping down on a chair, she lined the three boxes up side by side before rummaging through them. "Hey, my transistor. I'll be damned."

Sophie ignored the chortling as Eva continued to pull treasures from her past out of the boxes. Soon stuffed animals, year-books, clothes, and albums were strewn on the floor. She stepped over them gingerly to hand her mother a steaming mug of coffee.

"Jeezus, he even packed my weed." Eva held up a plastic

sandwich bag. "What the fuck? Crazy old bast... um... dude." She waved away the coffee. "I could sure as hell use a toke about—" She stopped at Sophie's sigh. "Oh, chill out. I'm not going to smoke it in the house."

"You're not going to smoke it at all." Sophie plucked the bag from her fingers. "I think you've poured enough crap into your body in the last twenty-four hours. Drink your coffee and give it a rest, okay?"

"Whatever you say... Leo." Eva went back to poking through her boxes. "What else is here?"

Sophie tossed the bag back into the nearest box, and Eva snaked a hand out to retrieve it. With an eye roll toward Henry, Sophie grabbed the weed, shoved it into her pocket, and knelt beside the biggest trunk. "It's got a padlock on it."

"Yeah, I noticed," Henry said. "Any chance you know where the key is?"

"Nope."

"Try the box of keys in his desk." Eva's voice was muffled as she pulled on a faded Hendrix sweatshirt. When her dark head popped out of the top, she gestured. "Second drawer down. In the back. God, I loved this sweatshirt. Still fits! Kinda."

Sophie rose in one smooth move and clambered over Eva's belongings. The box was right where she'd said it would be. Dumping a myriad of keys on the glass-top table, she sorted through them. Some had cardboard tags labeled in Papa Leo's heavy bold script.

"This should be fun." Henry picked up a handful of keys.

"Wait." She handed him a small brass one. "Try this. Label says, *Dish Trunk, attic*."

He fitted the key in the old lock. "It works." The padlock opened with ease, but when he tried to lift the lid, it was stuck fast.

"What do you need?" Sophie headed for the utility room.

"The biggest flat-blade screwdriver you've got and a hammer. Oh, and a rag."

She returned a moment later with the toolbox in hand. Eva was stacking albums and tapes back in the box, but stopped to watch as Henry first tapped around the bottom of the lid with a rag-covered hammer to loosen it, then pried it open with the screwdriver.

The odor hit them first. Dank and musty, it wafted out as he lifted the lid of the old trunk. Crumpled papers covered the top, and he pulled them out cautiously to reveal plates, cups, saucers, and bowls all wrapped in packing tissue. A metal pan of tarnished silverware nestled in one corner.

"It is dishes." Sophie frowned. "Why did he lock up a trunk full of dishes? That's weird." She lifted a saucer from the trunk and unwrapped it.

"Because he was a batshit-crazy, dotty old fart?" Eva sipped coffee, a smirk on her haggard face.

"I've never seen these dishes before." Once again, Sophie chose to ignore her mother, determined not to let the woman get to her. If she didn't rise to the bait, maybe Eva would get bored and go back to bed.

Henry stooped over the trunk, removing wrapped dishes and setting them on the floor. "Maybe they're family dishes. Might've come over from Italy or something." He straightened and glanced around at the dish-covered floor and then back into the now-empty trunk. "That's it. Just dishes and this pan of silverware."

"Oh God, these *are* family dishes. Just not my family." Sophie held out a white dinner plate that she'd unpacked. The plate was rimmed in gold and had a navy blue imprint in the center. But it was the lettering around the design that made her heart pound. "Look! Look at the name."

He took the plate and examined it closely. "Caroline Howe?"

He gave her a puzzled glance before recognition lit up his features. "Howe. Oh shit, we know that name."

"We do?" Eva lounged in the chair, fidgeting with her old radio. "I don't know that name. Who the hell's Caroline Howe? And why do we have her dishes?"

Already across the room, Henry set the plate down and sifted through his papers strewn on the table. "Here we go. Yup, his mother's last name was Howe. Dammit, that's all we've got though. No first name."

Sophie sprinted to the table and pulled Henry's laptop around. "I'm going to Google her." She typed in the name and scanned the list while he hovered over her shoulder.

"Geez, there's over a million hits," he said. "Well, she sure as hell isn't participating in any social media, so we can scratch the first nine hundred thousand."

"Hang on. Let me think." She wiggled her fingers above the keyboard. "There's gotta be another way to search."

"I know. Click back in my history. Let's find the page where I read that his mother was a Howe."

"Oh, that'll work."

"Whose mother?" Still sprawled in the chair, Eva perked up as Sophie and Henry's enthusiasm grew.

Sophie waved away the question as she swiped the track pad. Henry's warm breath on her neck was distraction enough.

"There!" Henry grabbed a chair and pulled it right next to Sophie's as he pointed to the screen. "That's the site." He leaned in so close she could smell his soap. "Ah ha. Gideon Howe. Okay, now Google him."

"Here we go, here he is." In spite of the proximity of Henry's lips to her neck, she managed to focus and read through the biographical information. "Inherited a shipping fortune amassed by his father during Reconstruction. Born in Newport, Rhode

Island. Married to Katherine Crawford in eighteen seventy-nine. Nine children." She turned to Henry. "God, prolific, wasn't he?"

"It would seem so. Does it name the kids?"

"Nope, dammit."

"Here. Do you mind?" He hesitated before reaching for the laptop, but she happily turned it over to him and watched with interest as he logged into a genealogy site.

"Oh, you're going for a census." She gave a big grin. "Great idea."

"Yes, they always listed all the kids' and their ages. Some even have birthdates." Pecking at the keyboard, his brows came together in concentration. "Okay, let's try Newport, Rhode Island. The 1900 census."

Leaning in, she scanned the list. "Um...no. Oldest child is Harriet. Born eighteen eighty-two. No daughter Caroline." Sophie sighed in frustration. Another dead end.

As she dropped into a chair, Henry reached across the table to grab his legal pad. His teeth worried his lower lip as he perused his notes. "Wait a minute. Sonny was born in 1901. Hmmm. Didn't the other site say that Sonny told people his grandfather Howe disowned her when she ran off with some Italian immigrant?"

Her heart began to beat faster again as she slid her chair closer and found the previous website. "Yes, it did. Maybe that's why he didn't mention her to the census taker—because to him, she *was* dead."

"Yes!" Henry let out a whoop as he clicked back to the census page, turning the computer so both of them could see it. "Okay, go back to 1890 and see if we can find her." His brow furrowed as he scoured the page. "Crap, no Gideon Howe listed in the Newport census in 1890. Wonder where they were."

Sophie's mind raced as they sat gazing at the screen for a moment. Suddenly she snapped her fingers. "Let's try Providence.

Maybe they lived in another seaport town since he was in shipping. It is the capital and a good place to have a business."

"Soph, you're a genius!" Henry kissed her soundly after bringing up the census page and finding their man listed with his family. "Here she is. Caroline Josephine, born 1880. Old Gideon must've moved his family from Providence back to Newport around nineteen hundred. So as far as the Newport folks knew, darling daughter Caroline died tragically young, and the family moved away from the painful memory."

"I've been to Providence. Those two towns are only about thirty miles apart." Sophie wasn't as confident as she stared at the map she'd Googled to confirm her suspicion. "They didn't move very far away."

"Good point," Henry agreed. "But even as late as nineteen hundred, thirty miles was a quite a distance. I read somewhere that a day's wagon ride was about ten miles over muddy, unpaved roads."

"Okay, I'm completely lost." Eva had hauled herself out of the cushioned chair on the screened porch and stood by the coffeemaker, draining the pot into her mug. "I'm making more coffee."

"Do you want some food?" Sophie dragged her attention away from the computer long enough to make the half-hearted offer. She'd almost forgotten her mother was present.

"No. I want to know what the hell you two are up to."

CHAPTER 21

Henry met Sophie's eyes over the top of the computer, and he raised one brow. Were they going to share what they suspected with Eva or not? It was Sophie's call, but with Dale out of the picture, it seemed harmless enough to tell her. If Leo had discovered the coins, maybe Sophie and her mom could find them together. It could even be a bonding experience.

Right. Like that'll ever happen.

"Well?" Eva fished a coffee filter out of the box before dumping several scoops of beans into the grinder and pushing the button.

"Um... Henry's just been doing some digging into the Todaros," Sophie replied. "You know, trying to see if the connection Dale made holds up."

"Don't believe a word that man says, missy." Eva wagged a finger in her daughter's direction. "*He's* never had any dealings with the Todaros. The guys after him are small-time loan sharks, not the mob. He's a damn drama queen."

"I wasn't talking about the today's organized crime rings. I'm thinking of what he told us about his grandfather running numbers for Todaro in the thirties."

"Oh. Well, maybe that's true. Bastard probably only stuck with me because I told him the treasure story and now he thinks the coins are here." Her features twisted as though she was going to break down, but with obvious effort, she controlled herself, shoving the box of coffee filters back into the cupboard. "So who's Caroline Howe?" Once the coffee was brewing, Eva plopped down at the table across from them, arms crossed under her ample breasts.

"She's the original Sonny Todaro's mother." Sophie didn't look up as she continued perusing the genealogy website.

Henry pulled his timeline out from under the pile of papers on the table and penciled in Caroline Howe as Todaro's mother. "Okay, so say he named the boat for his mother. A very touching gesture, by the way. Rather humanizes him, don't you think?"

"Sure does." Sophie smirked. "I feel so much better about all the bootlegging and prostitution and murder."

Henry glanced at her over the top of his glasses before continuing. "And now, we have the dishes with her name on them, which means Leo found that boat or at least some debris from that boat." He extended his hand. "Here, give me the computer, okay? I'll try to find out if it was ever registered anywhere or reported lost."

Sophie pushed the laptop toward him before rising and stretching. "Eva, you need to eat. Do you want me to make you something?"

Eva ignored the offer. "Did Dad find the coins?"

"We have no idea." Sophie said.

"But that's where you're headed with this, right?" Eva crossed her arms under her breasts, eyes focused on Henry. "Right, Dugan?"

He squirmed, his fingers poised over the keyboard as he tried to come up with key terms that would start a search for the *Caroline Howe*. Chewing his lower lip, he gazed at Sophie retrieving a carton of eggs from the refrigerator while her mother continued to stare at him. His hesitation was becoming awkward, so he proceeded cautiously. "We know Leo found dishes from a boat called the *Caroline Howe*. We know Todaro's mother's name was probably Caroline Howe. Past that, anything else is pure speculation."

From the kitchen, Sophie tossed him a smile as she whipped eggs together with a splash of milk.

Ah, okay, so we're not going to over-share with Eva. Got it.

He gave her the briefest of nods before typing *yacht registry* into Google as he avoided Eva's intense gaze.

"If he found the dishes, he found Todaro's boat, and if he found that boat, he found the coins. It's not a stretch." Eva sat up straighter and smacked her palm on the table, rattling pens and papers. "I knew it! I knew he'd found a treasure. He found those damn coins."

"Eva, just relax, okay?" Sophie poured the eggs into a skillet sizzling with butter and shoved them around with a spatula. "We don't know anything yet. We have a ton of research ahead of us."

"What kind of research?" Eva asked. "Can I help?"

Henry hesitated. "We need to figure out if the Caroline Howe was actually Todaro's boat, if she sank, and if he reported her missing. We'll be checking around the Web, maybe go up to the marine museum, libraries, newspaper archives, that kind of thing."

"So if Dad found Todaro's boat, then where do we start hunting for the coins?" Eva's green eyes, so like Sophie's, gleamed.

Henry was struck again at how different those eyes appeared when they glittered with avarice rather than with the humor, compassion, and sensuality he'd seen reflected in Sophie's eyes. The difference between mother and daughter still floored him, and he had to smile inwardly at his own naïveté. Eva wanted those coins as badly as Dale had, so Henry would trust Sophie's instincts about her mother. With a shrug he went back to his Web search.

"Do you think the Todaros have been searching for the boat and the coins all these years?" Eva accepted a plate of eggs and toast from Sophie.

"How would we know?" Sophie put a hand on Henry's shoulder as she reached for his coffee cup. "Want some more?"

"Please." Clicking on a yachting archives site, he took a shot and typed the boat's name into the search term box.

"It makes sense to me that they would. I mean, that's a helluva lot of money," Eva replied around a mouthful of scrambled eggs. "They wouldn't just leave it at the bottom of Lake Michigan."

"I'm guessing they probably didn't." Sophie carried two cups of coffee to the table. "Even if Papa Leo did find those dishes, that doesn't mean he found the coins. Todaro would've had people out searching for it as soon as he realized it had gone down."

"Okay, maybe. But what if they searched and never found it? Do you think they'd ever give up?" Eva's curiosity seemed to be running along the same line as Henry's own, but he let Sophie field the questions.

"I don't know," she said. "If Dale was right and those coins are worth millions, I suppose the search for them might've gone on through two generations."

"He was right," Henry said. "I checked. As far as I can tell, one did sell in the sixties, exactly like Dale said. It went to a collector in London through a coin auction in Toronto."

"What'd it bring?" Eva had set down her fork and leaned intently toward Henry.

"Two point four million, exactly what he told us."

"Wow." Eva released a whoosh of breath. "No way anybody,

especially people like the Todaros, is gonna let that lie at the bottom of the lake. No way in hell."

"That may be true," Sophie pulled a chair closer to Henry's. "But don't you think if Papa Leo had found that kind of treasure on the *Caroline Howe*, he'd have reported it? It would've been big—like a Mel Fisher kind of find. He wouldn't have known it belonged to Todaro, would he?"

"Maybe he found some evidence of Todaro down there." Eva's brow furrowed. "Or maybe he investigated the boat like Dugan here is doing. Except he went to the library or something. People did research long before computers and the Internet, you know. He wouldn't have shouted it to the world if he'd had inkling that it belonged to the mob."

"You think Papa Leo deliberately kept quiet about what he found because he figured out it belonged to Todaro and he was afraid?" Sophie's tone was doubtful.

Eva threw up her hands. "I'm only saying don't dismiss any possibility just because you believed your grandfather to be right next door to Jesus Christ. He wasn't, trust me, and anyway..."

Sophie and Eva's speculating became background hum as Henry stared in disbelief at the screen in front of him. There it was—Todaro's boat! *Seasprite (private motor yacht) built 1918 in Morris Heights, New York as a pleasure craft. Scrapped 1925. Salvaged and later renamed Caroline Howe, registered 1928 to Salvatore Todaro, Chicago, Illinois. Lost in a storm, November 1933.* Dale and his grandfather had underestimated Todaro's moxie—he *had* reported the boat lost, most likely for the insurance payoff.

He clicked on the *Caroline Howe* link and a grainy, black-and-white photo of the boat materialized. The picture was taken sometime in 1928, right after Todaro had had the yacht refitted. Henry zoomed in to try to get a clearer view. What an incredible boat. She was huge with a graceful white hull and teak decks and brass fittings. Todaro had spared no expense. Even the poor quality of the picture couldn't hide the lushness of the elegant craft. Scrolling down the page, several other photos displayed the inside of the boat—a beautifully appointed lounge, wide aft deck, and even a formal dining room. Henry sucked in a breath. "Holy shit!"

~

Sophie swallowed the sharp retort that had risen to her lips at her mother's words about Papa Leo. "What?"

Henry turned the computer toward her. "Here. I found the *Caroline Howe*."

Sophie peered at the screen filled with a yacht. A stroke on the touchpad took her through a series of photos that literally took her breath away. "Oh, my God, it's incredible!"

"Lemme see." Eva practically vaulted around the table and hung over Sophie's shoulder. "Christ, that thing must've cost a fortune."

"No doubt." Sophie couldn't take her eyes off the photos as she imagined the swarthy, dark-eyed Sonny Todaro walking the deck, smoking cigars in the lounge, and pouring expensive French wine at the elegant dining room table.

"I'll bet there were secret compartments down in the bottom where he hid the booze he was smuggling." Eva sat back down and picked up her toast. "Okay, Dugan, where do we go from here?"

Sophie's eyes met Henry's. *We?* He gave her a quizzical look but didn't say anything, so she answered for him. "We need to finish going through the stuff from the attic first. There's another trunk and about five more boxes. Maybe Papa Leo salvaged other stuff from the *Caroline Howe* besides the dishes. "

"Yeah, like the coins. Let's get busy." Eva forked the last of her eggs onto a sliver of toast and shoved it into her mouth before taking her plate and cup to the sink. She rinsed all the dishes and placed them in the dishwasher, then ran a sink of hot sudsy water to scrub the skillet and the griddle left from Henry's French toast.

"What do you think?" Henry asked, his voice masked by the sound of running water.

"Oh hell, I don't know." Sophie couldn't help being a little cynical about Eva's sudden vigor. She'd perked up since yesterday. Had she forgotten the huge fight she'd had with her boyfriend? Did the coins mean more to her than the man she supposedly loved?

Almost as if she'd heard her thoughts, Eva called from kitchen, "If the coins are here, I want to find them. It's the only way we can keep Dale from ransacking the place again and—" She stopped as Sophie whirled around to stare at her.

"Are you kidding me?" Fury boiled up in Sophie's throat as she shoved her chair back and rose.

Eva dried her hands and carefully hung the damp tea towel over the oven door handle. "Okay, yes. He told me he did it. That was part of the fight yesterday. I never knew it was him, honest, and I had nothing to do with it."

"Sure you didn't." Sophie stomped over to stand toe to toe with her mother. "Dammit, Eva. How could you let him do that? How could you let him trash my house? Papa Leo's house?"

"I'm telling you, I didn't know anything about it!" Eva straightened to her full height and looked Sophie in the eye.

Silence stretched like a thin taut thread between them before Sophie finally spun on her heel and marched back to the table. "He's never coming near my house again, got that? If he even so much as drives by, I'm calling the sheriff."

"Jeezus, do you think I don't know that?" Eva shivered and rubbed her arms. "I'm gonna shower and change. Yell if you find anything interesting." She disappeared through the screen porch, heading for the Sandpiper.

Releasing a frustrated breath, Sophie closed her eyes and fought the waves of anger that washed over her. More than anything in the world, she wanted to take all the crap on the porch back up to the attic and send Eva packing.

Henry got up from the table. "Soph, I hate to say this, but I'm guessing Dale won't give up. He's convinced you have those coins and he's on a mission to find them. If those damned things are here somewhere, we've got to find them and turn them in. That's the only way you'll ever be rid of him." He put an arm around her waist as they walked together to the porch. "So we need a plan."

His body pressed to hers gave Sophie some comfort, but the idea of Dale scoping out the cottages and maybe tailing them around town sent chills chasing down her spine. She turned and clung to Henry, taking strength from his broad chest and his strong arms enfolding her.

She didn't want to make a plan. She wanted to go back in time —back to before Eva showed up at her door. She wanted her summer back, the one where the most important thing she had to consider was which pair of shorts to wear. The summer where she settled into her home, painted the walls, and redecorated with flowery chintz and airy fabrics. The summer where she seduced Henry Dugan and they had lots of hot sex. *That* was the only plan she was interested in.

Her throat closed up as she leaned against Henry, inhaling his clean scent, pressing her mouth to the warm skin of his throat. His lips caressed her ear as his breath stirred the errant curls escaping her ponytail. With a sigh, she tipped her head back and his lips took hers in a fierce kiss.

Ah, yes...

This was how she was supposed to be spending her summer,

just like this. Not going through old trunks and boxes, searching for some treasure that Papa Leo probably never found. Not dealing with her long-lost lunatic mother or people coming to blows on her beach steps.

And certainly not clutching in fear over the possibility of being the next target of some cheap hood who believed she had an imaginary stash of gold hidden in her cottage.

CHAPTER 22

"That's it." Sophie stood up and rubbed her hands on the seat of her denim shorts.

Mid-afternoon sun warmed the screened porch where Henry was retaping the boxes she intended to keep, while Eva snored softly on the wicker settee. Like the others, the last trunk had contained nothing at all to do with the *Caroline Howe*. The boxes were full of books and old toys that Sophie had a vague memory of playing with on the beach as a child. One of the trunks held Nonna's summer clothes packed with a cedar sachet, and the other, several antique quilts and coverlets that she decided to pull out, launder, and use in the cottage. The outdated clothing she figured she'd donate to the local theater group, while the books and toys would go to charity or the trash.

She stacked the colorful quilts on a chair next to Henry. "These are nice, but otherwise, what a waste of time."

"You're sure you took all the stuff out of that big trunk and unwrapped every single dish?" Henry pressed the packing tape down on the top of the box at his feet.

"Yes, I'm positive." She jerked her head toward the trunk, its lock hanging open on the latch. "Take a look if you want, but I didn't find anything interesting in there. He didn't even use newspapers. He used that blank packing paper, so we can't date the find."

Henry walked over to the trunk and opened it. "Maybe there's a secret compartment or something." He peered at the lid, running his fingers around the inside edge.

"There's no secret compartment, Dugan, I checked." Eva squinted at them from her position on the settee. "And I told you, he found the coins when I was twelve. We can date the find."

"I thought you were asleep." Sophie stretched and looked at her filthy hands in disgust before giving Eva a sidelong glance. Her mother had given up the search after the first hour and curled up on the couch in the sun like a cat, so she was still clean. But Sophie and Henry were dusty and hot and sweaty. She wanted nothing more than to hit the beach and dive headfirst into the lake.

"Nah, I was just dozing." Eva made no move to get up. "Didn't get much sleep last night."

Sophie grimaced at Henry, who simply grinned before jerking his head toward the coffee table. "Look what else she found."

A packet of rolling papers had shown up, no doubt as her mother had been sorting through her own belongings. Sophie slid them off the table and stuck them in her pocket with marijuana she'd confiscated earlier. The last thing she needed was Eva getting high or sick on fifty-year-old weed. Surely that stuff got stale and lost its potency. Didn't matter—she was getting rid of it.

Her phone vibrated against her hip at the same time someone pounded on the kitchen door. She pulled her phone out. "It's Carrie."

"I'll get the door." Henry hurried out.

"Hey, Carrie." She stepped out onto the patio to take the call, holding the phone between her thumb and index finger to avoid touching it with her grimy hands.

"Sophie?" Apprehension laced Carrie's voice. "What's going on over there? I ran into Millie in the village and she said there was some kind of big ruckus at your place yesterday. Then you didn't show up for coffee this morning."

"I'm okay. It was Eva and her boyfriend. They had an argument and it got physical. We sent him packing." She closed her eyes, grateful for her friend's concern, but rapidly developing a headache over the fact that Eva's chaotic life had started spilling over into her own. Now she was the topic of village gossip? Good god, what next?

"Are they still there?" Carrie's asked. "I don't like this."

"I'm okay, Carrie, truly. Dale's gone, and I'm working on the rest of it."

"He's not gone, babe." Carrie's alarm came through loud and clear. "Jules and I saw him at the Grind this morning."

"Well, we can't kick him out of town, can we? Henry and I have been going through the stuff from the attic." She peered through the screen. Henry was coming back in with Earl Gibson hot on his heels. "Hey, Earl's here for some reason. I need to go. Don't worry about me, I'm fine... we're fine."

"Sophie, we have to talk. Jules and I are on our way."

"Carrie, no—"

"See you in a few."

"Dammit." Sophie shoved the phone in her pocket with a scowl.

It wasn't a good time for Carrie and Jules to come over—not when she was covered in attic dust and longing for a shower. Not with Earl here, and Eva lounging on the sofa in her miniskirt and tank top.

"Soph, Sheriff Gibson's here," Henry called.

She opened the screened porch door and Earl damn near fell over the boxes to get to her. When she looked over at Eva, she was sprawled on the settee, eyeing him like fresh meat.

Poor Earl's eyes were big as saucers as he shooed Sophie back out the door with a nervous glance over his shoulder.

Henry followed him out, stepping around to stand close to Sophie.

The old sheriff shuffled his feet and cleared his throat. "I thought I'd come by and let you know that Tony arrested Dale Case a couple of hours ago."

"What for?" Sophie put a hand on Henry's arm. "What's he done now?"

"Shoplifting at the Rexall. Nabbed some snacks, a bottle of booze, and a carton of cigarettes. Tony caught him down at the harbor after the cashier called 911." Earl tossed another uneasy look back toward the porch. "So how's she doin'?"

"Who knows?" Sophie shrugged. "Last night she was a basket case. Today, you'd barely know anything had happened."

"God, did he do that to her eye?" Earl cringed. "What's she going to do now?"

"I have no idea what goes on inside her head." She closed her eyes for a second, drawing closer to Henry's comforting warmth. "I want this all to be over. I want her gone, and I want my life back."

"Why don't you kick her out?"

"She's homeless, and I'm scared she'll go back to Dale and he'll beat her up again." Aware of how contradictory that sounded after just saying she wanted Eva gone, Sophie rolled her eyes and sighed.

Henry put an arm around her shoulders. "How long can you keep him in jail?"

"Not sure." Earl shrugged. "We're checking the database to see if he has any outstanding warrants. If not, we'll have to let him go on his own recognizance even if the drugstore presses charges, which they never do, dammit. Although this time, it isn't one of the village kids grabbing a candy bar."

"Eva confessed to us that he was the one who trashed the cottage," Henry offered. "If you can't keep him in for shoplifting, charge him with vandalism."

"It was him all along? I'll be damned." Earl gave Sophie a dubious look. "Will you press charges?"

"You bet I will!"

"I can probably keep him for a while longer if you do."

"I appreciate that, Earl." She reached behind her for Henry's hand. "I'm getting a little scared now that I've seen he's capable of violence."

"Is there anything we can do?" Henry's fingers closed over hers. "We're trying to figure out if Leo actually did find those coins. We've been going through his stuff. The mess on the porch is from the attic."

"You find anything?" Earl removed his hat and wiped his brow with the sleeve of his tan shirt.

Sophie led him over to a shaded seat at the table. "Can I get you some iced tea or something, Earl?"

"No, honey, I'm fine." Earl dropped into the chair with a grunt, while Henry took his place across the table. "Did you think you'd find the coins hidden up there in the attic?"

"Of course we didn't really think that, but we hoped," Henry admitted with a grimace. "We did find some dishes that may have a connection to the Todaros." He went on to explain as Earl took notes in the crumpled notebook he never seemed to be without.

Sophie only half listened as the two men speculated about the *Caroline Howe* and what her grandfather may have discovered under the lake. Fear and conjecture did battle in her head. Perhaps Eva was right. Maybe Papa Leo found the coins, researched the wreck, and kept the find hidden, afraid that if he announced it, the Todaros would come after him. Was it possible he sold one of the coins? Did he take it to the dealer in Toronto, who then sent it through an auction? If so, where did he keep all that money? It would've been close to a couple million dollars.

And what about the rest of the coins?

Assuming they were found on the dive in the late 1960s, Henry's Internet search revealed that only one had sold since the time Papa Leo may have had the gold in his possession. Where are the rest of them now?

Chewing her lower lip, she ran a mental tally on Papa Leo's will and the accounts he'd had back in Poplar Hill. They were all closed now since Sophie had moved to Willow Bay and opened new checking and savings accounts. The manager at the bank in town hadn't said a word about any accounts in Papa Leo's name when she'd deposited a rather sizeable cashier's check from the closing out of the estate and the sale of the house. She'd even helped Sophie establish a money market account with the funds. If he'd had an account at Willow Bay Bank and Trust, wouldn't they have contacted her when they heard he'd died?

The image of her grandfather toting a duffel bag full of cash suddenly danced in her head. How in the hell would he have made that work in this small town where everyone knew everyone else's business? Wasn't Carrie's worry about Dale proof enough of how fast rumors and gossip spread? Could he have brought a couple of million in cash into the bank, stuck it in a safety deposit box, and been drawing it out slowly all these years? What a preposterous idea. But on the other hand, how had he afforded all the new cars and trips and wine and—

"Don't you think so, Sophie?" Henry's voice interrupted her rampant thoughts.

Sophie blinked. "I'm sorry. What?"

"Don't you think if it were true, Leo would've told you before he died?" Henry gave her a quizzical look. "I mean, this is big... huge, and he knew he was dying."

"Well, that seems reasonable to me." Earl rubbed one hand

over his face. "Those coins are worth a lot of money. I looked them up on the Web last night. One sold not long after Leo quit diving in the late sixties. I distinctly remember when he stopped because he sold his tanks and gear to my nephew who was sixteen at the time. I thought my sister was going to kill him. She was scared to death of Pete diving."

"That doesn't prove anything," Sophie said.

"That's not all." Earl paged through his notebook. "I also remembered that was about the same time we started renovating the lighthouse, and your grandpa was one of the biggest contributors. We even ribbed old Leo about hitting the lottery 'cause he was top donor three years running. He backed off giving money. Started volunteering, but it seemed like every time we had some emergency need, he would fork over the cash to cover it."

"What do you mean?" Henry asked, a frown furrowing his brow.

"Well, like 'bout fifteen years ago, the boiler went out. Leo put up the money to replace it. Before that, when the seawall started crumbling, Leo footed the bill for the new steel wall. I was the board treasurer at the time, and that was a damn big expense. He just wrote me a check and told me to get it fixed, but he always told me to keep his gifts quiet."

"You believe he found those coins on that last dive, don't you?" Her question came out in a whisper.

She didn't want to hear his answer. If he said yes, it meant her mother was right. And not only about the treasure, but also about Papa Leo hiding the coins—that he knew what he had and didn't turn them over to the government.

Did that make him a criminal? No better than Dale or... or even some mobster like Todaro?

"I freakin' told you things changed after that last dive, missy." Eva appeared on the patio, her hair sticking up in back from lying on the sofa. "But you didn't believe me. Now, maybe you will. He found that goddamn gold." Smirking and barefoot, she padded over to plop down in the chair next to Earl's. "Hey, Earl."

"Hello, Eva. How're you doing?"

"I'm holding up." She crossed her leg, letting her short skirt ride even higher on her thigh. "Did I hear you say you got Dale in the lockup?"

"Yup. He was shoplifting."

"Little jerk." Eva barked a short laugh. "Keep him there, okay?"

"Do you want to press charges for that?" Earl pointed to her injured temple.

Eva's eyes dropped to her hands folded on the table, "Maybe I'll stop by later on."

"I could keep him a while longer for battery and if we add the vandalism…"

"You told him about that?" Eva glared at Sophie and Henry.

"Of course." Sophie's hackles rose at her mother's tone.

Earl stood up and plopped his wide-brimmed hat back on his bald head. "I'll let you guys work this out. I'll be around if you need me."

"I can't believe you ratted him out." Eva seethed, shoving her chair back and stomping across the patio to the beach steps. "Goddammit, Sophie."

Sophie wasn't at all sure she could handle much more of the woman's company. One minute she felt sorry for her and the next, she wanted to smack her silly. Instead, she walked Earl to the door, where he gave her an awkward pat on the shoulder.

"It's all gonna sort out, Sophie." he said. "You come in and sign a complaint this afternoon and then I can keep Dale under lock and key, okay?"

"Okay. Thanks, Earl." She started to hook the screen door behind him, but then caught a glimpse of Julie's little BMW at the corner.

As much as she loved her friends, she only wanted to shower and open a bottle of wine with Henry, who'd been uncharacteristically quiet during her confrontation with Eva.

She washed her hands and dried them slowly as she wandered out to the living room, keeping an ear out for the sound of Julie and Carrie's arrival. Eva was gone and Henry was still sitting under the umbrella on the patio, lost in thought. No doubt he was regretting ever accepting her invitation to come to Willow Bay to write his novel. Damn sure he hadn't gotten any writing done in the past few days.

"Hey, Soph! Where are you?" The screen door at the back of the cottage slapped shut and Julie and Carried rushed in.

"Come on," Julie brushed past her, heading for the patio. "We're going for a walk. We gotta show you something."

CHAPTER 23

Henry lingered on the patio after Carrie and Julie had blown through and grabbed Sophie with a brisk, "We're taking her for a walk," from Jules. Drumming his fingers on the table, he made a concerted effort to empty his mind, which had been going full steam ahead for the past few days. He pressed his palms on the cool stone surface of the table and breathed deeply... twice. Then again.

Okay, so clearing his mind wasn't working. Instead he let the computer geek kick in and made a mental punch list of the current state of affairs.

Dale was in jail for the foreseeable future, particularly if Eva pressed battery charges and Sophie pressed charges for the vandalism. Although Eva had taken off and was probably down on the beach smoking and pouting, she had clearly made herself at home in the Sandpiper. Carrie and Julie had spirited a sapped and puzzled-looking Sophie down to the beach as well. Leo had found something of Sonny Todaro's at the bottom of the lake, but it was dishes, not gold, and his own curiosity was so aroused, going back to his writing would be futile.

How had this happened? All he'd expected to do when he arrived in Willow Bay was write. To finish the book.

Instead, he'd gotten caught up in the chaos Eva brought with her from Florida. He should be pissed. He hadn't written a single damn word on his novel since his delicious and nerve-wracking supper with Sophie a few nights earlier. But he wasn't angry. He wasn't sure what he was feeling anymore. Irritated with Eva and Dale, for sure. Intrigued by the idea of solving an eighty-year-old shipwreck mystery, absolutely. Fascinated with the town of Willow Bay and drawn to the grey-blue expanse of Lake Michigan, unquestionably. Most of all attracted to Sophie Russo. Undeniably involved with Sophie Russo. He grimaced and laid his head on the tall back of the teak chair, closing his eyes against the afternoon sun.

Oh, hell. Okay, falling in love with Sophie Russo.

He didn't even realize he was holding his breath until it all came out in one giant whoosh as his mind wandered back to the very beginning of his relationship with his favorite editor. It had been an odd situation from the start because all their communication had been e-mail or telephone calls. But it worked. Talking on the phone with her was the best because she had an incredible voice, warm and vibrant; she caressed him with it. When she laughed, the sweet sound made him so happy, he tried to make her laugh whenever they talked.

And boy, did they did talk! About everything—not just work and careers—she became a confidant, someone he trusted with his inner thoughts and feelings. She was the first person he called when he made the decision to divorce Kristie because he knew he'd find sympathy and concern, not the we-told-you-so heckling he'd gotten from his own family. When he decided to take the sabbatical to write his novel, she supported him fully. She knew him. Before they ever met in person, she knew him.

He knew her, too. The pain in her voice when she called to tell him of her grandfather's passing made his own heart ache. Her relationship wasn't exactly a taboo topic, but she rarely discussed it, until the guy split. She opened up one night after the rat had moved out, pouring her heart out as he'd sat in his office at ETT Press, sipping bourbon and wishing he could hold her. That was the night he realized his own marriage was over. When she'd mourned the lack of intimacy and fun in her relationship, it struck a chord. He was fifty-one years old, married to a selfish child, and his best friend was a middle-aged freelance editor he'd never even laid eyes on.

When they finally met in person a couple of weeks ago, the immediacy of the attraction between them had been inevitable; it was the depth of his feelings for her that shook him to his core. He'd always fallen for much younger women like Kristie—who was twenty years his junior—probably because it was easy. He could focus on his career while she spent his money. He was a middle-aged cliché.

But Sophie was different. More mature. She got his jokes. Kristie simply stared at him, uncomprehending. Sophie recognized the music he loved. Kristie had never even heard of Bob Dylan or Jefferson Airplane. He and Sophie shared a common culture that harkened back to the days before smartphones, texting, and selfies, all of which happened to be Kristie's favorite pastimes. Sophie's warmth, her intelligence, and her self-deprecating humor drew him in. Her interest was in him, not his money, and part of him was unsure how to handle that.

He gazed out at the grey-green lake glistening in the sun, seeking its calming effect, and contemplated whom he could call to hash it all out. He wanted to talk to his best friend. He gave a small snort of disgust, never believing that he'd be a victim of what his younger sisters would probably refer to as Hubble Gardiner syndrome. He'd never been crazy about the movie, *The Way We Were,* but the three girls had watched it endlessly one summer after they'd discovered the DVD in a $5 bin at the video store. It was their "girls' night in" movie. How ironic that he was in Katie Morosky's shoes—needing to talk to his best friend about his lover, except his lover was also his best friend.

The theme song from the movie slithered into his head like an earworm and he jumped up from the table, humming Bob Dylan's "Forever Young" with determination. He paced to the beach steps, gazed out across the sand, and caught a glimpse of Eva, ankle-deep in the surf. His heart speeded up and fear gripped him, but as he watched, she turned and headed toward the steps.

Walking back across the patio he noticed the vents in the crawl space on the Firefly were shut tight. It was summer, they should be open. He glanced over at the Sandpiper, but didn't see any vents in the single row of foundation blocks. Curious, he made one entire circuit around the rental unit and realized that cottage was sitting on a concrete slab while the Firefly had been built on a crawlspace... unless there was a basement under there.

He tried to remember if Sophie had ever mentioned a basement, but he didn't think so. Besides, all the mechanicals for the cottages were in their utility rooms, identical except that the Firefly's was bigger and contained a washer and dryer. No, it was just a crawlspace. Itching for something to do, he made his way around the Firefly and opened the vents, four in all, finishing up as Eva appeared at the top of the steps.

"What're you up to, Dugan?" She plopped down in a chair and pulled her hair back, securing it with the rubber band she always had on her wrist.

"Just opening the crawlspace vents. They should be open in the summer."

"How do you know that? Do you own a house wherever it is you live?" She pulled another chair closer, kicked off her flip-flops, and settled her feet in the seat.

"San Jose. I have a condo, but I was raised in a house and my dad was very handy." Henry debated the wisdom of a getting-to-know-you-conversation with Eva, but decided to go for it. Maybe she would reveal something new. "Hey, I was thinking about some wine. Want to join me?"

"Where's Sophie?" Eva eyed him suspiciously.

"She and her friends went for a walk on the beach." He headed for the house and returned a few minutes later with a chilled bottle of Riesling and two glasses, along with a package of crackers and an unopened chunk of smoked Gouda he'd scrounged from Sophie's refrigerator. Setting it all on the table, he pulled a corkscrew, napkins, and a small knife from his pocket.

After he opened the wine, he poured and offered one to Eva, who accepted it and touched his glass with hers.

"To Sophie," she said.

His shock at her toast must have been written all over his face because Eva gave a sharp bark of laughter before she sipped her wine.

"What's the matter?" she drawled, not seeming in the least defensive. "Why shouldn't I drink to my own kid?"

"You two haven't been getting on all that well." Henry avoided her eyes, focusing instead on opening the cheese and cutting off a few slices.

"We're damn different, that's for sure." Crumbs scattered as Eva tore open the package of crackers. She brushed bits of cracker off her lap. "Doesn't mean I don't care about her. She's my daughter, for God's sake."

He made a sandwich out of two saltines and a slice of cheese as he tried to decide how far he could go. Oh, hell. What difference did it make what he asked her? She'd probably lie anyway. He went for broke. "Why'd you abandon her?"

She finished her glass of wine and set it down by the bottle, indicating with a jerk of her head that he refill it.

He did and then downed another cheese and cracker sandwich before she finally answered.

"They were never going to let me be her mother."

"What do you mean?" Intrigued, Henry drained his wine glass and poured himself another. He decided to play a little dumb in the hope that she'd open up. "You are her mother."

"I gave birth to her." Eva grimaced. "But she was their do-over."

"Do-over?"

"A chance to have the daughter they really wanted. Not the sorry mess of a girl I'd become."

"What happened?" He handed her a piece of cheese and a couple of crackers. If they were going to be finishing the entire bottle of wine—and it seemed they were—she needed to eat.

She munched for a moment. "They wanted a perfect little lady —a straight-A student who played the cello and went to Sunday school. Who wore frilly dresses and dated the captain of the football team. Instead they got me."

"What was so wrong with you?"

"I was… a square peg." She gave him a wan smile and accepted more cheese and crackers. "A little hippie who loved electric guitars, motorcycles and fast cars, and even faster boys."

"Did you…" He hesitated, trying to find a kind way to ask the question. "Did you ever wonder about Sophie?"

Eva's response was immediate and clearly straight from her heart. "Only every day." She shook her head. "But I knew she was safe and loved. And I knew if I came back, it would only cause problems for her because I wasn't ever going to be what *he* wanted me to be. Every so often, I asked him for money. It was how I checked on her because he sent me pictures when he sent the money. I have them all in an album. Baby pictures, school pictures, graduations, and vacation pictures. He always sent a picture."

"That was nice of him." Henry wasn't sure what to say.

"Ya think?" Eva laughed grimly. "I'm thinking he was just reminding me that she was his. But it didn't matter. I got to see her grow up and become a woman, so it didn't matter why he did it."

That didn't sound like the gracious, kind man Sophie had described to him on more than one occasion. "Sounds to me like he only wanted you to know she was okay."

She shook her head and her tone was adamant. "He turned her against me and never let me forget it."

"Where've you been all these years? Why didn't you contact her when she grew up?" Henry knew he was getting close to being plain nosy, but she seemed open, so he topped off her glass and kept pushing. "I think she would've loved to have known you."

"Nah." Eva pulled a crumpled pack of cigarettes from her skirt pocket and lit up, blowing the smoke over her shoulder. "By the time she was old enough to think for herself, they'd brainwashed her against me. Too much time had passed. I've been trying to make a living, keep body and soul together. She had her own life. She didn't need me."

"So what really brought you up here?" Henry rose, found the mussel shell ashtray, and set it on the table next to her elbow.

"Thanks." Silently, she smoked the cigarette down to the filter, taking deep drags between sips of wine.

Henry drank his wine and waited, hoping he hadn't crossed a line. That she wouldn't shut down and stop talking.

"The truth?" Eva finally said on breath of smoke.

"Why not?" He gave her a smile. "What've you got to lose?"

"I figured now that he was gone, I might be able to make some kind of connection with my daughter." She eyed him, obviously trying to judge whether or not he was buying it.

"So the treasure had nothing to do with it?" It was a logical question and at this point, Henry was in too deep not to ask.

"What treasure?" She gulped the last of her wine and reached for the bottle. "We haven't found jack-shit."

"What happens if we do find it?"

Eva splashed some more wine into her glass without looking at him, no doubt anticipating his disapproval. "You've got money, Dugan. You have no idea what it's like to have to think about what you're willing to do for a meal or a warm bed."

Henry swallowed the guffaw that rose to his lips, nearly choking on his wine. She was seriously playing the poor-me card? No way. "Come on, Eva. You just admitted that Leo sent you money for forty-five years. And you told us that you've been working in the food industry forever. I seriously doubt you ever had to sell your body for a meal." Disgusted, he shoved his chair back, prepared to leave.

"Okay." She threw her hands up. "Okay, so Dale convinced me that Dad had found the coins."

"How did you meet Dale?"

"I was tending bar at the track in Hialeah and he wandered in one night a couple of years ago. Swept me right off my feet."

Her smile reminded him of an older, much more worn version of Sophie's. At one time, Eva Russo must have been a very attractive woman, but hard living and bad choices had taken their toll. He quirked one brow and nodded, encouraging her to go on.

"Like we told you, one night we got to talking and discovered our connection to this place. The more I thought about it, the more I realized that Dad must've found those coins. It's the only way he could've gotten the kind of money he spent." She paused to light up again, sucking the smoke into her lungs with such vigor it made Henry's chest hurt.

"Is it possible that Dale sought you out?" Henry straightened the plastic wrapper from the cheese and pressed it back around the chunk that was left. "I mean, maybe he had this all figured out before he walked into the bar."

"You don't think it was my amazing looks and sunny disposition that attracted him?" A hint of Sophie's wry humor showed through. Somehow it made him like Eva better.

"That's not what I'm saying…"

"Yeah it is, but don't worry about it." She stubbed out the cigarette. "Hell yes he tracked me down. I'm convinced he and his father, and probably even his grandfather, have all been up here countless times diving for that wreck. I may not have a bunch of fancy degrees, but I'm not stupid, Dugan. The Case family has been obsessed with those coins since the boat got lost in the thirties." She tipped the wine bottle first into his glass and then into hers, emptying it.

"I never thought you were stupid, Eva."

She gave a little too-casual shrug. "Way I figure it, if they are here, why not try to find 'em? Nothing wrong with getting rich." Then she met his eyes over the remnants of their snack. "Besides, it was a chance to… to get to know Sophie a little."

CHAPTER 24

C arrie and Julie headed down the beach so fast Sophie was practically jogging to keep up. "Where are you guys taking me?"

"To the lighthouse," Jules called over her shoulder. "Get a move on."

"The lighthouse? But I'm all dirty and sweaty. I can't show up at the lighthouse like this." She hated grumbling but all she really wanted was a shower, a glass of wine, and Henry.

"It's closed, so nobody's gonna see you." Carrie slowed her pace enough for Sophie to catch up.

"Then why are we going?"

"There's something you need to see." Julie turned with a little impatient gesture. "Come on."

Sophie was getting breathless and her legs ached from getting up and down a hundred times as she and Henry had emptied boxes and trunks. Whatever this was, surely it could've waited for morning.

"Why didn't we just drive?" Receiving no reply, she quickened her pace as the red roof of the lighthouse came into view. Soon, they were clambering up the stairs from the beach.

Julie led the way across the picnic area and through the parking lot to an outbuilding that had once housed the Willow Point lifesaving station, but was now the gift shop and offices for the restored lighthouse. Sophie glanced around the empty parking lot, surprised not to see Gus Whittier's ancient Woody parked in its usual spot down near the road before she remembered Julie mentioning his going out to California to meet his new great-granddaughter. Gus had been night watchman at Willow Point lighthouse for as long as she could remember, and along with Papa Leo, was part of a fivesome that got together for poker every Thursday night in the summer. Most often they played around the big table in the kitchen of the Firefly with Sophie acting as their personal server.

The guys' assumption that she'd bring them a beer or nuke the nachos on poker night should have offended her feminist sensibilities, but they were sweet, courtly old gentlemen. They always teased her gently, making her feel like a young girl instead of a boring forty-something spinster. Were the other four still playing? Had they found a replacement for Papa Leo? She shook her head, swallowed the ache in her throat, and followed Carrie and Julie.

The building was locked up tight, but Jules had a key and she flipped on the lights as they stepped into gift shop.

"Okay." She brushed her hands together briskly. "Now you already know that your grandfather's name is on the plaque as a big donor to the lighthouse restoration fund."

"Yup." Curiosity trumped tired and grumpy as she saw the eager expressions on her friends' faces.

"You may not know that I'm the new treasurer for the Friends of the Lighthouse board. Just took office in March."

"And I'm the new volunteer coordinator," Carrie added with a grin. "So, get ready. I'll be signing you up for something here pretty soon."

"Okay, sure." Sophie nodded. "I'd love to help out. But why are we here?"

Julie crooked one manicured finger and headed for the offices in the back of the building. "After you told us about Leo possibly finding a treasure at the bottom of the lake, I went through some of the old books." Fluorescent lights hummed and flickered on as she hit switches on their way down the hall. Sophie followed them into a cramped office. The desk was covered in leather-bound ledgers.

Jules reached across the piles to grab the one that lay open on the blotter. "Take a look at this, babes."

The entry she pointed to made Sophie's stomach clench. "Holy shit," she said, nearly breathless. "A hundred and sixty-five thousand dollars? Somebody just handed over a hundred and sixty-five thousand dollars?"

Jules nodded. "It was when Earl was treasurer, and from what I can tell, it paid for the entire steel seawall that was installed later that year."

"What year is this?" Sophie ran her finger across the row to check the date. "Hm. 1982. I was thirteen." She snapped her fingers. "I remember when that new seawall went in. The cliff was eroding and falling into the lake. Papa Leo spent hours down here sandbagging before they finally installed the seawall."

"Well, he also installed a buttload of money." Carrie settled into a chair in the corner of the cluttered office. "We think he probably found the coins, honey. That's why we wanted to show you this."

"What are you talking about? It doesn't say *who* made that donation, and Papa Leo sure didn't have that kind of money." Sophie stared at the ledger page, but her brain simply couldn't engage. Earl had mentioned that Papa Leo had been a big donor to the seawall fund, but seeing the actual amount was earth shattering. Did this mean Eva was right? Papa Leo had found the coins and he'd sold at least one? That had to be the answer. Where else would he have gotten that kind of money? She squinted as the numbers blurred on the page and her eyes began to burn. How could he keep such a secret? Was this what he was trying to tell her the night he died? She blinked back tears. Maybe she really didn't know him at all.

"There's something else you need to see." Julie took the ledger from her hands, set it down, and led Sophie behind the desk. "The people who've had this office have all been anal as hell and kept every scrap of paper ever generated over the last thirty-five years the restoration effort has been underway. I went down to the basement and found the box from the year he made this big donation." She laid three faded Xerox copies out on the desk.

"What are these?"

"Photocopies of checks that Leo wrote to the foundation that year." Jules pointed to one. "This first one is from February of that year and it was drawn on a bank down in Indiana. So was the one he wrote in November that same year. See? One for a thousand and one for five hundred."

Sophie nodded, trying to make sense of the evidence before her. Papa Leo's tidy handwriting made her heart ache even more.

"But look at this one." Jules laid the last paper on top of the other two.

Sophie's heart sank even further. It was the big check—the one for a hundred and sixty-five thousand dollars, and Papa Leo had written it.

"It's drawn on a bank in Traverse City." Jules said. "And check this out, your grandmother's name isn't on the account and she was alive then, wasn't she?"

"Yes, she died about two years later, when I was fifteen." Sophie held up the paper. "I've never seen this account before.

But these," she indicated the others with a brief nod. "They're from the account he had for years at our bank in Indiana."

"Exactly!" Carrie slapped the arm of the chair. "All you need to do is go to that bank in Traverse City and see if Leo has an account there. Sophie, there could be a fortune just waiting for you."

"And I'd bet anything there's also a safety deposit box," Jules added.

Sophie couldn't even speak as she stared at the photocopy. It was Papa Leo's name on the check, his handwriting, his firm signature.

How on Earth...?

Suddenly her legs didn't want to hold her up anymore. She clutched the edge of desk with a gasp. Pain wracked her chest as she sucked in breath after breath, unable to find enough air.

"Oh, damn, Carrie, she's hyperventilating." Jules reached back and pulled the desk chair against the back of Sophie's knees. "Sit, Soph." She pressed Sophie's shoulders and held the chair as she sank into it, fists pressed to her aching chest.

"Do you have a paper bag?" Carrie leapt up, scanning the room hurriedly before grabbing a large manila envelope from the top of a file cabinet. "Here." She hurried around the desk, scrunching the top of the envelope. "Take this." She shoved it into Sophie's hand. "Breathe into it."

"Take regular breaths, Soph." Jules smoothed Sophie's hair back from her cheek and tucked the strands behind her ear.

The envelope smelled of eraser dust and copier toner. Sophie breathed into it as normally as she could, but she couldn't stop shaking. Her fingers tingled and she was so lightheaded, she feared she might actually be having a heart attack. After a few minutes, her breathing improved as she inhaled and exhaled into the crumpled envelope. At last she took several breaths without

the envelope and felt better—more normal. Or at least as normal
as devastated could feel.

She bent at the waist, folded her arms on her knees and rested
her forehead on her arms. Carrie and Jules rubbed her shoulders
and back as the tears began to seep out of her eyes. Swallowing
hard, she couldn't speak. If she tried to speak, she'd either puke or
burst into hysterical crying. Neither one seemed like a good
option.

When she finally raised her head, the tears were streaming
down her face and she rubbed her eyes with her fists like a child.

"Hush now." Carrie gathered her into a hug. "It's okay."

"He lied to me," Sophie choked out. "My whole life, he lied
to me. Why? Why would he do that?"

"Maybe he believed he was protecting you," Jules offered as
she rotated in place and scanned the tiny office. "Dammit,
where's my tissue box? The girls in the gift shop must've
borrowed it again. Hang on." She scurried out.

"Protecting me?" Sophie leaned back from Carrie's embrace.
"From what?"

"Maybe he figured out who the boat belonged to," Carrie said.

"You think?" Sophie grasped onto the heartening thought,
mostly because she couldn't bear the idea that Papa Leo could've
been so duplicitous.

"Maybe."

"Of course! That has to be it. He was worried the mob would
figure out he'd found their lost treasure." She rose, wiping her
cheeks with the back of her hand. "So he hid everything and
didn't tell a soul about it. Apparently, not even Nonna. He was
trying to keep us safe."

"Sure." Carrie was quick to agree, obviously wanting to ease
Sophie's pain. "He could've researched the find, too, and realized
who the boat belonged to—that makes sense."

"Yeah." Sophie bit her lower lip. "But he had to have sold at least one of the coins. How else would he have so much money? That means he stole money from the government. My Papa wouldn't do that."

"Look." Carrie crossed her arms over her breasts and gave Sophie a stern stare. "Doesn't maritime law say that anything salvaged from the bottom of the sea, or the lake in this case, belongs to the person who found it? If that weren't true, that Mel Fisher guy who found the *Atocha* would've had to return everything to Spain or wherever it came from. The people who've been diving on the *Titanic* should be sending all the artifacts they're recovering to the families of the victims. But are they doing that? Hell no. A lot of that stuff's in a traveling exhibit that's been to nearly every museum in the country."

"But the coins were stolen from the treasury."

"So what?"

"I don't know." Sophie wasn't at all convinced. "There's probably some law. We need to look it up."

"I'm going to bet old Leo already looked it up."

"Then why did he keep it a secret?"

"Probably because of the Todaros," Carrie said. "Wouldn't you have kept it quiet?"

Sophie sniffed and rubbed her palms on her cheeks again as Jules appeared in the doorway.

"I can't find them." She nodded at the desk. "Just use a blank piece of paper. Kinda rough, but hey, better than your shirt."

"Oh, wait, I think I've got a paper towel here." Sophie reached in her pocket and pulled out the tattered paper towel and Eva's bag of weed. The packet of rolling papers dropped to the floor. "Dammit, I forgot I had this."

"Is that grass?" Julie stooped down to retrieve the rolling papers. "What are you doing with marijuana?"

"Eva found it in her stuff from the attic." Sophie held up the ancient plastic zipper bag. "I confiscated it."

"God, how old is that shit?" Jules snatched the bag, shook it, and sniffed.

"At least as old as me." Sophie watched with amusement as Jules opened the bag and stuck her nose into it.

"Huh." Jules thrust the bag of weed at Carrie. "Smell it. It still smells like grass."

"Of course it does. It is grass." Carrie held the bag gingerly between two fingers.

"I mean maybe it's still good." Jules raised one brow and grinned.

"Oh, holy shit, Jules. We are not smoking forty-five-year-old marijuana." Carrie zipped the bag shut and tossed it to Sophie. "Especially not here, in a public museum."

"We're not? Why not?" Sophie couldn't believe the words that came out of her mouth. Her friends gazed at her, one clearly aghast, the other clearly delighted. "I mean, what could it hurt? I doubt it has any strength left. Let's give it a try."

"Have you lost your mind?" Carrie asked.

"I've never smoked grass before. I want to see what all the fuss is about." Sophie blew her nose on the tattered paper towel and pitched it in the wastebasket. "Besides, a little high sounds pretty damn good right now." She took the rolling papers from Julie. "Do either of you know how to do this?"

"I do," Jules said before returning Carrie's horrified look with wink and a grin. "Okay, I confess. I tried it with Ryan and bunch of his fraternity brothers once when I went down to visit him at school. It was before he got accepted to med school."

"You did drugs with your son?" Carrie gasped.

"I had a couple of tokes on a joint in the basement of a frat house. Geez, Caro. Chill out. We need a way to light up." Jules dug in her desk drawer and came up with a long butane grill lighter before she led the way out of the office. "Come on. Let's do this outside. That way we won't stink up the gift shop."

"Do you think these papers are still good?" Sophie's heart pounded. This was just crazy enough to feel good and with all the other kinds of crazy that had been going on lately, she wanted—no, needed—a little escape.

"It's just tissue paper," Jules replied breezily as she relocked the building. "They should be fine."

"I do not believe this." Carrie lagged behind as Jules and Sophie rushed to the picnic tables and set up shop in the evening shadows.

"Okay, all you do is…" Jules spilled a couple of papers out of the packet and carefully rolled the joint, twisting the ends like a pro. "Ta-da!"

"Tony's gonna come by and arrest the lot of us," Carrie moaned as she settled on the bench across from Sophie.

"Quit being such an old lady." Sophie stuck her tongue out. Julie's sense of fun was always contagious and Sophie was particularly susceptible this evening. "Light it up, Jules."

CHAPTER 25

Sophie drew in a deep cleansing breath, letting the cool breeze off the lake fill her lungs before releasing it, slow and measured. She imagined she was in yoga class, counting the seconds, making each inhalation and exhalation exactly the same length. Relaxed. So tranquil, even the hard wooden surface of the picnic table felt as cushy as giant pillow. She couldn't remember a more peaceful time, at least not in the recent past. She opened her eyes.

The stars!

"Look at all the stars!" The words sounded squishy in her ears. "There's a million of 'em." The sun had just dropped into the horizon and the sky was purplish-blue with dusk, but the stars were already appearing. They seemed to have been tossed across the heavens by an unseen hand.

"Mm hm." Carrie murmured from her spot on the bench below Sophie. "Little tiny stars... big shiny stars... hey, that rhymes..."

"Sophie, get up." Julie tugged at the sleeve of her T-shirt. "Come on, twirl with me."

"No, I don't wanna twirl." Sophie was perfectly content to

remain on the table, gazing at the incredible Michigan sky. "Here." She scooted over to make room for Julie, only vaguely aware of the possibility of splinters. "Lie down with me. Look at the sky."

"Okay." Jules settled on her back, her arm brushing Sophie's. "But if I look at the sky, you have to twirl, deal?" She passed the joint, now neatly clipped into a bobby pin Jules had found in her desk. "Take this. It's almost gone."

"I can't. I'm dizzy." Sophie accepted it anyway and took another hit, basking in the dreamy state the weed had induced. The stuff had been pretty dry and it burned up fast. Jules had rolled four—or was it five?—joints before they felt anything at all, but wow, who knew ancient marijuana could create such a lovely high? Was it actually the weed or was it simply that she'd never smoked before? She frowned. Or was it that she needed to cut loose, to get away from her life and her mother and mysteries she didn't understand. And Henry…

Ah, Henry. The one thing in her life that made sense. Warmth flooded her insides and she sighed deeply.

"What's the giant sigh for, Soph?" Jules elbowed her none too gently in the ribs.

"Ouch." Sophie squealed, but when she glanced at Jules, it suddenly occurred to her that Henry didn't really make any sense, either. What the hell was *friends with benefits* anyway? Whoever thought of that? How was she supposed to make love with the guy and not fall in love with him? How did that work?

"How does what work?"

Sophie didn't realize she'd spoken aloud until Jules repeated it. She closed her eyes, remembering Henry's hands and Henry's lips as she tried the form the words to explain her confusion. But the words wouldn't come. She was too relaxed and he was too sexy to discuss, even with her dearest friends.

Besides, the stars were winking at her, and the scent of the

water and the roses that climbed up the side of the lighthouse
wafted on a delicious breeze that lifted her bangs from her forehead. She handed the miniscule piece of joint down to Carrie.
There was an actual name for the end of a joint. She'd read it
once. Oh yeah, a roach. Like the bug. Ugh. But that made the
hairpin a roach clip. Did they actually sell real roach clips or did
everyone who smoked have to improvise. What else would work?
Tweezers. A paper—

"Evening, ladies. Whatcha doin'?"

Sophie tipped her head back, astonished at the sight of
Maestro Liam Reilly's broad form silhouetted upside-down
against the pinkish light from the parking lot. Rolling over, she
bumped her knees on Carrie, who'd sat up just in time to avoid
having Sophie's feet thump onto her belly. Sophie swallowed the
puff of grass she'd just inhaled and Carrie dropped the roach on
the sand and ground her heel into it.

"Hi, honey." Carrie gave him a tremulous smile.

"Liam, babe!" Julie sat up and spun around, her legs swinging
off the edge of the table. "How's it going, dude?" She elbowed
Sophie in the small of the back with a muttered, "Breathe, idiot."

Sophie released the smoke on a choked cough and Julie
reached back to pound her on the back. Head swimming, Sophie
blinked at Liam, who stood at the end of the table, arms crossed
over his vast chest, one brow quirked, a small smile playing on
his handsome face.

Carrie rose, one hand on the table. "We were… um… we were
just… um… enjoying the stars."

Liam nodded. "The stars, huh?"

"Yeah. Little stargazing, you know…" Sophie agreed, unsure
whether her legs would hold her up if she tried to stand. Probably
better to get her bearings here on the table for a minute or two.
"Then we were going to head back to my place." She cocked her

head in the general direction of the cottages and saw the Lombardy poplars whiz past.

Whoa.

"Look at that sky, Liam." Julie hopped off the table, stumbled, but caught herself. She made her way over to Carrie's husband. "Isn't that amazing?"

"Amazing." Liam agreed, grabbing Julie as she tilted back to stare up at the heavens. "So what have you girls been smokin' out here?"

"Nothing." Jules and Carrie responded in unison, sounding like a pair of guilty teenagers.

Their feigned innocence gave Sophie an attack of the giggles. When Julie and Carrie both glared at her, she bit her lip and clamped her teeth shut, but she couldn't hold it in. Clapping a hand over her mouth, she turned away as peals of laughter escaped.

"Doesn't smell like nothing." Liam steadied Julie against the table and walked around to the other end where they'd left the bag of weed, the papers, and the grill lighter. Pulling his phone from his pocket, he turned on the flashlight app and gave the bag a sniff. "Are you kidding me? Where'd you get this nasty shit?"

"It's old," Carrie said. "Very old."

"It's like antique grass, so it's not really illegal, right?" Jules offered.

Sophie kept her head down until Liam reached out to take her chin in his hand and shine the light in her eyes. It hurt, so she closed her eyes and turned her head away. "Stop it. Turn off that damn light. Go away."

"Yeah, Liam. Go away." Julie swung around and extended her hand to Sophie. "You're harshing our buzz. Okay, Soph, now let's twirl."

Sophie jumped down and clasped Julie's hands. They spun

together in a rather lopsided circle that only lasted a few seconds before they both fell onto the sand in a giggly heap.

Liam sighed. "Come on, ladies. I'm taking you home."

"Nooo…" The word came out in a sing-songy whine, which surprised the hell out of Sophie—she hadn't whined since she was fifteen years old. She and Julie rose, clutching each other for balance. "I like twirling. I forgot how much I like twirling."

"Twirl!" Julie cried and they gripped each other's forearms and danced. "Come on, Caro. Twirl with us."

Pocketing the paraphernalia, Liam strode to Carrie. "Nope. We're done twirling for tonight. Carrie, let's go, babe." He took her gently by the bicep and led her to his car, calling over his shoulder. "Come on, you two. Getting stoned up here on this cliff is about the stupidest thing I've ever seen. Sheesh. One of you could've fallen down on the rocks and been killed, for God's sake," he ranted as he opened the car door.

Wow, was he ever a grump. Who knew? He always seemed so nice whenever she saw him in the village or visited Carrie. Sophie scowled as she watched him carefully belt Carrie into the front seat of his SUV, but when she started to follow, Jules held her back.

"Lookit," Jules whispered and pointed. "The lights are making a halo around his hair. That's so cool."

Sophie stared as Liam's red haired glitter in the parking lot lights. "Wow. It's like an aura."

"He's tall." Jules clutched Sophie's arm. "God he's a big guy. Don't you think he's a big guy?"

Sophie narrowed her eyes at the tall man headed toward them. "Yup. I like big guys. They're cuddly… like teddy bears. Not like real bears, of course. Real bears probably wouldn't want to cuddle."

This clearly struck Jules as hilarious. Giggles bubbled out as she shook Sophie's arm, but Sophie pulled away. "What? Why are you laughing? That makes me sad. Bears are furry and they look so loveable, but you have stay in your car at the dump or they'll come after you."

"Sophie, Julie, come on." Liam took each of them by the elbow. "Let's go home."

"I can walk up the beach. It's not very far." Sophie slipped in the sand, but Liam's hold kept her from falling on her ass.

He tightened his grip. "Why don't you let me drive you?" He opened both back doors and guided them in. "Buckle up now." Sliding into the driver's seat, he tossed the weed in the console between him and Carrie.

"Hey, you can't keep that. It's mine." Sophie protested. Could he keep it? Did he have the right to keep her weed? Well, technically, it wasn't her weed. Hm. "If I confiscated it, it's mine, right?"

"Yup, and if I confiscate it, then it's mine." Liam grinned at her in the rearview mirror as he started the engine. "See how that works?"

"Oh yeah." Sophie nodded, seeing the perfect logic in his words, but failing to make the clip end of the seat belt fit into the holder. Jules reached over and snapped it in. What a nice person she was. "You're a good friend, Jules. I love you."

Julie shot her a dazzling smile before shouting, "Hey, big guy, you gonna turn us in?"

"Shh… shush!" Carrie turned around and pressed one finger to her lips. "Don't holler."

"No, I'm taking you all home," Liam replied. "And listen up. Anybody who pukes in my car will be cleaning it up themselves, so if you feel sick, say something."

"Whaddya think we are, a bunch of kids?" Jules kicked the back of Liam's seat. "We're not gonna barf. Grass doesn't make you barf. We're fine. Aren't we fine?"

"We're fine." Carrie and Sophie answered in unison.

"Yeah, you're fine all right." Liam shook his head, turned in a wide circle, and pulled away from the lighthouse.

Henry glanced at the clock in the corner of his screen and then out the French doors. The patio lights had come on against the encroaching darkness. Sophie and her friends had been gone nearly three hours. Carrie had said they were going to the lighthouse, but he had no idea how far that was or whether it was safe for them to walk back up the beach in the dark.

Eva had gone into the Sandpiper a couple of hours ago and he hadn't heard a peep from her since, even though he'd assumed she might come looking for supper. Lord knew there wasn't anything much in the kitchen over there. He'd basically existed on popcorn and cold cereal until he'd started eating with Sophie.

Where the hell was that woman anyway? He was kinda perturbed that she hadn't returned yet, although he had no idea why he was so upset. It wasn't like they had any kind of commitment to each other. She was free to do whatever she wanted, but wouldn't simple manners suggest that she at least call him? He stared moodily at his cell phone and then tapped the screen and dialed her cell. It went immediately to voicemail.

They still had to load all the stuff back into the attic and he sure as hell wasn't going to lift that damn dish trunk by himself. It was heavy. Now he was wandering around the Internet looking for some mention of the *Caroline Howe* while his stomach growled and he longed for a beer. He was fucking sick of wine. He shoved his chair back from the table, opened the fridge and stared, as if just gazing into the cold would magically turn the bottle of wine sitting there into a well-constructed lager.

Lights flashed in the kitchen window and gravel crunched outside. He knit his brows as he unhooked the screen door and watched a man help Sophie out of a big SUV. She twisted away and leaned in the back window before accepting the guy's assistance to the door. Henry smelled something vaguely familiar as he held the door open and Sophie dropped a kiss on his lips as she passed through.

"Hey, baby." She sauntered unsteadily into the kitchen.

"Hi." The man extended his hand. "Liam Reilly."

"Henry Dugan." He let the door rest against his backside as he shook hands. "What's up?"

"Found these three up at the lighthouse, a little worse for wear, so I thought I'd bring them home."

"A little worse for wear?" Henry's curiosity was raging and he glanced in at Sophie, who was ransacking the refrigerator. "Is she okay?"

Liam just grinned. "She's fine. Nothing a good night's sleep won't fix. I'll let her explain. I need to get these other two home. 'Night."

"Thanks." Henry gave him a nod. "Oh, hey, I'm a big fan, Maestro."

"Yeah?" Liam's white teeth gleamed against his salt-and-pepper goatee. "Back atcha, Henry. Your books saved my ass more than once."

"Glad to hear it." Henry smiled.

"Thank you, Liam." Sophie flew out of the kitchen right into Liam's chest, winding her arms around his neck and giving him a smacking kiss on the cheek. "You're just the best, you know it?"

"Yeah, I know it." He unwound her arms and set her next to Henry, who caught her as she began to waver. "Get some sleep, Soph."

"Yessir." She saluted and Henry leaned back to avoid being elbowed in the glasses. He yanked the screen door shut and watched for a moment as Liam drove away with his other two charges.

What the hell?

Sophie scampered back to the fridge, pulling out cheese and a bowl of strawberries, before *ooh*ing and *ahh*ing over a dish of hard-boiled eggs. "Egg salad!" She gave him a toothy grin. "I'm going to make egg salad."

"Are you *high*?" He stepped behind her and sniffed. Yup, the odor of weed permeated her clothes and when he tugged her away from the fridge into the overhead light in the kitchen, her pupils were pinpricks. "Jesus! You *are* high."

"Only a little." Sophie gave him a pout that ordinarily would've been cute as hell, but at that moment, he was sorta irritated.

"What were you thinking, Sophie?" Henry gave her a little shake. "Don't tell me you smoked that nasty shit your mom found in her stuff. Who knows how old that crap was? It could've turned toxic."

"It didn't, I assure you." Her grin was a little lopsided. "We were kinda surprised it had any power left in it. It was pretty dry though."

"Thank God you're okay." Henry released her and began gathering up his notes and shoving them into his bag. "Frankly, I was kinda worried. It was getting dark, and I don't know anything about this area or if you were safe or not. A call would've been nice."

"I didn't have my phone with me; it's right there charging." Sophie pointed to the bar. Her eyes narrowed and she threw up her hands. "Sorry."

"Yeah, well, next time, take your phone, okay?"

"Okay, *Dad*."

He gazed at her, standing there, adorable in her snug T-shirt with dark tendrils of hair wisping around her face. The streak of dirt across her cheek made her appear about fifteen instead of forty-five. Finally, the utter silliness of the situation overtook his frustration and he burst out laughing, "How many times do you suppose this scenario played out in this very kitchen forty-odd years ago?"

Sophie grinned. "Probably more than we can imagine. Is it even possible for us to be working out Eva's déjà vu here?" She turned back to the fridge. "I'm starving!"

"I'll bet you are," Henry replied with a wry smile as he finished packing up his notes and laptop. "I vaguely remember the munchies from my college days."

"Is that what this is?" Sophie set the dish of eggs on the counter. "I've never smoked grass before, but I've read about the munchies. Do you want some egg salad?"

"I don't think so, but thanks." Henry gave her quick hug. He was too exhausted to eat. The only thing that sounded good was a hot shower and cool sheets. "I'm going to go get in the shower. You'll be okay out here?"

She attempted a rather uncoordinated wink, but her pupils were starting to respond to the light, so she was probably coming down.

She was going to crash good and hard in about an hour or so —he'd seen it happen plenty of times years ago with his roommates at San Jose State. He'd smoked a little weed in college, but the idea of sucking smoke into his lungs bothered him, so beer had become his drug of choice, although he rarely got smashed. Oh, he enjoyed a nice buzz as much as the next guy, but he hated how he felt the day after a drunk. So not worth it.

"I'm okay. Go shower." She clutched the edge of the counter and then straightened and blinked before looking him in the eye. "See? I'm okay. I'll be in soon, I promise. Just gonna have some... you know, some food."

CHAPTER 26

Sophie eyed Henry's behind as he sauntered down the hall. Man, he had a nice ass. And not just for a middle-aged guy. He plain had a good butt. She shook her head. She was still starving. Tugging open the refrigerator again, her eyes lit on the bottle of Riesling. Egg salad on toast, strawberries, and a glass of ice-cold wine—the perfect supper. Yanking the cork out, she poured a generous glass, slugged it down, and poured another before she started peeling and dicing eggs. Man, she was thirsty. Did grass dehydrate you? The squeak of the screen porch door caused her to miss the egg she was cutting. For a second, she just stared as her injured thumb turned the cutting board red, but then the sting caught up to the slice.

"Oh, shit." She grabbed a paper towel and held her bleeding digit over the sink. "Damn, damn, damn." Cold water made it feel mildly less painful, so she let the stream run over it.

"What's going on?" Her mother, dressed in a long, fuzzy robe, strolled into the house without even knocking. Over the purple shiner, she wore a pair of wire-rimmed glasses perched on her nose, no makeup, and her black hair was clipped up off her neck.

"Who did I see pulling out a couple of minutes ago? What happened?"

"I cut my thumb." Sophie's voice caught as she swallowed the lump in her throat.

"Oh, God, you're a mess. Let me see." Eva clearly had gotten a good look at the bloody cutting board. Gently, she pulled Sophie's hand from the water, wrapped it in a dry paper towel, and held it up to the light. "It's a clean cut, sweets," she said. "Here, we'll put a butterfly on it and wrap it up. You'll be okay."

"It stings." Sophie blinked back tears. How stupid to cry over a cut thumb. And why did it feel so damn good to have someone else there even though that someone was Eva?

Please, don't let me be having an I-want-my-mommy moment.

Because she didn't—not really. Not at this late date.

"I'm sure it does." Eva's tone was as soothing as she led Sophie back to the hallway bathroom and first aid. Working with the smooth efficiency of an emergency room nurse, Eva had the thumb bandaged in no time while Sophie sat mutely on the edge of tub, dejection setting in as her head began to pound.

"Do you want to tell me what happened here?" Eva pressed the final tab of a Band-Aid into place.

"Not particularly." All Sophie really wanted was to go to bed. "Thanks for the first aid, Eva. I'm going to bed."

"Nuh uh, not so fast, sister." Eva grabbed Sophie's arm, spinning her around as she exited the bathroom. "Do I smell grass on you?"

"Cripes!" Sophie shook her off and stormed to the kitchen. "What the hell? First time in my entire life, I let loose a little, and suddenly, I'm being treated like a delinquent teenager. I'm forty-five fucking years old. If I want to smoke a little weed with my friends, I think I have the right to do it. And *you* certainly have nothing to say about it!"

"Well, it *is* illegal in Michigan." Eva nudged Sophie aside with her hip and took over the egg salad with practiced ease, dumping the bloody egg pieces into the trash. "And if you were smoking the grass you took from me, it's a miracle you got any kind of high at all. That shit's older than you are. Go sit down. I'll do this." She jerked her head toward the table and washed the cutting board before dicing up the rest of the eggs.

"It's illegal in Michigan?" Sophie grabbed her glass of wine and dropped into a chair. "That's interesting coming from you."

"I'm surprised it didn't just burst into flames—I imagine it was dry as dust." Eva blended mayonnaise and mustard into the diced eggs, shook some salt, pepper, parsley, dill, and paprika into the mixture, and popped a couple of slices of bread into the toaster.

"Hey, that's exactly how I make egg salad. Dill was Nonna's secret ingredient," Sophie said gulping the last of her wine. Her stomach rolled slightly and she debated the wisdom of eggs and mayonnaise, but it sure looked good.

"Where do you think I learned to make it?" Her mother tossed a smile over her shoulder, and Sophie suddenly saw Nonna standing there.

Dear lord.

In that moment, Eva looked so much like her grandmother, Sophie's heart ached. Her words left her as she stared at her mother bustling around the kitchen, gathering up a plate and fork, and rinsing and hulling strawberries before sprinkling them with just a touch a sugar.

"I'm a damn good cook, kid, and I learned it all from my mother. She was an amazing cook. Could produce a gourmet meal from the simplest ingredients." Eva set a plate down in front of her. "You've really tied one on, didn't you? Eat something. You need some food to counteract the wine. I'm betting you haven't eaten all day." She poured herself a glass of Riesling and sat down across from Sophie.

"I've eaten," Sophie mumbled and stared at the plate of food, which looked delicious, but somehow her stomach was rebelling at the thought of putting anything inside it. Two big glasses of Riesling after getting high probably wasn't the smartest move she'd ever made. Neither was sleeping with her best client, come to think of it. Or letting her mother into her life. Or trying to make a big mystery where one most likely never existed in the first place.

All in all, her recent choices had sucked.

"Where's Dugan?" Eva's gravelly voice interrupted Sophie's self-flagellation.

"In the shower," Sophie replied before forking a strawberry into her mouth. She tilted her head toward the hallway. Sure enough she heard the sound of water rushing in the master bathroom.

"Ah. Why aren't you in there with him?"

Sophie scowled and took a bite of egg salad sandwich. It was delicious, dammit, just as she knew it would be. She ate in silence. No way was she going to get into a girl-talk moment with her mother, especially not over her relationship with Henry.

"You two are a cute couple." Eva took a sip of her wine. "How long have you been together?"

"We're not together."

"Really? Coulda fooled me." Eva gave her a raised eyebrow. "I Googled him last night on my phone. He's freakin' rich."

"He's a client." The food was calming her stomach and Eva's egg salad was even better than her own. It had to be the spices—Nonna never measured anything and neither had Eva. Sophie measured everything when she cooked and followed recipes to the last word. She never wanted to mess anything up. True enough when she was in the kitchen, but apparently, it didn't apply to the rest of her life, which it seemed to her was about as messed up as a life could get. Single, middle-aged, all alone in the world except for a wacked-out mother who was a virtual stranger, and now she was screwing her best client.

Yeah, right, go ahead and think of him as just a client.

If what they'd shared was purely casual sex, it was pretty amazing casual sex. She'd had no idea making love could be that intense. Tom had certainly never made her all her bells and whistles go off, and her only other sexual experience was when she was sixteen. Danny Mason in the back of his father's station wagon. God, after that experience, it was a miracle she hadn't opted for a convent.

No, she was kidding herself if she thought what she'd enjoyed with Henry was only sex.

I'm in love with him.

And why not? He was smart and successful, attentive, funny, and kind. He'd been endlessly patient, giving up his writing time to help her try to figure out the treasure and handle her mother. He'd acted like a man in love. Hadn't he?

Oh, hell, it'd been so long since she and Tom had fallen in love, would she even recognize a guy in love? But Henry had gotten worried when she'd disappeared and came home stoned—because he cared so much? Why wasn't he sick and tired of all the freaking drama? She certainly was. Nope, he'd just hung in there… like… like a guy in love.

"Hey?" Eva snapped her fingers in front of Sophie's face.

"What?" She jerked her head up.

"Are you going to talk to me?"

"No." Her head pounded and her stomach was queasy, so Sophie shoved the plate aside and stood up. "Thanks for supper. I'm going to bed." Ten feet from the bedroom, her stomach roiled violently and she barely made it to the bathroom.

"Holy shit, child." Eva swept into the lavatory to place a hand on her daughter's head and hold her hair back while Sophie wretched miserably.

Resting her cheek on the cool porcelain of the bathtub, she fought back tears. Was it wrong to be so grateful that the woman who'd ignored her since her birth was here, stroking her head and murmuring little comforts?

"Here, baby..." Eva wet a washcloth and smoothed it over Sophie's face, then filled a paper cup. "Sip, swish, and spit."

Sophie pulled herself up off the rug and did as her mother asked.

Eva pressed her hand into the small of Sophie's back. "Come on, let's get you to bed."

Sophie allowed her mother to lead her to the bedroom door as if she were a child. Henry, wrapped in a towel with his hair damp and sticking up from the shower, took over from there, exchanging a knowing look with Eva that Sophie chose to ignore, because she couldn't even make rational sense of why the two of them suddenly seemed... chummy? Not possible. Exhausted in every conceivable way, she leaned into the curve of Henry's arm as Eva patted her shoulder.

"Thanks, Eva." she murmured. Her legs were lead weights and she could barely keep her eyes open.

"Goodnight, kid." Eva said softly. "Get some rest."

CHAPTER 27

Sophie squeezed her lids shut at the sunshine streaming through her bedroom window. It took all her energy to slowly open one eye. The bedside clock blinked twelve, which meant that at some point in the last day or so, the power had gone out. How had she missed that? When she stretched under the covers, she realized she was alone and still dressed in the shorts and T-shirt she'd had on the day before.

Sitting up, she winced at the relentless pounding in her head. Her teeth felt like they had fur growing on them and down by her feet, the sheets were grainy. She stretched and swung her legs over the side of the mattress, gazing in disgust at her crumpled clothing and dirty feet.

Ugh.

The events of the previous night came flooding back— smoking Eva's grass, twirling with Jules in the picnic area at the lighthouse, being dropped at home by a rather bemused Maestro Reilly... and did she really eat egg salad with her mother?

And oh, Lord... how much wine had she consumed? A vague memory of Eva holding her hair back while Sophie vomited played in the back of her mind. Did that actually happen? The foul taste in her mouth seemed to indicate that it had.

And Henry.

Gah! Henry!

It was all coming back. The poor guy had tucked her in, dirty feet and all. And had she grabbed him when he slipped in beside her? Heat suffused her cheeks as she recalled Henry's grin as he gently removed her hands from his butt... and elsewhere, rolled her to her side, and wrapped one arm around her. *Oh crap...* She popped out of bed, then put a hand on the post at the foot when a wave a dizziness swept over her. *Okay, deep breaths.* She closed her eyes and steadied her shaky legs before facing herself in the bathroom mirror.

Holy cow!

She looked like hammered shit—hair tumbling around her shoulders in a riot of tangled curls, black smudges of mascara under her red eyes, and dry, chapped lips. A quick shower and teeth brushing brought her closer to semi-human. Wrapped in her short fuzzy robe, she pressed her hair into a towel as she padded out to the kitchen to start a pot of coffee. A chime sounding puzzled her for a moment before she remembered her cell phone still charging on the bar.

She checked and found a text from Henry.

ARE YOU OKAY THIS MORNING?

Where was he? Was he just checking in on his way out of town? She couldn't blame him if he was.

Butterflies flittered in her belly as her fingers hovered over the keys. Finally she took a deep breath and typed.

WHERE ARE YOU?

Please, please let him respond... and don't let the answer be AT THE AIRPORT.

The phone vibrated against her palm before it chimed.

WALKED UP THE BEACH TO THE GRIND.

Sophie heaved a sigh of relief and checked the time—nine-thirty. What were the chances he'd run into Carrie and Jules? Probably pretty slim. She doubted they'd made it out of bed any earlier than she had. Quickly she thumbed a response.

I'M COMING. WILL YOU WAIT FOR ME? PLEASE?

JUST PICKING UP MUFFINS. I'LL BE BACK IN A FEW.

NO, STAY. I'LL COME THERE. HANG ON.

She gulped down coffee and a piece of toast to keep the dry heaves away, then swiftly dried her hair and used blush and mascara to gain some semblance of normal. Lingering in front her closet for a few seconds, she debated between capris and a striped top or her yellow flowered sundress and a pair of sandals. The dress was pretty and she needed all the feminine armor she could don to face Henry after last night's debacle. Who knew what he was thinking. She was surprised to realize how much she wanted him and that she wasn't above using her womanly wiles if a simple apology didn't put them back on an even keel.

Before she headed out, she stopped by the desk to grab a manila envelope from the bottom drawer. The attorney had given it to her when she left Indiana. It contained several copies of Papa Leo's death certificate, his birth certificate, and a copy of his will. If all went as she hoped, she and Henry would be on their way to the Traverse City First Bank and Trust before lunch. She truly wanted him along for the trip because she had no idea what she'd find at the bank. Her stomach was in nervous knots for more than one reason.

She glanced at the Sandpiper as she latched the screen porch door. No sign of Eva this morning, which was fine with Sophie. The previous night's display of maternal instinct had affected her more than she cared to admit, but truth was her mother was an enigma that she simply didn't have the emotional energy to deal with at the moment. First she had to apologize to Henry. Then she could figure out what to do about Eva.

She scooped up her keys and cell phone, dropped them in her purse, poured herself a to-go cup, and shut off the coffeemaker. At the last minute, she turned to grab the Mercedes keys from the hook by the kitchen door and toss them into her bag as well. No sense in handing Eva a golden opportunity. Thankfully, Dale was still in jail and she was fairly sure Eva couldn't hotwire a car.

During the drive into town, she rehearsed and re-rehearsed what she wanted to say to Henry. He'd been so kind last night—worried because she'd been gone so long and he didn't know where she was. Even though his sense of humor had kicked in as soon as he saw she was okay, she was still embarrassed at her own behavior.

But when Sophie found Henry in the coffee shop, sitting at a table outside on the patio, her well-practiced words left her. He was studying the newspaper, glasses sliding down on his nose, his longish hair lifting in the cool breeze off the harbor, sun glinting off the streaks of silver. His shorts showed off his sexy, muscled thighs and his polo pulled a little over his broad shoulders.

Good Lord, he was delicious... He glanced up and caught her eye as she threaded her way through the other tables. His smile was shy, almost tentative, which made her feel even worse.

"Henry, I'm so sorry," she blurted before she even sat down.

At the same time, he said, "Soph, don't be silly. You have nothing to be sorry for."

"No, I do." She yanked off her sunglasses and held up one hand. "I was a dope. And you've been nothing but kind and gracious. Please forgive me?"

"For what?" He shook his head and her stomach clenched. "It's okay. What you do is your own business, and you've had a lot to deal with." The smile that hadn't quite reached his eyes suddenly lit up his whole face, and he nodded at the chair across from him. "Are you going to join me... friend?"

For a moment, she hesitated. *Friend?* Was he sending her a

message? Was that all they'd ever be? Friends with benefits? If she wanted more, she had to speak up. Or show him. With a mental shrug, she pulled the chair closer, sat down, and went for broke. She took his face in her hands and pressed her lips to his, putting all her emotion into that kiss.

Sophie's kiss surprised Henry so thoroughly that for a couple of seconds, he couldn't muster a response. But then he kissed her back, delighting in the coffee-sweet taste of her. He'd woken up before dawn, checking on Sophie before creeping out of bed to go over his notes about the Todaros, the sunken yacht, and the possibility that Leo Russo *had* found a fortune in stolen gold coins.

Last night, when he wasn't sure where she was, he'd seriously contemplated just driving back up to Traverse City and getting on a plane. He'd even priced flights, but every time he got as far as clicking the PURCHASE button, he stopped. Maybe because this was different from the aggravation he'd felt over Kristie's drama, which only made him want to get as far away as possible. This time he didn't want escape. He didn't want to leave Willow Bay. He didn't want to leave Sophie. The fact was all he wanted was for the sun to rise so he could wake her and tell her how much he wanted more. That shocked the hell out of him.

Henry was in love and for the first time in his life, it felt right. It felt good, and he was aching to pull Sophie Russo into his arms and never let her go again. He welcomed all the drama and chaos and how she leaned on him. She needed *him*, not his money and not what he could buy for her, and by god, he needed her. A grown-up woman. The warm, funny, intelligent, seductive maturity that was his Sophie. He deepened the kiss and put his hand on the back of her head to keep her lips locked on his. She wound her arms around his neck and opened her mouth to his seeking tongue.

"Well, if this isn't as disgusting a PDA as I've ever seen." A familiar voice above their heads startled them apart. Julie Miles stood there, smirking, hands on her slim hips, sunglasses pushed up on top of her head. Carrie Reilly grinned over her shoulder as Julie continued her teasing tirade. "You have a damn cottage. Hell, you have *two* of them. Couldn't you spare us and the entire village this display of unbridled lust?"

Sophie's laughter sent a spark through Henry's veins as he released her and she gazed into his face, her expression so full of wonder, and yes... love, he nearly grabbed her again. The interruption was untimely as hell because they surely needed to talk, but the village gossip mill probably wasn't the best place anyway.

Carrie and Julie brought two chairs over, sat, and put their coffee and muffins down. "Looks like we got here just in time, Jules. They could've gotten carried away and then who knows what would've happened." Carrie laid out a napkin and fork for each of them.

Henry grinned, but kept one arm around Sophie, his thumb stroking her shoulder and down her arm. "So I see you two survived last night's little excursion."

I'm fine." Julie said, digging into a huge blueberry muffin.

"Me, too." Carrie attacked her own pastry with relish. "Soph, where's your food?"

Sophie snuggled closer to Henry. "I had toast and coffee at home."

"You look a little green around the gills," Jules cocked her head and gazed at Sophie. "Did that pot make you sick?"

"Um, well..." Sophie hesitated. "It wasn't that. It was probably the wine I had later."

Henry leaned back to give her a long look. *Wine.* So that was why she seemed a bit green around the gills (he liked Jules's description!) when Eva brought her to the bedroom last night. She looked gorgeous this morning, though, in a yellow sundress that showed off her luscious curves and the beginnings of her summer tan.

"Don't ever mix wine and pot, kid." Jules said. "You're too much of a lightweight for that."

"I won't be mixing pot with anything ever again." Sophie shuddered.

"Well, the problem probably was the wine, not the pot." Carrie said and then giggled. "Poor Liam. We really made an interesting night for him, didn't we? He laughed his butt off when we got home. I swear every time he looked at me, he cracked up."

"Yeah, Will howled when you guys dropped me off, but we did have a fine time when he finally stopped laughing." Jules gave the group a broad wink. "Getting high sure cranked up my libido."

"Apparently, I missed a golden opportunity by taking a shower last night instead of staying in the kitchen with you," Henry murmured and his breath stirred the curls over Sophie's ear.

Another expression of utter delight passed over her features, and she looked like a kid who'd just been given a pony for Christmas. The reaction warmed him all over. They needed to get out of the village and go someplace where they could talk... and touch. *Definitely touch.* He started to make an excuse for them to leave when Jules spoke up, asking a question that completely threw him.

"So are you going to the bank today?"

CHAPTER 28

"I'm nervous," Sophie whispered to Henry as they sat in the manager's office at Traverse City First Bank and Trust. "Really nervous. What am I doing here?"

"Finding out the truth." Henry placed one hand on hers on the armrest. "It's going to be okay."

"Maybe I don't want to know the truth." She grimaced as her heart rose in her throat. "What if Eva's right and I never knew Papa Leo?"

"Look." He turned in his chair and laced his fingers with hers. "I think your grandfather had a secret, and he needed to keep you safe. If he did find the coins and somehow figured out who they belonged to, I don't blame him."

"But he could've told me." She sat back, clutching his fingers. Henry's quiet strength was the only thing keeping her from bolting for the door. "I would've understood, even helped him."

"What if he sold one of the coins and kept the money?" One blond brow quirked as he dipped his head to peer into her face. "It's clear you have an issue with that. Would you have understood?"

A long pause later, Sophie took a deep shuddering breath.

"Yes... yes... absolutely." She put as much conviction in her voice as she could muster—more for herself than for Henry. All the evidence she'd seen pointed to the fact that Papa Leo had found Sonny Todaro's lost coins. Eva's comments aside, Sophie knew deep inside there was no other way he could've afforded all the luxuries she'd always taken for granted.

How could she have been so blind? She'd lived a protected life in that little college town, going from her grandfather's arms right into Tom's. Never questioning for a moment how Papa Leo afforded all the vacations, the beautiful cars, the expensive wines, or her college education.

She'd never asked how he managed to maintain three homes —to pay the taxes and upkeep on the cottages here and the house in Indiana. She hadn't even considered the fact that the money he spent on the two cottages far exceeded anything he'd ever charged in rent. She'd been a naive child her whole life, blissfully unaware in that safe, secure little existence. She allowed Papa Leo to treat her like damn princess and never asked a single question.

Heat rose to her cheeks as she stared at the manila envelope in her lap. What must Henry think? Did he see her as a spoiled brat? She wanted to explain to him how it was—only her and her grandfather for so many years. How she'd stayed with the first man with whom she'd ever had a serious relationship and how things were in the intimate culture of a small Midwestern college town.

She turned to him, opening her lips to speak when a dapper, gray-haired man stepped into the office.

"Hello, I'm Jim Evans, Ms. Russo." He extended his hand first to Sophie and then to Henry, who rose slightly and offered his name.

Evans settled into a big leather chair behind his massive desk. Sophie couldn't help feeling a bit like she was in high school again, sent to the principal's office for being out of class without a hall pass. The bank manager folded his hands on top of the desk blotter and gave them a smile. "What can I do for you today?"

"I'm here to close out my grandfather's account." Sophie straightened her spine and squared her shoulders in an attempt to project confidence. "He died in January and this is the first chance I've had to get here. We're actually summer residents in Willow Bay, so we don't get up in the winter much, although I've just recently moved up here, so I guess I'll be here all the time now..." She stopped herself, aware she was babbling.

"Do you have the account number?" Evans asked. "I also need a death certificate and some identification from you."

Sophie drew out the necessary paperwork, including the will stating that she was Papa Leo's sole heir. She also handed over her driver's license and a slip of paper with the account number she'd taken from the photocopy of his check to the Friends of the Lighthouse Foundation.

The manager laid each item on his desk, perusing them silently for several minutes, occasionally glancing up at Sophie and then back down at the papers. Her stomach clenched even tighter as the clock on his desk slowly ticked the seconds away.

At last he sat back, tenting his fingers and tapping them against his chin before he spoke. "Ms. Russo, first, let me express my condolences at the loss of your grandfather. He was a good man and one of our best customers. Actually, I've been anticipating your arrival. I checked on Leo back in April when I hadn't heard from him for a few months and I saw the obituary online."

Sophie's heart sped up and she tried to speak, but her mouth was so dry her tongue refused to cooperate. *This guy knows!* Did Papa Leo confide everything to him? She simply stared at bank manager.

"Sophie—may call you Sophie?" He opened a drawer in his desk as he spoke.

She glanced at Henry before nodding and choking out, "Of–of course."

"Leo was in late last August and told me about the cancer. He knew that it was his final summer up here." Evans pulled a packet from his desk drawer. "He gave me this for you." He set a small yellow envelope on the desk between them. Across the front in Papa Leo's spiky handwriting were the words, *For Sophie Russo —upon my death*. The manager gave her a small smile. "He said you'd know what to do with it."

She reached for it and then jerked her hand back, not at all sure she wanted to open it. "What's in it?"

"I imagine the key to the safety deposit box he has here at the bank," Evans replied. "And possibly a note for you. Otherwise, I have no clue. Open it and find out." He rose. "I'll go check on the account balances while you do that."

Sophie nodded numbly as he left the office, closing the door quietly behind him. The bank manager had a computer on his desk. He could have checked the balance right then and there, but obviously he felt she needed some privacy to open the packet. She did, because Papa Leo had a secret life.

Holy shit.

She dropped back in her chair, suddenly weak. Henry gave her elbow an encouraging squeeze, but still she hesitated, reeling at the news that her grandfather had a safety deposit box she didn't know existed. She wasn't sure she was prepared to deal with its contents. The one in Indiana had held the usual stuff—marriage and birth certificates, Nonna's death certificate, car titles, and other personal papers—all the things in the manila envelope she carried with her today. Nothing unusual.

"Go ahead, Soph, open it," Henry said softly. "It's time."

It really was foolish to be so afraid. She already knew what she would find in the box—the coins and probably some cash. Opening it would be almost anticlimactic. The mystery was solved, and she could stop wondering whether or not Papa Leo had found Sonny Todaro's stolen gold. Obviously, he had, and like any other normal human being, he'd turned the find to his advantage. So why did that thought make her heart ache so terribly? Had he really done anything wrong? It wasn't like *he'd* stolen the coins from the Mint.

Just get over yourself and open the damn envelope.

She took it, tore off the top, and shook the contents onto the desk. Out fell a safety deposit box key and a folded sheet of paper. Next to her, Henry sucked in a breath and when she looked over at him, his eyes were wide. Clearly, he was fairly popping with curiosity. She unfolded the note, which was very short considering everything she'd been through the last few days. She read it and then handed it to Henry. There were no secrets from him anymore, they were in this together.

My darling girl,

This is a key to a safety deposit box that contains a treasure I found on a shipwreck in the lake many years ago—gold coins that I discovered had been stolen from the Mint during the Depression. My research showed that the boat belonged to a man named Sonny Todaro—there's plenty of information about him on the Internet if you get curious, but suffice to say, he was a bad sort.

According to maritime law, the coins were salvage and thus mine to do with as I pleased, so I have no regrets about using one to make our life a little bit easier and sweeter and to help out those around us in need. I sold only one coin, but that was all I needed to sell. It would've been too risky to use any of the others. You'll find the rest in the box—the dealer paid in cash to avoid a trail the government or anyone else could follow. Understand why I had to hide it from you, Soph. It was too dangerous not to.

I've had this secret for so many years and in spite of the money, it's been an albatross around my neck. Find a way to return the coins to the Mint. Don't let them weigh you down the way they did me. The world is much smaller than when I first discovered them, and the Internet makes them very easily traceable today, so be careful. Leave them in the bank until you hand them over.

The rest of the money is yours. Use it as you see fit, share it, enjoy it, and if you're inclined to help out your mother when she calls, there will be extra sapphires in your halo when you join me heaven.

Find your own life and live it with gusto, my Sophie, and remember I'm always with you.

Your loving Papa Leo

When she handed the note to Henry, her hand was trembling so hard, he held it for a moment before releasing his hold on her to read what Papa Leo had written.

So there it was. Surely this was what he was trying to tell her the night he died. And Eva was right all along. That thought didn't burn as hotly as Sophie had believed it would earlier. After all, Eva had been there when he found them. She'd watched it all play out. For once, she'd told the truth.

Henry passed the note back to her with a small triumphant smile. "So, there you go."

"This must have been what he was trying to tell me right before he died."

"No doubt," he agreed and then said, after a moment's hesitation, "Do you want to go open the box now? The manager's slowly making his way back. Probably giving you some time."

Sophie drew a deep breath. "Let's see what the balance is in the account first. If the coin sold for over two million at auction, Papa Leo must've gotten way less than that from the dealer." Figures bounced around in her head as she tried to calculate roughly how much of probably a million and half might be left if Papa Leo had been spending it since the late sixties or early seventies. Surely not too much was left. "Do you think he put it all into an account here?"

"No. Remember he said the coin dealer paid in cash so there'd be no paper trail for anyone to follow. I Googled it last night—a million dollars will fit in an attaché case, a couple of million will fit in an average-sized duffel bag."

"You Googled how much cash would fit in a briefcase? Seriously?"

He shrugged. "Just trying to figure every angle. Hell, a million bucks in hundreds will fit in a standard microwave oven or the bottom two crisper drawers in your fridge."

How incredible that Henry had followed every possible path with just a laptop and a willingness to sit and do the research. She'd been so distracted by Eva and Dale and her despair about Papa Leo keeping secrets, she never could've focused on that kind of digging. Henry Dugan was a geek of the first order, but he was her geek and she was glad to have him with her. She threw her arms around him and hugged him just as Jim Evans tapped on the glass door.

"Ms. Russo?" He opened the door a crack.

"Come in, please." Sophie waved him in and he perched on his desk chair before he laid a piece of paper in front of her.

"This is the current balance in your grandfather's accounts."

"Accounts?" She quirked one brow. "Plural?"

"He had a checking account, a money market, and six CDs. The amounts are listed there."

Henry gazed at the paper and then whistled softly. "Wow."

The checking account had just over five thousand in it, the money market, about one hundred fifty thousand, and the certificates of deposit were for twenty-five thousand each. *Holy cats!* Sophie gulped. There was over three hundred thousand dollars total in the accounts.

"Do you mind if I ask him a question, Soph?" Henry touched her shoulder.

"No, not at all."

Henry pointed to the list of CDs. "How long ago did he take out the CDs?"

Evans cleared his throat and then gave a little laugh. "Every other year between nineteen seventy-five and nineteen eighty-five."

"That means these are well over their face value." Sophie said.

"That's right." The manager agreed with a brisk nod. "Each one is a ten-year CD, and Leo let them roll over. The interest on them is considerable. You're quite a well-to-do woman, Ms. Russo. We'll need to change the names on them, of course, if you decide to stay with us, but it's all yours now."

"Okay." Sophie swallowed hard, trying to absorb what he was saying, but was unable to take it all in. "Could... could we get into his safety deposit box first? The key was in the envelope, just as you said."

"Come with me." Evans rose and led Sophie and Henry to the vault at the back of the bank.

CHAPTER 29

Sophie grasped Henry's hand as they walked while butterflies fluttered in her stomach. What would they find in the box? Papa Leo's letter hadn't even hinted at how much cash was left. Shaking, she signed her name where Evans pointed, gave him the flat metal key, and held her breath as he knelt and opened the largest-size safety deposit box.

It was heavy. She could tell by the way the manager hefted the weight of it when he carried it to a private cubicle next to the vault.

"Just come out when you're done." Evans slipped away as Henry closed the door behind him.

"Still nervous?" Henry asked.

"Yeah, but more excited and a little frightened to see the coins." She chuckled as the absurdity of the situation suddenly hit her—in all her very ordinary life, she'd never imagined anything like this. It was too unreal. "Henry, the coins are in here," she whispered.

"I know." He planted a hearty kiss smack on her lips and then gave her a little nudge. "Open it already."

She lifted the lid of the gray box. At first she thought it was empty, but then Henry tipped it slightly from behind and a stack of faded Xeroxed papers and a small hide-bound notebook encased in a cellophane envelope, fell to the front. The edges were crumbling and water stained. Sophie picked it up, careful of the bits of leather that rained down when she open the envelope. The cover was embossed with the word JOURNAL and a couple of the letters still had traces of gilt in the curves.

Henry reached in to pick up the stack of fifty or so Xerox pages and they both gasped to see that he'd uncovered two neat rows of currency.

Sophie put one hand out, drew it back as if something had bitten her. She couldn't even breathe and her heart nearly pounded out of her chest. She stared at the rows of faded bills and when she looked up, he, too, was staring, obviously also speechless. Then his eyes met hers. For some reason, they both seemed unwilling to touch the money.

At last, Henry got brave and picked up one of the packets of bills, which were wrinkled and soft, as if they'd been left in someone's pocket and gone through the washing machine. He fanned through the package. "These are all hundreds." He reached for another one. "And these are twenties."

Sophie picked up one up gingerly and the dried-out rubber band snapped when she fingered the cash. Hers were all hundred-dollar bills. It certainly looked and felt real, but she knew good counterfeiters could make phony bills look completely authentic. The date on the top bill was 1929 and as she flipped through them, she saw that they all were from 1929.When she picked up another packet, they were also hundreds, but dated 1930.

"These are from the Depression, Henry. This is old money."

"That's our time frame." He rubbed his face thoughtfully and a streak of dirt appeared on his cheek. "Do you think it's real?"

"No idea." Sophie was still reeling, as she counted and discovered there were about fourteen packages of bills in ten-, twenty-, and one-hundred-dollar denominations. "These aren't numbered consecutively — maybe it is real."

"If it is, it has to be part of what they found on the Caroline Howe, but Dale never mentioned cash." Henry's mouth twisted as he gazed at the box. "Unless his grandfather didn't know about the cash, only about the gold."

"Wouldn't cash have disintegrated being in the water like that?" Sophie dropped the packets back into the box then brushed her gritty hands together with a grimace.

"Money's made of cotton and linen fibers, not actual paper, so even if it did spend time underwater, it would probably dry out and look fine." He held a bill up to the light. "Ship captains used to wrap stuff in oilcloth and keep it in a watertight locked trunk or safe. I'm guessing your granddad found it in the wreckage with the cash and coins in it." He sorted through the bundles on the table. "Money can survive underwater. I saw an exhibition once about a boat that sank in the Columbia River in the late nineteenth century. There was cash and coins, even a leather-bound notebook from one of the passengers." He pointed to the journal. "A lot like that one."

"If Todaro was running liquor on the Great Lakes during Prohibition, doesn't it make sense that there would be cash onboard? A lot of cash?"

"Yup, it does."

"What are the papers?" Sophie jerked her head toward the pile of old Xerox copies.

"Looks like copies of pages from an old diary or something." He tugged off the rusted paper clip and began reading aloud, squinting at the bad copy of faded, scrawly handwriting. *November 25, 1933. Lat/Log: 45-25'54" N Longitude: 084-59'31" W. Unloaded last of sold cargo tonight and collected last of payments. Will get underway tomorrow a.m. under heavy cloud cover. Skeleton crew, gave rest of men shore leave until midnight.*

Message from S.T. asking for E.T.A. If weather holds, should be in Chicago by Wednesday."

"Hang on." Sophie took up the leather journal and untied the thongs. The first page read, JOURNAL, and below that, *Presented to Captain Franklin T. McGuire from his loving wife, Belle, Christmas 1932.* She turned the ragged pages, trying not to destroy the book in the process, but the edges of the paper crumbled in her fingers. "Dammit. This is so delicate," she said as she held it toward Henry. "Here, compare the handwriting. See if what you've got are copies made from this, okay?"

"You're right. Looks like I've got Xeroxed pages from that journal." Henry glanced from the book to the papers in his hand and back again. "So, we've got a journal from a boat captain. Check the last entry if you can do it without destroying the pages."

"It's November 28, 1933, but the ink is so faded, I can barely make it out."

"Apparently, Leo made copies of the captain's log, probably because the pages were tearing." He flipped through the stack of papers and quickly came upon the entry for November 28, 1933. "Ah, yep, here it is. *Lat/Log: 44-37'48" N/Longitude: 086-14'55" W. Temp. dropping. Snow in the clouds. May not make Sheboygan, so will head south to Muskegon and put in there to wait out storm.* What do you want to bet those coordinates are somewhere damn close to Willow Bay?"

"Did he copy the whole journal?"

"Nope, looks like he only did a few days in November up to the last entry on November 28. The rest of the pages appear to be stuff he probably printed from microfiche of newspaper archives. It's articles and information about... let's see here." He fanned the papers. "Okay... hmmm... this is about the double eagle coins... um... and these are shipwrecks along the shore here... oh crap, here's that same picture of Todaro that we found on the Web today. Yeah, it's his research."

"Didn't the yacht registry website say the *Caroline Howe* was lost in a storm in November 1933?" Her voice wavered as her hand trembled with excitement.

"Not a specific date, but yes, November 1933."

"That's got to be it, don't you think?" Sophie clasped her hands together. "Papa Leo discovered the *Caroline Howe* and a chest full of money and gold."

"It looks that way." He nodded, staring down at the fragile journal sitting on top of the layer of bundled cash. "But where's the gold?"

Sophie tipped the box again. Another ten or so bundles of cash fell forward and behind the cash was a Ziploc bag containing a worn leather pouch that appeared soft, but was stiff and brittle when she touched it. Coins clinked when she shook it, and when she opened it, a musty odor wafted up. The coins slid out into her palm—nine shiny twenty-dollar gold pieces in perfect condition. The water hadn't harmed them one bit.

"Oh my God," Henry breathed as she poured the coins into his open palm. He turned them over, examining each one before handing them back to her.

She laid them on the table where they gleamed in the overhead lights. "What am I going to do with all this?" Sophie's head was spinning. Honestly, she'd figured she'd find an account with money in it, but she'd never expected the cash. Papa Leo must have come in the bank several times a summer and made deposits of cash. Did the bank never question the large sums? She had no idea how all this worked. Now that it belonged to her, what the hell was she going to do with it? Were the old bills worth more than their face value? Was it even legal to keep money in a safety deposit box? She fell back into the chair, suddenly too shaky to even stand.

Henry gave her a quick worried glance and then scooped up the coins and put them back in the leather pouch. He resealed the Ziploc before stuffing it deep into the safety deposit box. Then he started packing the bundles of money back into the box. "You look pole-axed, Soph. Want to get out of here? Let's just go do the business with the manager and worry about this stuff later." He stopped, a handful of bundles mid-air. "I mean unless you want to count all this right now?"

"No, no, no. Let's do it later. I want to go home." Sophie was grateful for his take-charge attitude. She didn't have an ounce of take-charge left in her. More than anything, she wanted to get out of the bank and back to the Firefly with the journal and the Xeroxed pages.

The money wasn't going anywhere.

Sophie had tucked a couple of the old bills in her purse before they closed up the safety deposit box. She planned to look up some history on them when they got home, but she couldn't stop thinking about where they'd come from, whose money it was. Her handbag on her lap seemed to hum against her thighs as they drove home. That was ridiculous of course. Exhaustion was making her loopy. So what if it was once payoff for illegal booze? The money had no magical energy—it was just antique bills that Papa Leo had found at the bottom of the lake. Nothing more. But she kept both hands wrapped firmly around the handle of her bag.

"What are you thinking?" Henry took his eyes off the road that curved high above the shore long enough to give her a curious smile. "You're awfully quiet over there."

"Just... kinda... overwhelmed, I guess." The breeze off the lake that swept through the car was cool in spite of the afternoon sun heating the windshield. She lifted her chin to let it waft through her bangs and gave him the best grin she could muster, in a weak attempt to convey how grateful she was to have him with her. "Got a little more than you bargained for when you rented a summer place from me, didn't you?"

"In more ways than one." He reached his hand out to tuck a lock of hair behind her ear—just a gentle touch that sent fireworks racing through Sophie's veins.

She stared at him as he focused once again on driving. So this was love—what she had longed for all her life. This overpowering happiness. Not the silly infatuation over guys in school or the logical, follow-the-next-step, almost brotherly relationship she'd had with Tom for so many years. No, Henry was passion, aching desire, and laughter, friendship, contentment, hope, and insatiable curiosity about what was next.

She didn't want to only be friends or colleagues or even friends with benefits, she wanted happily-ever-after. And she wanted it to start right now. "Henry." She said it so softly she wasn't sure he'd heard her over the road noise.

"Mm hm?" He flipped on his signal and slowed for the turn onto Beach Road.

"I love you." It probably wasn't the most opportune time or place for that particular declaration, but as she gazed at him, the words simply came out. She couldn't hold them back any longer.

Henry's blue eyes were huge behind the wire-rimmed glasses. He stopped the car dead in the middle of the intersection and threw it into Park. A furrow appeared between his brows as he stared at her for a long moment, his expression so full of tenderness that Sophie almost forgot to breathe. Then he pulled her to him and their lips met and clung.

"I love you, too, Sophie."

"You do?" She grinned as warmth radiated throughout her body.

"Dear God, yes, woman," he replied fervently. "Let me get

you home and I'll show you exactly how much." After another soul-stirring kiss, he put the car back in gear and headed up the gravel road.

Sophie shivered in anticipation. It didn't matter anymore what Papa Leo had done with the coins or how much money was waiting for her in the bank or even what she was going to do with all of it. All that mattered was—

Oh, holy shit.

Sophie sucked in a breath, turned in her seat, and pointed. There in the gravel parking area behind the cottages was a beat-up brown Honda. Dale was back.

CHAPTER 30

Henry put one hand on her leg. "Call Earl."

"Already dialing." Sophie held up her cell phone. "How the hell did he get out of jail?"

"We didn't go in to press charges." Henry scowled. "Maybe Earl couldn't hold him any longer. Or maybe somebody bailed him out."

"She wouldn't dare." Sophie knew exactly where his mind had gone. But the door to the Firefly was open and she could see the kitchen through the screen door. Her gut told her Dale was in her house, probably ransacking it again.

"Benzie County 911, what's your emergency?" The dispatcher's voice, loud enough for everyone on the road to hear, blared in her ear.

"I need the sheriff at 74 Beach Road." Sophie turned down the volume.

"Excuse me, ma'am? Speak up please. What's your emergency?"

She blew out a frustrated breath, then spoke in measured tones. "There's a break-in in progress at 74 Beach Road. I need the sheriff now."

"What's your name, ma'am?"

"Sophie Russo. It's my house."

"Is that where you're calling from?"

"I'm outside. Just tell Earl to get out here, please?" The dispatcher's plea to stay on the line disappeared as she tapped the screen and disconnected the call. She gazed at Henry. "What do we do?"

"Well, we don't actually know that anything bad is going on in there." Henry chewed his lower lip. "Hell, they could be screwing each other's brains out over at the Sandpiper for all we know."

"Please don't say that." Sophie rolled her eyes. "Earl's going to be pissed if we go in there, but if he's roughing her up again, we need to stop it."

He took a deep breath and unsnapped his seatbelt. "Okay, wait here and I'll go check it out."

"Excuse me, no." Sophie opened her door. "We're in this together, Dugan."

He gave her a long look and then shrugged. "Okay. Let's go in." He moved in front of her as they approached the stoop. "I'm sure he knows we're here, so let's just walk in like nothing's wrong. That might put him off-guard."

The screen door slapped shut behind them and Sophie called out, "Eva? Are you in here?"

"Sophie, get out—" Eva's cry was cut off by the sound a sharp slap.

"Ah, here she is, the lovely Miss Russo." Dale's gravelly voice came from the kitchen where he sat at the table in front of Henry's laptop, one finger on the trackpad. "And Henry, old man. How are you?" Dale's slumped shoulders and good-ole-boy accent was magically gone. He'd shaved, his hair was neatly combed, and he was dressed in pressed slacks and a sport coat.

Fury rose in Sophie's throat at his cavalier attitude, at his very presence in her home. "What are you doing in my house? I told you never to come back here again."

"*I'm* the owner of those gold coins, Sophie dear." Dale's previous mousy affect had also disappeared. Somehow he seemed bigger, more confident. "Would you care to hand them over to me?"

"Are you crazy? Get the hell out of here, Dale. I don't have them." She slid her hand into the pocket of her dress, feeling for her cell phone.

"Really? Your dear little mother says otherwise." He glanced over his shoulder and a chagrined Eva appeared from the living room with another man, this one tall and built like a football player. Sophie's breath caught in her throat when she saw that he held Eva's arm behind her and that he had a gun in his hand.

"Eva?" Her heart pounded at the trickle of blood running from the side of her mother's mouth. "Are you okay?" She leveled an angry glare at Eva's captor. "What did you do to her?"

"She's fine." Dale jerked his head toward the chair next to him. "Sit down."

"No thanks, we'll stand." Henry gave the gunman a dismissive glance, but stepped closer to Sophie.

"Sit." The word was quiet, but Dale slammed his fist on the table, making the computer jump. "And put your cell phones on the table."

The henchman shoved Eva into a chair. He stood behind her, one beefy hand gripping her shoulder, the other holding the gun on Sophie and Henry. Eva squirmed in his grasp, but stopped when he tightened his hold and gave her a hard stare. "You two do as he says," he snarled.

Sophie sat and laid her phone on the table.

Henry grabbed the chair closest to Sophie's, spun it around, and rested his arms on the back. His expression was a study in nonchalance, as he placed one hand on Sophie's shoulder.

"Keep your hands where I can see them, asshole." The gorilla waved the gun in Henry's direction.

Instinctively, Sophie ducked, but Henry didn't move or remove his hand from its reassuring position. Instead he tightened his grip on her.

"My hands are right here. Are you blind?" he asked with a quirk of one brow.

"Yeah. I see 'em, asshole." The man scowled before aiming his gun once again. "Just no sudden moves."

Dale eyed Henry for a moment. "Your cell phone, please."

"You need to make a call, use Sophie's. It's right there in front of you."

"*Your* phone. Now."

"Give him the goddamn phone, asshole." The ape's rough voice sent a chill through Sophie. She leaned into Henry's warm touch.

"Your repertoire of intensifiers is rather limited, isn't it?" Henry tossed his phone on the table far enough away from Dale that he had to stand to retrieve it.

"Thank you. Let me introduce you to my brother, Roy." Dale said, reaching for Henry's phone and then Sophie's. "Say hello, Roy."

"Ma'am." Roy nodded and extended his hand.

Sophie ignored it as Dale turned on both phones and checked the call logs.

"You called the sheriff." Dale gazed at Sophie's screen with a sigh. "That was stupid."

"Instinct." Henry's cool tone belied the tension in his fingers. "When we saw your car, what else could we do?"

"What a shame." Dale tossed the phone to Sophie. "I imagine that bumbling Barney Fife is on his way, so Sophie, call them back and tell them you were mistaken."

"Hell, no." Sophie raised her chin defiantly.

THE SUMMER OF SECOND CHANCES

"Make the call or Roy puts a bullet through your mother's head." Dale made the threat so calmly that only Eva's gasp of horror assured Sophie that she'd heard him correctly.

"He'll do it. Call off the sheriff, Sophie." Eva cried. "Please!"

Sophie looked over at Henry, who simply raised one brow and nodded. Gritting her teeth, she made the call, hoping against hope that Earl would put two and two together and realize that when he released Dale from jail, her place would be the bastard's first stop.

"Thank you." Dale's smile reminded her of a snake. "Now, why don't you hand over the coins, then Roy and I will be on our way?"

Henry's hand trembled on her shoulder. He was scared too, in spite of his cocky demeanor. Somehow that heartened her. Frightened meant he'd be cautious and not take any unnecessary chances.

"Ah, the coins." Henry pursed his lips. "Sadly, we don't have them."

"Dugan, you idiot. Tell him where they are." Eva's voice rose as she dabbed at the blood on her cheek with her thumb.

"We don't have the coins, Dale. We couldn't find them," Sophie said.

"Well, it appears you've certainly given it the old college try since I left. I've been looking at your notes. At this point, I think you may know more about the Todaros than I do." He tapped the trackpad on Henry's laptop and brought up the website with details about the first Sonny Todaro. "Your Internet history has been a fountain of information."

Eva moaned and the gorilla—Sophie couldn't think of him as anything else—cuffed her ear.

Henry let out a disgusted sigh. "Could you ask your... your brother to stop hitting Eva?"

"Roy, leave her alone, okay?" Dale said before shutting the laptop with a soft snap. "Now, why don't you guys simply tell me what else you've discovered and maybe between the three of us, we can figure out the rest? That way, you can get on with your summer vacation, and I can take my property and leave this godforsaken town."

"If you've gone through my notes, as I see you have—" Henry nodded toward the mess on the table and floor. Their research had been neatly stacked earlier that morning; now papers and open notebooks were scattered across the kitchen floor and table as if someone had swept them away in a fit of anger. "—then you know everything we know. Besides, legally, those coins, wherever they are, belong to the U.S. government, not you. They were never supposed to be circulated."

"What a noble idea." Dale reached into his pocket and pulled out a pack of cigarettes. He tapped one out of the pack and lit it. "You don't mind, do you?" He inhaled deeply, before blowing a waft of smoke over his shoulder. "Those coins are *mine*. My grandfather picked them up at the Mint and my family's been looking for them for damn near eighty years. Now I know for a fact that they went down with the *Caroline Howe*. I also know for a fact that your grandfather found them."

"What makes you think that?" Sophie swallowed hard as her stomach lurched. Keep him talking. That was the trick. If they could buy some time, maybe Earl would get here. "I only *suspect* he may have found something in the lake a long time ago, but I don't know for sure. He never told me anything."

Dale sighed and folded his hands together, resting them on the table. "You really do think I'm stupid, don't you? I assure you I'm not. My family has been diving these waters for years searching for that damn wreck. And we've been watching this area of Michigan for years as well, waiting and hoping some local diver might discover it. Our divers actually did find the damn wreck, probably just a few days after Sophie's granddad. It was obvious someone had already been there and our gold was the only thing missing from the wreck."

"How could you possibly know when that gold disappeared from the wreck?" Henry's question seemed quite reasonable to Sophie. "Anyone could have found it any time after the ship went down. Are you trying to tell us that you've had people here watching the town for eighty years? Paying attention to every diver that went under the lake?"

"That's exactly what I'm telling you." Dale's light gray gaze never left Henry's face. "We have people in the dive shops, on the tourist boats, working on the newspaper. Hell, my cousin Dave works in the maritime museum. Do you think we'd let over twenty million in gold just slip through our fingers?"

"Okay, I admit it. I'm impressed by your family's tenacity," Henry said.

Sophie couldn't believe how serene he remained in spite of Roy shifting his gun between him, Eva, and Sophie. Her body quaked with terror, and she gritted her teeth to keep from screaming. Somehow Henry managed to sound as if he was in a conversation with a friend over a beer.

"Well, Henry, that's just the kind of people we are." Dale's smile revealed yellow teeth. "We don't forget. Ever."

"So what made your family think it was Leo who found the gold?" Henry asked.

He was buying time, he had to be. Surely he wasn't keeping this thug engaged simply out of intellectual curiosity.

Maybe he thinks Earl will come anyway and he's giving him time to get here. That's gotta be it.

That was smart. Sophie slid over in her chair so that her back pressed against Henry's side, absorbing warmth and a small amount of courage as he squeezed her shoulder again. They'd be okay. Surely Earl would be roaring up any moment with Tony. Officers with guns, that's what they needed.

Come on, Earl, figure it out and move your ass!

Her mind whirled as scenario after scenario flew through her head, each one grimmer than the last. She blinked, trying to focus on the conversation between Henry and Dale.

"It wasn't tough." Dale was saying. "He was a greedy fool. He took one of the coins to a dealer in Toronto to sell it. A connection there let my dad know it had gone on the market. We'd been waiting a helluva long time for one of them to surface. That kind of news travels fast in numismatic circles. Collectors pay attention to coins as rare as those. And old Leo Russo suddenly started spending money. A lot of it."

"What makes you think he sold a coin all those years ago? It could've been anything," Henry said, tightening his arm around Sophie.

"*I* didn't think anything. Back then, I was a teenager attending a Catholic prep school in Florida. My main concern was how to sneak booze into the dorm. Oh, and girls. But my grandfather and my father had been searching this area for years."

"So now what?" Sophie tried to force the fear out of her tone and replace it with scorn, but her voice trembled. They were walking a verbal tightrope. They just needed to keep him engaged until Earl arrived, but one wrong step could piss him off, and they'd be in big trouble. "You've suddenly developed an interest in old family legends?"

"Not legends." He dropped his cigarette butt in the coffee cup she'd left on the table earlier that morning. "Facts. Scores to be settled. Your grandfather stole from us. We just want what's rightfully ours."

"If Leo did find anything in the lake, the law says it's salvage." Henry gave Dale a cockeyed grin. "But, I tell you what, if we ever do find those coins, she'll send you a check, okay?"

"Fuck the law." Dale didn't raise his voice, but the intense look in his eyes made Sophie lean farther away from him as he continued in the same deadly quiet tone. "Now, we're going to sit here until you tell me what I want to know. I'm thinking I can probably encourage you to start talking if I allow Roy over there to put a bullet in your mother's knee."

Roy lowered the gun, pointed it directly at Eva's trembling leg, and cocked it.

"No!" Sophie cried as Roy took aim. "Wait. Listen. We found some old cash and the captain's journal from the *Caroline Howe* in some stuff from the attic."

Henry drew back and stared at her, obviously aghast that she lied so boldly to a guy holding a firearm, but what else could she do? It didn't matter how she felt about her mother, she certainly didn't want her to get shot.

Dale held up one hand. "Hang on, Roy. We're getting somewhere. How much cash?"

"I didn't count it."

"Where is it?" Dale was practically drooling.

"Out on the screened porch. I'll go get it." Henry offered, rising from his chair.

"No, Roy'll go get it." Dale reached behind his back and pulled out a gun of his own. "You stay put."

Sophie didn't know anything at all about handguns, but this one appeared every bit as big and deadly as Roy's. She reached for Henry's hand as he plopped back down. Her stomach turned over, and she swallowed hard to keep from dry heaving.

Dear god, where was Earl? Had she misjudged the old lawman's curiosity that badly? It was a lousy ten-minute drive from town to her cottages. Seven, if you exceeded the speed limit, which he certainly should've been doing. But she still didn't hear the wail of sirens in the distance.

Maybe they'd already scoped out the situation and surrounded the cottages. Maybe they were out there, just waiting for an opportunity to storm the place—perhaps even watching for a signal from her or Henry.

She glanced around, planning an escape route should bullets start flying. Their best bet was to slide under the table. She could shout at Eva to join them.

Roy brought the weathered wooden dish trunk in and heaved it up onto the table, right on top of Henry's laptop.

"Um, do you mind?" Henry tilted his head toward the computer. "Could you get that thing off my laptop, please?"

"Oh, sorry, asshole." Roy jerked the computer out and tossed it on the floor with a wicked smirk in Henry direction.

"Jesus, it's eighth grade all over again," Henry muttered under his breath. "What a dipshit."

"Do you think Earl will come anyway?" Sophie whispered.

"Dunno. Guess we'll see," Henry murmured, his breath coming hot and shaky on her neck as his fingers tightened on hers.

Dale looked up from pawing through the trunk. He'd tossed loose packing paper and dishes aside as if they were so much trash. The pan of flatware hit the floor with a clatter and clang. "Jesus Christ, this is nothing but old dishes. Where's the cash and where are the fucking coins?"

"The coins weren't in there," Henry said. "We haven't seen them."

"Really?" Dale grabbed his gun and fired at Eva's knee.

Eva howled and curled up on the floor, writhing in pain.

"You bastard!" Sophie ran to her mother, grabbing a dishtowel from the counter before turning her over gingerly. Blood was everywhere.

"Take it easy, now. Let me help you." Grimacing, she staunched the flow as Eva lay whimpering and clutching her leg. Fortunately, Dale was a crappy shot or Eva had moved because the bullet seemed to have missed her knee and gone right through the fleshy part of her calf. "Lie still, Eva. Stop squirming."

Henry scurried around the table, but the gorilla tackled him, dropping him to the floor with a loud *oomph*. Henry was a big guy, but Roy was younger and easily had fifty pounds on him. He yanked Henry up by his shirt and deposited him in a chair before giving him a swat on the back of the head. "Sit down, butt-wipe."

Ransacking her memory for the first aid training she'd learned in Girl Scouts, Sophie worked fast, keeping an unobtrusive eye on Dale as she wrapped towel around the wound and applied pressure.

What kind of an animal just ups and shoots an unarmed woman?

When she peeked again, Dale had his gun aimed at Henry's head.

"Want to try it again, Dugan?"

Henry winced as his eyes moved from Eva and Sophie to Dale. He had to be struggling with what to say. What did it matter? The gold wasn't important anymore, and obviously, Dale had gone completely off his rocker. He'd have no qualms about putting a bullet through Henry's head. Tears of terror and frustration burned her eyelids. "Your fucking gold is in a safety deposit box in a bank in Traverse City, okay?" she shouted, choking back a sob. "Henry, can you come and help me get her to the sofa?"

"Stay put, asshole." Roy slapped Henry back down into his chair. "She ain't gonna die. It's barely a flesh wound."

"How do you know it's in the bank?" Dale kept his gun trained on Henry, who was staring down the barrel, a lazy half-smile on his face that puzzled Sophie.

"We just came from there." Henry replied. "We saw it ourselves."

Sophie helped Eva to a sitting position, leaned her against the cabinets, and then gathered more towels to make a cushion for her wounded calf. The bleeding seemed to have slowed, but they needed to get her to the ER. What if the bullet was still in there?

Dale gave a frustrated growl, glanced over his shoulder at Eva, and with a short nod to Roy, set the gun down on the table. He threw Henry and Sophie a look that dared them to touch it before he stomped out onto the screened porch, mumbling to himself. Sophie's eyes locked with Henry's as they both gazed at the weapon Dale had abandoned. If she moved quick and quiet, she could probably grab it.

Henry shook his head so minimally, she almost wasn't sure what he was trying to tell her. She tossed him a wide-eyed look, then furrowed her brow in a question, but Roy caught the exchange.

"Don't even think about going for that gun, you dumb bitch, or I'll put a bullet right through your boyfriend's head. Got it?" He tapped Henry's temple none-too-gently with the business end of his own pistol.

Henry jerked his head away. "Okay, that's it. I'm done."

He's done? Fear rose in Sophie's throat. *What the hell does he mean, he's done? Henry, don't be an idiot!*

In one fluid movement, Henry rose, knocked the gun out of Roy's hand, kneed him in the balls, and then landed a punch right in the big man's solar plexus.

Roy howled and fell to his knees, clutching his crotch, while Henry picked up the pistol and swatted Roy on the back of the head with it.

"Get the other gun, Sophie." Henry shoved the big man over onto his belly and placed one foot on his back. "Don't even think about moving... asshole." He mimicked Roy so perfectly Sophie had to look twice as she grabbed Dale's gun.

"What the fuck's going on in here?" Dale cried. He stormed into the kitchen but stopped dead at the scene before him.

"Have a seat, Dale." Sophie indicated a wooden chair with the gun.

He sighed, shook his head, and threw up his hands as he dropped into the chair. "Of course. Why the fuck not?"

"Here, tie him up with this." Eva pulled an apron from the drawer next to her and held it out from her spot on the floor. "Dale, you stupid bastard."

A couple of swift knots later, Dale was tied to the chair and cursing like a drunken sailor at Eva. Sophie stuffed the damp dishrag in Dale's mouth before she retrieved another apron from the pegs in the utility room for Henry to bind Roy. Just as she turned to grin triumphantly at Henry, a siren wailed out on Beach Road.

CHAPTER 31

"You've got everything, right?" Sophie fussed over the small trunk of the Mercedes, rearranging boxes and her mother's suitcases.

"What?" Eva drawled as she leaned on her cane near the back fender of the car. "You afraid I'll forget something and come back to haunt you again?"

"That's it," Sophie agreed with a wicked smile. "I'm just making sure because once you're gone, you're gone, woman." She beamed at Henry, who carried the last box from the Sandpiper and stowed it in the backseat of the open roadster. The hard top was stored in Noah's barn and Eva had decided to leave it there—possibly it was her way of letting Sophie know she intended to return one day.

"Very nice, daughter. This is the thanks I get for taking a bullet for you?" Eva's weathered features softened as she smiled at Sophie.

Sophie couldn't help but notice the physical changes the months of summer had wrought in her mother. She'd toned down the cosmetics considerably; although her mouth was still of slash of red lipstick, the heavy eye makeup had eased into more neutral tones and her hair was cut into a cute pixie style that took off at least ten years. She was wearing clean jeans and a denim jacket over the faded Woodstock T-shirt she'd found in her attic boxes. Her nails were shorter and simply buffed, and she'd exchanged the ratty flip-flops for a sturdy pair of walking shoes that supported her healing calf.

"Um… you took a bullet for *me*?" Sophie shut the trunk and walked around to grin at Eva. "Man, this story gets bigger every time you tell it."

""That's how I remember it." Eva chuckled and tucked her psychedelic painted cane between the bucket seats.

"You always seem to forget the part where you brought the bad guys with you." Henry came up behind Sophie and slipped an arm around her shoulders.

"Well, then you tell it, Dugan. You're the big fancy writer." Eva reached in her bag and then gave a disgusted sigh. "Why did I ever let you talk me into quitting? It's times like these you really need a cigarette." She tossed the bag in the passenger seat and extended a hand to Henry. "Give us a hug, Henry. I'm outta here."

"Your lungs are thanking you, I promise." He released Sophie to give Eva a warm hug. "You drive safe and let us know where you are, okay?"

"I'll keep you posted." Eva clung to him for a few seconds. "Once I sell my place in Venice, I'm thinking Texas or maybe New Mexico. Someplace warm and dry and as far away from the Case family as I can get." She turned to Sophie. "Well, kid. This is it."

Sophie gazed at her for a moment before opening her arms to embrace her mother. "Take care of yourself, Eva," she whispered around the lump in her throat.

"It's been good to get to know you, Sophie. You've turned into a fine woman—I'm proud of you." Eva's voice choked. "Well, crap, seems like I oughta have some motherly words of wisdom here." She trembled in Sophie's arms. "Hey, I know. Hang on to Henry—he's a keeper. Stay well and be happy, okay?" She pressed a kiss to Sophie's cheek, gave her another quick squeeze, and slid behind the wheel of the open roadster. "Admit it. You're gonna miss me a bunch."

Sophie could only nod as she bit her lower lip, then took a deep breath "So long, Eva."

"So long, baby! See ya around, Dugan!" Eva waved vigorously as she gunned the Mercedes and peeled out of the parking area.

Sophie sighed deeply. Her feelings about her mother had become so conflicted, especially in light of Papa Leo's note. One part of her wished she could go back to the good old days when ignorance was bliss. But another part remained intrigued by her mother—a vagabond life so different from Sophie's sheltered choices. Would they have built a real relationship if Eva had decided to stay in Willow Bay? It seemed as if they'd made a tenuous beginning this summer, but perhaps it wasn't Eva's nature to stay put. Papa Leo most certainly understood that and apparently, he'd accepted his daughter for who she was and loved her the best way he could.

"You really are going to miss her, aren't you?" Henry said as they watched the little car disappear down the gravel lane in a cloud of dust.

She bit her lower lip and gave the question serious consideration before answering slowly, "Yeah. I am. Logically, I shouldn't miss her one bit, but I will. Maybe this is another legacy that Papa Leo left me, you know?"

"You mean the care and feeding of your wayward parent?" Henry gave her a wry smile.

"Exactly." She remembered all the times her grandfather had rescued Eva. "He was always there for her, sending checks all over the country, wherever she happened to be at the moment. He never complained or expected an explanation, he just sent the money. And here's something about me that you may not want to know. I'm ashamed to admit I've always harbored resentment about his generosity."

She flushed and couldn't look Henry in the eye, so she bent down to pull a weed from the garden along the parking area. Then she straightened and tossed the bit of vegetation aside. If they were going to try to make a go of this relationship, maybe he needed to know this darkest part of her soul. Maybe it was time to get it out—to release it all and move on. "It wasn't about the money; the money was insignificant. It was because I thought Eva was a crappy daughter and she didn't deserve Papa Leo's graciousness." She swallowed the lump that was forming in her throat again. "She... she didn't deserve his love."

"She was his daughter," Henry replied softly.

"She was." Sophie blinked back the tears that burned her eyelids. "And I'm her daughter, but she abandoned me." She swiped her palms across her cheeks. "Now though, I kinda wonder if she did what she believed was best for me at the time. She was sixteen and had a wild streak in her that she was too young to tame. Who knows what would've happened to me if she'd taken me with her when she left? She knew Papa Leo and Nonna would keep me safe, raise me well... love me."

"My mom told me once there's nothing fiercer than a parent's love." Henry said. "I've never had kids, so I can't speak to it, but on some level, it had to have hurt her heart to leave you."

"I spent all of my life trying to make up for her behavior by being the perfect daughter to Nonna and Papa Leo." She put up a hand. "Don't get me wrong, I loved them so much and I wanted to be there for them. But I stayed in Poplar Hill, went to college there, drifted into a relationship with Tom there, and made a career that kept me at home. I think subconsciously, I didn't want to leave them the way she did. The thing is, I resented the hell out of her for that and it grew in me like a nasty virus. I let it keep me from loving anyone wholly because I was afraid they might leave me."

She folded her arms across her belly to ease the ache there as she paced from the cars to the stoop and back again. She couldn't seem to shut up. She glanced up at Henry, not knowing what to expect. But his expression was gentle and warm as she poured out a lifetime of bitterness.

"Do you see? I blew it with every man I ever dated. I was sure they'd leave eventually because I assumed that people never stayed for the long haul. I believed I wasn't worthy of the forever kind of love. I drove them away or I picked guys I knew had no staying power. In spite of how my grandparents loved me." She searched for the right words. She needed him to know, to understand. "This summer, for the first time in my life, I went into a relationship not expecting to get hurt or be abandoned—not expecting anything at all. And for the first time in my life, I fell madly in love." She met his gaze straight on. "I want you, Henry Dugan, more than I've ever wanted anything in my life. But if you aren't up for a middle-aged, perimenopausal mess of a woman, I don't blame you."

Henry reached for her, stroking his hands down her arms before tugging her into his embrace. "Oh, my love, I'm not going anywhere. Can't you see that? You're stuck with me." He kissed her hard and then kissed her again as if to emphasize the point. "Frankly, I'm rather looking forward to middle-aged and peri-menopausal. I'm so over young, bratty chicks. You're the first woman in my life ever who's wanted me for me, the first one who doesn't give a damn about my net worth. I've searched forever and you were right here, working beside me, all along."

Sophie threw her arms around his neck and pressed her lips to his, getting lost in the magic of his kisses and caresses.

When they came up for air, he tipped her chin back with one

finger and gazed into her eyes. "So Eva? The car? The account you set up for her? You're all good with it?"

"Yes. It's all good. Obviously the car means way more to her than it does to me. Besides…"

"Besides… what?"

"I have a confession." She shivered as he explored the curve of her ear with his tongue. "Mmmmm…"

"What kind of confession?" he asked, kissing her throat. "I love confessions. Especially from beautiful women."

"Hmmm?" Lost in the touch of his lips on her skin, Sophie closed her eyes, allowing herself to sink into the warm haven of his arms.

"Confess." His whisper stirred the hair on her cheek and sent goose bumps chasing up her arms. He grasped her wrists and held them behind her back. "Come on, tell me."

She twisted in his hold, fake-struggling while he pulled her closer—so close she could feel his heart pounding. "I can't drive a stick."

"What?" He leaned back, his brow furrowed.

"I can't drive a stick," she repeated. "That's why I let you drive the Mercedes home from the motel."

"You're kidding." He chuckled. "I thought you were just being nice to me."

"Nope. I never learned."

"So, what were you planning on doing with the Benz?"

"Maybe sell it to Liam." She shrugged. "Or learn to drive it. But I think it's best that I gave it to her."

"Okay, I see I have my work cut out for me with you, Ms. Russo." He released her and led her to the stoop. "I'm starting a list of things I need to teach you and driving a manual transmission is going on it. But first, come inside? I have something for you. A gift."

"A gift?" A tingle went through Sophie as he herded her into the Firefly. "What kind of gift?"

"Something I made myself." Henry was being mysterious as he sat her down in a barstool and grabbed his iPad from the table. He sat on the stool next to her, placed the tablet in front of her, and pushed the button to make the screen come to life. The page showing was a Word document and Sophie smiled as she read aloud, "*Shipwreck Summer* a novel by H. J. Dugan." She clasped her hands together in delight. "Oh, Henry, you finished your book! How wonderful!"

"Nope, I wrote a new one." Henry gave her a wry smile. "Somehow the story about my great-grandparents got stalled, but as we worked through all the research about the coins and the Todaros and got deeper and deeper into the mystery, well, that story just about wrote itself."

"Is this what you've been doing ever since Dale was arrested and the Mint guys came and got the coins? Writing a new book?"

"Yep—for the last three months." He peered at her over his glasses. "It's a real how-I-spent-my-summer-vacation story."

"Can I... may I read it?" Sophie was dying to stroke her finger over the screen and get to the first pages of the novel.

"Sure. It's ready for my editor." He touched the screen and the next page appeared—the dedication page—and the words there literally took Sophie's breath away.

For Sophie, will you marry me?

"Henry?" Sophie's heart skipped a beat as she gaped at him. "Are you... are you proposing to me?"

"Sure looks like it." Henry's eyes grew tender as he tugged her toward him until she was standing between his legs. "I'm crazy in love with you and as amazing it is to this old geek, you're in love with me, too. So, let's get married."

"But... but... where will we live? What about your job and your life in San Jose? I've never even met your family." Her words tripped over one another. "Henry... we–we can't just up and get married." She stopped to gaze at him as he sat there, a big smile on his handsome face. "Can we?"

"Of course we can. People do it all the time." His expression turned deadly serious. "Screw the friends-with-benefits thing, Sophie. I want you. I want it all. Say yes."

"Yes." She didn't hesitate another moment. "Yes, I'll marry you."

"Now?" He drew her closer.

"Right now?"

"Sure. Why wait? We know we belong together. Besides we're not getting any younger."

"Hey." She gave his arm a playful smack. "Speak for yourself, Dugan."

"Well, we do have a lot of lost time to make up for." When he nuzzled her neck, his beard tickled and sent shivers up her spine.

"Okay, let's do it." Sophie laughed out loud as joy bubbled up inside her. It was the most impulsive thing she'd ever done in her life, and yet nothing had ever felt so right. "As soon as possible."

"Great. We'll get a license tomorrow and find a justice of the peace. Carrie and Julie can be our witnesses." He cupped her cheeks in his palms and touched his lips to hers, feather-light at first and then with more passion as she opened her mouth to his. When he broke the kiss, he leaned his forehead against hers. "Everything else, we'll work out as we go along," he said, his breath ragged. "Hell, we can live in both places—San Jose and Willow Bay. People do it all the time."

"That's true." Sophie's heart overflowed and she wound her arms around his neck. "Carrie and Liam have a house here and an apartment in Chicago, and so do Julie and Will."

"Well, there you go." Henry let his hands slide over her back, then down to cup her behind as his lips came down on hers again in a kiss that turned her inside out.

"I love you, Henry J. Dugan." She touched his beard and ran her thumb over his lower lip. "Hey, what's the *J* for?"

"James." He caught her thumb between his teeth and nipped gently. "Henry for my great-grandfather, but Mom read *Daisy Miller* while she was pregnant with me, thus, Henry James."

"Henry James. Seriously?" Sophie chuckled when he nodded. "You were destined to be a novelist, weren't you?"

"I guess we'll know after you read this." He kissed her again before easing her out of his arms and pushing the tablet toward her. "Here. I'll make some coffee."

The scent of freshly ground beans filled the cottage as Sophie curled up on the sofa with Henry's iPad and began to read...

Once More From the Top

What do you do when the one who got away…comes back?

Carrie Halligan never regretted the choice she made sixteen years ago to raise her son Jack by herself in Willow Bay, Michigan. A successful photographer by day, at night Carrie satisfies her musical passions by playing piano at a hotel bar, maintaining a balance that works for her and Jack. Walking away from Maestro Liam Reilly without telling him she was pregnant with his child may have been the hardest thing she'd ever done, but it was definitely the right thing.

When Liam shows up in town to perform a benefit concert with the local symphony, however, Carrie's carefully crafted life spins out of control. After sending Jack to summer camp, she realizes she can't keep Liam in the dark forever. Telling the truth to the man she once loved more than life itself isn't near as hard as spending time in his presence and realizing that the years haven't diminished his power over her heart. Will her lie be too much to get past, or will the spark of passion between them overcome everything?

Available at: Amazon | Barnes and Noble | Kobo | Smashwords

Sex and the Widow Miles

His life ended. Hers didn't.

Beautiful and aging gracefully, Julie Miles was looking forward to retirement with her husband, Dr. Charlie Miles, in their idyllic Willow Bay, Michigan home. But when Charlie dies of a heart attack, simply getting out of bed becomes a daily struggle. Desperate for a change of scene, she leaves her home to stay in her friend Carrie's unoccupied Chicago apartment.

Her handsome and younger new neighbor, Will Brody, seems to enjoy his assignment to keep an eye on her, and Jules can't help but be flattered. She embraces life—and sex—again, until the discovery of a dark secret shatters her world once more. She knows her feelings for Will are more than casual, and he's made it clear he wants her, but how can she ever trust a man again when her perfect life turned out to be a lie? Determined to get to the bottom of it all, Jules goes in search of the truth and discovers that there's always a second chance to find real love.

Available at Amazon | Barnes and Noble | Kobo | Smashwords

Saving Sarah

She thought she'd never feel safe again. She was wrong.

When Sarah Bennett's abusive ex hunts her down in Chicago, her friends spirit her away to Willow Bay, where she hopes to begin again with a different identity. But terror keeps her holed up, unable to start her new life.

Deputy sheriff Tony Reynard never expected to be staring down the barrel of a gun when he enters Sarah's apartment to finish up some handyman work, but that's how the fiery little redhead greets him, and he's beyond intrigued.

After an intervention by her loving friends, Sarah becomes involved in a project to turn an old mansion into a battered women's shelter. The women work together to renovate the house, along with the help of the townspeople and the delectably handsome Tony, who is a true renaissance man. Tony vows to bring Sarah back to life and love, but knows he needs to move slowly to win her heart.

When her ex tracks her down once more, Sarah must find the courage to protect her friends and her new love from his wrath.

Available at Amazon.com | Barnes and Noble.com | Kobo | Smashwords

ABOUT THE AUTHOR

Nan Reinhardt is a *USA Today* bestselling author of romantic fiction for women in their prime. Yeah, women still fall in love and have sex, even after 45! Imagine! She is also a wife, a mom, a mother-in-law, and a grandmother. She's been an antiques dealer, a bank teller, a stay-at-home mom, a secretary, and for the last 20 years, she's earned her living as a freelance copyeditor and proofreader.

But writing is Nan's first and most enduring passion. She can't remember a time in her life when she wasn't writing—she wrote her first romance novel at the age of ten, a love story between the most sophisticated person she knew at the time, her older sister (who was in high school and had a driver's license!) and a member of Herman's Hermits. If you remember who they are, *you* are Nan's audience! She's still writing romance, but now from the viewpoint of a wiser, slightly rumpled, menopausal woman who believes that love never ages, women only grow more interesting, and everybody needs a little sexy romance.

Visit Nan's website: www.nanreinhardt.com
Facebook: https://www.facebook.com/authornanreinhardt
Twitter: @NanReinhardt
Talk to Nan at: nan@nanreinhardt.com